SECOND STANZA

MEG NAPIER

NAPIERPRESS

First and foremost, as always, to my family: my husband, who gives me boundless love, support and encouragement; my children, who bring me joy and gently make me aware of how much I still need to learn; my sister, who has always been my greatest cheerleader and dearest friend, and my mother, who promotes my books far and wide in spite of my addiction to four-letter words. And thanks to my brother, who helped me in my early—still struggling—meanderings into the modern era of online existence.

And to friends, relatives, even kindly strangers, who pick up this book out of a generous spirit: I hope you find time to read it someday, and I hope it keeps you up late in suspense and ultimately brings you wonder and joy.

"I realize then that it's not enough to know what someone is called. You have to know who they are."

Gayle Forman, **Just One Day**

"What's in a name? that which we call a rose
By any other name would smell as sweet."

William Shakespeare, **Romeo and Juliet**

AUTHOR'S NOTE

I am a voracious, demanding, and enthusiastic reader (and audiobook listener). I'm also impatient and at times intolerant, and one of my pet peeves is authors who create needless difficulties with characters' names. So I feel I must warn you: names change in this book. There is a reason, and a good one, and I'm pretty sure that once you get caught up in the story, you'll agree. And yes, there is violence within, but I think you probably realized that when you saw the cover. Thank you so much for coming along for the ride.

PROLOGUE - MARCH 2013

The acrid smell hit her the moment she stepped out of the car. The house was gone, and all that remained were piles of indeterminate burned wreckage.

"Oh my God, Jackie. This is unbelievable. It's like something out of a horror movie. Please tell me we're at the wrong address."

Jackie couldn't speak. What she was seeing—Rose was right. It looked like something out of a bad movie. It wasn't real. It could not be real.

"Are you sure he was here? Maybe he came and went, and he's back at your apartment, recharging his phone. I'm sure that's it."

Rose's voice carried on, but Jackie could only stare at the indescribable pile of mangled rubble that had been Leo's mother's house. *His house*, when he wasn't at school.

He had left her bed yesterday morning after a call from his mom woke them. Jackie had tried to ignore the conversation, still clinging to the hope that it wasn't time to get up.

But as soon as the call ended, he leaned over and kissed

her, softly at first, but then more deeply, pulling her out of her sluggishness.

"I have to go." His words sounded hoarse, as if he were fighting a cold. "My mother says the furnace is making a funny noise, and she thinks she smells gas."

Jackie could feel his erection pressing against her thigh. She wanted to pull him down on top of her and lose herself in his passionate lovemaking and then fall asleep once more in his arms. Why was he catering to his mom on a Saturday morning?

She tried to tug him down. "She should call the furnace company or the gas company. It might be dangerous."

"You're right. But she always likes me there when strange repairmen come to the house. I've got to go."

He kissed her again, with an almost bruising intensity, and Jackie wrapped her arms around his neck. "Ten minutes. Then you can go."

He pulled back and turned, facing away from her, and sat on the edge of the bed, breathing hard.

"I've got to go now. I'm sorry. I love you."

He stood, picking up his jeans as he moved toward the bathroom. Jackie wrinkled her brows in frustration. He was seriously choosing a noisy furnace over sex?

A minute later he was heading for the door, not looking at her. But he turned just as his hand touched the doorknob.

"I am sorry," he whispered. "I love you."

"I love you, too," Jackie said to the closing door. She stretched and blew out her breath in a sigh. She didn't want to get up yet, but she was awake, and she knew from experience that she was unlikely to fall back asleep.

She made her own way to the bathroom and then came back, frowning at the mess around her. They had returned home late from an a cappella concert the night before and then cuddled together on the bed while Leo sang his own songs to her, strumming softly on the guitar.

The guitar had been carefully placed in the corner, but everything else in the room was tossed helter-skelter, including Jackie's clothes, their backpacks, and assorted sweatshirts.

A day and a half later, Leo still hadn't returned. Jackie texted first on Saturday afternoon and then in the evening— just a friendly *hope everything's ok*. There was no answer, but Jackie told herself not to worry. His mother could be intense at times.

By noon on Sunday, Jackie was chewing on her lip and compulsively checking her phone, unable to concentrate on her schoolwork. She and Leo texted constantly in the hours they weren't together, sharing comments about their classes, other students, the way the sunshine glittered on a puddle— everything. But now there was only silence.

Both rooms of the apartment were eerily empty, and an odd chill filled Jackie's center. By 4 p.m. she was pacing the hallway of their apartment suite, alternately peering out the peephole and rechecking her phone. She called Rose, her only close friend with a car, and begged for a ride to Leo's mother's house in Ruckersville, about a half-hour away from Charlottesville.

But all that was left was a mound of barely identifiable debris and the suffocating smell of things not meant to burn on a sunny weekend in March.

"The police said it was a gas explosion."

The voice was harsh and raspy, and Jackie turned to see an older woman standing there, a cigarette dangling from her fingers.

"We thought the whole place was being bombed. The boom just came out of nowhere, and all our houses shook."

"Did . . . was anyone . . . do you know if the people inside survived?"

"God, no. Not a chance. The fire trucks and cops were here for hours, but nobody came out of there alive, that's for sure."

"So Mrs. Jorgensson . . .?" She had to know, had to ask about Leo, but her throat was caught in a vice.

"Was that her name? Strange people, them. Standoffish. Never stopped to say hello, and those blinds were always shut tight. Like she thought she was too good for these parts. Her kid sometimes nodded or smiled when he passed by, but that was it."

"Leo?"

"That the boy? Mighty fine-looking young man, for all they acted like they was too good for us."

There was no air. Jackie couldn't see, couldn't hear, couldn't breathe. But this uncaring bitch was her only source of hope.

"He was here? Are you sure? Maybe he left."

"Nah." She shook her head. "I saw him drive up in that blue car of his at about 8:30. I was out on the stoop, grabbing a quick smoke. I'm not supposed to light up inside now that Andy's on oxygen. And the explosion couldn't have been more than twenty minutes later, cause I was getting eggs out of the refrigerator, and I ended up dropping the damn things on the floor. Right mess they made, too."

The ugly, unkempt woman made a snort of disgust, as if some broken eggs were a greater calamity than the death of a mother and son.

"You can kinda make out the wreckage of their cars in the back if you squint through all the dust."

"Do you know where they took them? Their bodies?" Her voice choked on the horrifying words.

Mrs. Obnoxious Busybody spat out her breath in a *'why*

should I care?' manner. "Who knows? The whole street was blocked for hours with police cars, fire trucks, and ambulances. Even the Dominos guy had trouble getting to our house with pizza, and that was after six."

Jackie turned away, unable to listen to another word from the heartless creature. She stared at the horror in front of her. Had they burned to death? Choked on smoke or gas? Or had her beautiful Leo been crushed by collapsing debris?

> *My love will never leave you.*
> *Hold me tight and say the same.*
> *I'll forever sing my song for you*
> *and cry that morning came.*

He had written those words just a few weeks ago and sung them to her again only Friday night. How could he now be dead?

The sight in front of her faded and was engulfed by black with only pinpricks of light. She was dimly aware of sharp objects cutting into her knees and Rose's voice calling her name, but all she could think was *Leo*. Her Leo was gone.

CHAPTER ONE

> "Come on. Say you'll go. You keep
> promising you'll go out with us and
> then you never do."

Jackie stared at Nadine's sixth insistent text of the afternoon. She had another hour of work, at least, and wanted to go home afterwards and curl up with a glass of wine and the book she was reading. Or maybe she'd watch one of the shows she had queued up and habitually ignored.

Multiple question marks appeared, and a minute later, colorful fireworks shot across her phone screen.

> COME OUT AND HAVE FUN WITH US!

The words screamed at her, and she caved. Maybe if she went out and pretended to have fun, Nadine would let up for a while.

They had come on board the company at the same time two years ago: Nadine recruited from a nation-wide grocery chain and Jackie from an online dating program she had worked hard to promote but never tried herself. Now their desks were a strong Skittles throw away from each other in a large suite on the third floor of Home Pantry's ever-burgeoning corporate headquarters.

But the company prided itself on keeping its workers happy, so all offices were encouraged to shoo employees out by 7 p.m. on Thursdays and 6 at the latest on Friday nights. Given that this was the early start of a holiday weekend, it seemed everyone in the building was eager to shut down their computers and hit the bars. Nadine loved Austin's dynamic nightlife and ceaselessly badgered Jackie into joining her.

She'd go out tonight, dredge up her acting skills, and then maybe Nadine would give her a pass for a few weeks.

CHAPTER TWO

"I think that'll do it."

"Holy fuck, Jake. Thank you. Even a few minutes more without connection, and I'd have had to close down for the night. There's no way a 'cash only' system could've kept up. Can you hear the hordes down there already?"

The whole neighborhood could no doubt hear the noise downstairs. Texas Tango was one of Austin's hottest watering holes, and the Thursday night crowd was making its pleasure known.

"No problem," he said, smiling at the look of utter relief on Danny's face.

As someone who avoided crowds and parties with near religious doggedness, Jake had been amazed by Austin's dedication to fun. Since he had arrived in the city seven years ago, neither horrific heat waves, record-breaking ice storms, nor a pandemic had succeeded in tamping down the city's indefatigable spirit.

Not a place he'd voluntarily choose to visit on a busy night, Texas Tango was his landlord's son's baby, so when Danny's frantic text had arrived just before six saying the bar's computers were down, he had rolled his eyes and headed over. He still had work he wanted to get done, but his IT position at Home Pantry allowed him maximum flexibility since much of his work could be done from his laptop or the elaborate computer set-up in the apartment he rented from Danny's father.

It had taken him a little over an hour to find the bug, sweep Tango's systems, install new malware protection, and reboot, allowing the restaurant/bar/dance hall to once again process credit cards.

"Seriously, man. I really owe you. You'll stay, right? The place is hopping, and anything you want to eat or drink is on the house."

"Thanks, but I've got to get going."

"It's only 8:30. The party's just getting started down there."

"Yeah, I know. But I have work to do at home."

Danny looked at him as if studying an unknown specimen in a zoo.

"No wonder my dad loves having you live upstairs. When that young couple lived there before you, he hated them coming and going at all hours, and then he really hated it when their baby came along. He's happy as a clam with you there, and I'm happy cause I don't have to keep running over there every time his cable goes out or he forgets his Netflix password. And now you saved my ass once again tonight."

He clapped a hand on Jake's shoulder, and Jake forced himself not to freeze up.

"My pleasure," he said. He moved to pick up his backpack from the corner of the small office where he had dropped it when he arrived. At the time he had been aware of music playing below. Now the whole floor vibrated with the sounds of heavy rhythms and the raised voices of probably over a hundred people.

"Come on, Jake. At least have something to drink. We've got almost every beer you can name, and our margaritas are excellent, even if I do say so myself. And, of course, our barbecued ribs are the best in the state, which pretty much means the best in the world."

Jake smiled and shook his head.

"Thanks. I'm not much of a party animal. And I had some food before I left the office."

Danny shrugged. "Whatever you say. Maybe you want something to go?"

"Nope. I'm good, thanks. I'll use the restroom on my way out and be home early enough to not wake your dad. Take care."

He made his way downstairs, Danny right behind him. They emerged into a hallway from a door marked 'private,' which Danny locked once they were through. The hallway was a decent size, with light fixtures shaped like sombreros hanging from above and doors marked 'Señor' and 'Señorita' on either side.

With a final "Thanks again, man," Danny moved towards the crowd and Jake headed into the men's room, grateful there was no line as there was for the women's restroom. He was surprised Danny hadn't followed the rest of the city in converting them both to unisex bathrooms, but as long as he didn't have to stand in line, he was happy.

Coming out, his entire body froze in shock.

She was standing there. Right there, in line for the bathroom.

Move, he said to himself. *Put your head down and move.*

"Hey, Jake, is that you?"

He ignored the friendly greeting and turned in the opposite direction, heading towards the bedlam on the main floor instead of the door beyond the restrooms he could have used. It said 'Emergency Exit,' but this was not the first house

5

call he had made to Texas Tango, and he knew the bouncer kept an eye on the exit's camera but only came back there if someone seemed to be skipping out on their tab.

Far better to deal with the crowd than risk meeting her eyes.

He had seen the name Jacqueline Bourne on the staff list. Seen it, stopped breathing, and then convinced himself that there were probably hundreds of Jacqueline Bournes in the world, just like there were likely a thousand people with the name Jake Carpentero. He had resisted the temptation to check her out, find out if it could possibly be the same Jackie. *His Jackie,* who could never again be his Jackie. The unlikelihood was too great, and he was a man who didn't believe in happy coincidences or second chances.

Yet despite his absolute certainty that the Jacqueline Bourne who worked in marketing at Home Pantry—he had checked that much and no further—was not the same Jackie he had known, the woman standing outside the bathroom was unmistakable, and she was with a Home Pantry employee he did know.

His one abbreviated glance had recognized Nadine Perrera but zeroed in on the tall, beautiful woman standing next to her. Somehow, in that one quick glance, his eyes had noticed the wavy light brown hair worn just below her shoulders and the tiny, port-wine stain birthmark high on her left cheekbone. The woman in line had been holding her hair up, off her neck, obviously fighting the heat, while she chatted in line with her friend. That spot was unique—a blemish on an otherwise near perfect complexion that had always made his Jackie self-conscious.

He had found it both distinctive and beautiful and had often started his kisses there, telling her it was his spot to claim as his own, especially as she usually went out of her way to cover it with her hair. Of course he hadn't known the term 'port-wine stain,' or even the word birthmark, but he was adept at hiding what he didn't know. That he most definitely had not known the words in Swedish was one of the far too many secrets he had had to keep from her.

That same Jackie, the girl he had loved so deeply, and whose heart he knew he had broken, was standing in line for a bathroom in Austin, Texas. Why was the East Coast English major, whose dream had been to publish the books she had already written and to spend her life writing more, living in Austin and working as a high-level marketing manager for a global food delivery service?

His Jackie. When he had first seen her name, and noted its departmental identification, he had been relieved. It was definitely a different person. The Jackie he had known and loved would not be spending her life working for the pseudo-beneficent monopoly on its path towards international dominance.

But this woman—who could most definitely not be *his* Jackie but who somehow was, all the same—was standing in line with Nadine Perrera, someone he knew for certain was in marketing at Home Pantry. He had recloned her laptop only a month ago.

Fuck, fuck, fuck, fuck, fuck. He pushed his way through the swarms of dancing and laughing young people, desperate to reach the front doors. Outside was almost as bad, the outdoor seating area and barbecue grills taking up half the block, with groups of hot, sweating people waiting in line to join the mayhem.

He had to get home, had to think. Had Jackie seen him? Was there any chance at all she might recognize him? He didn't think so. He was vigilant about dyeing his hair and eyebrows and always shaved carefully so that no lighter than expected facial hair might attract notice. The surgery to his nose and cheekbones had been aggravating and painful, and he was still occasionally surprised by the image he saw in the mirror each morning. But until tonight he had been confident no one from his past would ever put him together with the young man who had attended college in Virginia.

Would the two women discuss seeing him? He had met with Nadine at a coffee shop during a particularly infectious week of the lockdown when they were both working from home. She gave him her company laptop, he gave her a loaner iPad, and they had chatted for a few minutes. The next week she came up to his fourth-floor office to pick up her laptop, and they chatted again. Or more accurately, she had been friendly and outgoing, saying he should join her and other young singles from the company when they went to happy hours and the like. Jake had nodded politely and kept his eyes on his own multiple screens, offering inconsequential "uh-huhs" and "maybes" when the conversation required them.

"I'll add you to the group chat if you'd like. Give me your phone and we can get each other's contacts," she effused, holding out her own phone. At that point Jake had been forced to pull out one of his carefully constructed asshole personas.

"Thanks, but my girlfriend gets jealous real easily."

"Oh, she can come along! Lots of us bring significant others."

"Yeah, but she thinks my work is too all-consuming as it is. Thanks anyway."

Somehow, despite his best intentions, he had eventually caved to her unwavering warmth and enthusiasm, reluctantly putting his number into her phone. He could, and probably would, ignore any invites, so what was the harm?

They had ridden in an elevator together one time after that, and she had, again, been bubbly and friendly, even asking after his imaginary girlfriend and giving a happy wave when she got out.

What would Nadine say about him to Jackie? How likely was it that Jackie had seen him? He had turned away instantly, and now he wished with every fiber of his being that he could be a fly on one of those stupid sombrero lamps, just staring at her and drinking her in.

His bike was locked to a stand on the next block, and as he walked the perennially bright street, the thudding of his heart overtook the receding noise from Texas Tango.

Jackie was here. Here in Austin. *He had to go*. Had to leave quickly. If she recognized him, realized he was alive and tried to make contact, his cover could be blown, and her life could be in danger.

Her life.

He couldn't risk that. Couldn't risk her. Knowing she might be in danger had been *the* deciding factor in persuading him to go along with the plan his mother and their handler had concocted nine years ago. A plan he had hated from the get-go.

But oh God, she was so beautiful. Still so achingly beautiful, and seeing her, the memories of all they had been to each other swept over him like an avalanche. He wanted to hold her tightly in his arms and never let her go, to kiss that sweet, purple mark and sing to her. Music and lyrics had poured out of him while they were together, but after that fateful day, he had never cared enough to buy a new guitar. He knew the words to the Don McLean song, but for him, the music had died the morning he left Jackie.

He rode his bike, the side streets eventually leading him away from the worst of downtown to a more civilized area where single family homes were interspersed with small apartment buildings and free-standing cafes, bakeries, and ice cream shops. During one of his extremely infrequent conversations with his mother, he had joked that there were probably as many places to get ice cream in Austin as there had been in her own hometown. She laughed and told him to think of her the next time he indulged. She would be consumed with worry if she thought his cover had slipped.

He reached the adobe style house where Danny's father now lived alone except for Jake. The second story had been converted into a small apartment with an outside staircase at the side of the house leading to a separate entrance. It suited Jake's needs perfectly. Mr. Riga was pleasant but not talkative, bothering Jake only occasionally with minor issues. Two weeks after Jake had moved in, the landlord had knocked on the door and apologized with obvious embarrassment before holding out a pill bottle.

"There was somebody new at the pharmacy, and they put one of these damn tops on the bottle that no one can open. As if we had little kids crawling around at our age. The regular pharmacist knows better."

Jake had opened the bottle easily, but Mr. Riga's eyes had gone wide staring at the array of computers on Jake's two desks.

"You must know a lot about all this stuff," had been his apt assessment. "Maybe sometime when you have a minute, could you look at my computer? I can't find any of the instructions I thought I saved about paying my damn bills. I got a call the other day saying our account was overdue. It was probably a scam, but I can't remember where to look to check if I paid or not."

Jake had gone down then and there, helped the old man find his online files, and printed out a sheet with some simple instructions and his own cell phone number in bold.

"Just call me if you need anything. It's no problem."

After that their hellos had been a lot more friendly, and Jake didn't mind the visits to his landlord's apartment. Mr.

Riga was always grateful and never pestered him with personal questions. Mrs. Riga, while she lived, had tried to fuss over him, but she hadn't seemed to mind when Jake declined her sporadic invitations to eat with them. Jake had no clear memories of his own father, but he hoped that if his mother ever needed help, there would be a friendly person nearby she could trust.

After Mrs. Riga's death, Jake made an effort to check in with his landlord more frequently. He liked the man and felt kinship with his solitary existence.

Now his eyes darted around his small, orderly living quarters. It would take several hours to wipe his desktop and work laptop, and he could then get his essential personal belongings packed into a few bags and be on the road before dawn.

Fucking A. He forced himself to stop for a moment and try to assess the situation logically. The fight or flight instinct had been hammered into him the way other children learned their ABCs. But at this moment, was he being practical or irrational?

There was *probably* no need to run off like a startled cockroach. She most likely hadn't even seen him, could not possibly have recognized him, and . . . He stared sightlessly around the apartment, his thoughts vacillating like a ping pong ball.

Should he run? Was it safe to stay? Would he be putting her in danger by staying?

She couldn't have recognized him. He kept repeating the words to himself. But he had been absolutely certain that the Jacqueline Bourne working in marketing was not his Jackie.

He hissed. She was *not* his Jackie. He had to stop thinking of her as his. He had given up any claim to her when he had abandoned her so ruthlessly and most likely broken her heart.

11

Get your shit together, he admonished himself. *Just try to think rationally for a minute.*

He sat down on the edge of his bed, the back of his bent head cradled between his clasped hands.

Think it through! Even if she had seen him, he was not the fair-haired young man she had known. Nadine had called his name: *Jake.* Jake Carpentero was an Hispanic-American computer specialist with dark hair and firmly sculpted muscles. He had grown up in Texas but spoke Spanish fluently. He had excellent work evaluations, lived a quiet life, and was liked by his landlord. Absolutely nothing in that description could be linked to a Swedish-American boy from Virginia.

If he ran, there would be questions. Valued, responsible employees didn't just drive away in the dead of night. If he needed to leave, he had to plan it out strategically in a way that made sense to a casual observer.

He felt a momentary pang for the hole his absence would leave in his landlord's life. His son would have to step up and do more. It had been a mistake to allow such a close relationship; Jake was never meant to be important to anyone.

He raised his head and blew out a long, exhausted breath. What would a real Jake Carpentero do?

Jake Carpentero would need to begin a reasonable job search. He needed to find a position that matched his qualifications in a city far from Austin. Once he found one, he would invent personal reasons for needing to move. It wouldn't be hard, and he would do it in a way that would raise no red flags.

He stared at his meager possessions. Nothing of sentimental value, and only the computers had any real monetary value. He was a two-dimensional figure all-around. The only uniquely personal thing about him was the tiny foolish tattoo he had drunkenly chosen on the fifth anniversary of his "death." He rarely drank, but that night, alone in a town half a country away from the only woman he had ever loved, he had let his discipline slip. Too many tequila shots, followed by shots of vodka when his caution had yielded to his buzz, and he began a self-pitying whine-athon with the artistically-inked bartender.

When the helpful gentleman told him that his friend's tattoo parlor was less than a block away, Jake had pushed himself off the stool and swayed down the street. "Ace" had been closing up, but at Jake's pathetic supplication, he glanced at the drawing Jake had made on a cocktail napkin and shook his head in pitying acquiescence.

"I'm only doing this as a favor for Dave and because I'm intrigued by your idea. That and the fact that it won't take too long."

Thank God he had retained enough sense to make sure the tattoo was where no one would ever see it.

A horrible longing crept up his insides, and he felt tears come to his eyes, much as they had on that long ago night. He had resolved the morning after to put her out of his mind, to focus only on the life he was now living, but seeing her tonight broke down the barriers he had struggled to keep erect.

Jackie had been everything to him. But he needed to remember what was truly important. Because of what he had done—what he allowed to be done to him—she was alive and had built a new life for herself.

He was alive, too, but the hard truth he ruthlessly ignored had slipped its leash tonight and was now staring him in the face. He was alive, but his life was empty. Why the fuck had he even bothered to escape the gas explosion?

A knock at his door crashed through his misery. He squeezed his eyes shut, and his arms rose instinctively to cover his head and block out the sound, but the knocking continued. *Jesus Christ.* As much as he cared for the dear man, he didn't know if he had it in him to handle his lonely landlord again tonight.

"Jake? Jake? Danny just called. He said you dropped your phone on the way out of his office."

He glanced towards his backpack, confused. The outside zipper compartment where he always stuffed his phone was only partially closed.

Goddamn fucking hell. The night had just gone from bad to worse.

CHAPTER THREE

"I'm sure that's Jake. We need to go after him and get him to join us."

Jackie raised her eyebrows at Nadine.

"I'm not going anywhere. I've already been standing here ten minutes just waiting to pee. If you want to go chase after some guy, you go ahead."

"He's not just some guy. He's Jake, from work."

"Is that like Jake, from the TV commercial?"

"No! He's one of the tech wizards at work. You know—those guys on the 4th floor who make all the magic happen."

Jackie's eyebrows went up again.

"Magic? Has he cast a spell on you?"

"Oh, for heaven's sake, Jackie. Pretend you're a normal person for a change, instead of a 50-year-old librarian! He's a nice guy, and he knows a lot about computers. He had to do something or other with my work laptop, but then when I went to pick it up, he helped me with my phone, and I put him in our group chat—you know, the one I keep trying to make you part of, but you won't, cause you're such a stuck-up pain in the ass. And besides, he's cute."

"I'm a stuck-up pain in the ass?"

Nadine obviously recognized the hurt in Jackie's voice, even above the brain-numbing noise of the restaurant. She pulled Jackie in for a quick hug and gave her a reassuring smile accompanied by a resigned shake of the head as she released her.

"Of course not, dummy. You just don't know how to relax and have fun."

Jackie returned the smile with its own degree of resignation.

"I'm here, aren't I?"

"Yes, but if we have to wait much longer for this bathroom, you're going to be telling me it's time to leave. Anyway, back to Jake. He seems like a nice guy, but I think he's lonely. He said he has a girlfriend, but I'm not convinced. He was with Danny, just now, so I'll ask him."

"Who's Danny? And do you know everyone in this building?"

Nadine laughed.

"Not yet, but the night's young! Danny's the owner of Texas Tango."

"What's Texas Tango again?"

"Oh my God! You're impossible. We are *in* Texas Tango!"

Jackie made an embarrassed grimace.

"I knew that. Sorry. It's just so loud, and there are so many people."

"Which is why we come here! Oh, thank God." The last words came as two women moved out of the door marked 'Señorita.'

They pushed their way in, and the noise level subsided slightly as the door closed behind them.

"Why does a place this big have such a tiny bathroom with only two stalls?"

"Remind me to ask Danny when I go to try to find Jake."

Jackie laughed. She'd rather be home, but Nadine truly was a force of nature unto herself.

An hour later she checked her phone for the umpteenth time. How soon could she attempt her first 'I'm going to head out' without Nadine telling her it was too early?

They were crowded in an area halfway between the bar and the band amidst a large group of young people from Home Pantry. Empty margarita and beer pitchers, empty glasses, and mostly empty plates covered the small high tables.

"Who's gonna come with me to the bar to get refills?" Nadine yelled above the noise. "It might take hours for a waitress or waiter to get back to us."

One of the young women from purchasing volunteered, and they gathered up handfuls of empties and took off. Jackie plastered a small 'I'm happy to be here' smile on her face and pretended to gaze with interest at the crowds of people. A few were dancing, some were singing, many were drinking thirstily, and Jackie felt like an alien sent down to observe the human race.

What the hell was she doing with her life? She didn't want to be here, but she didn't particularly want to be anywhere else, either. Except maybe home with a book, and what kind of life was that?

She loved reading and had once wanted nothing more than to scribble her own stories to share with the world. But the urge to put personal ideas down on paper had shriveled up all those years ago. Now she kept her mind safely relegated to the cozy world of historical mysteries and romances. Pain suffered on the foggy streets of London or on battlefields where brave young men fought Napoleon was sufficiently remote to leave her interested but uninvolved.

"Come dance."

Jackie's eyes widened. What was his name? *Shit.* He worked on the same floor, in the same giant web of cubbies and cubicles. Mike? Miguel? Manny? Manny, that was it. He had asked her about joining him for lunch a few times, and she had always demurred politely. But she really didn't feel like dancing.

"Come on." His tone friendly, he reached down and grabbed her hand, pulling her away from the table she had been guarding and further into the crowd of gyrating bodies.

She could do this. She was a big girl. One dance, and then she'd find Nadine and escape.

She tried. Sorta. Moved her legs and hips. A little bit. Looked up at Manny and smiled. A fake smile that made her cheeks feel weird. He apparently didn't notice and reached to gently pull her hips toward him. She resisted, keeping the false smile on her face. He pulled a little more, and she stepped back forcefully and tread directly on another woman's foot.

"Hey, watch it," the young woman huffed, giving Jackie the stink eye.

"Sorry," Jackie mumbled, and the woman rolled her eyes.

"I'm really thirsty. I'm going to go see if I can help Nadine with those beers," she yelled at Manny, who was still moving his shoulders, arms, and even his head in enthusiastic rhythm to the music.

He shrugged and nodded, seemingly unhurt by her desertion—or maybe he was just eager for more beer himself.

Jackie looked around, eyes wide and her breathing now uneven. She'd had enough. She spotted Nadine and whatever-her-name-was from purchasing over by the bar, talking to two men. Maybe that was Danny and the mysterious Jake, not from the TV commercial. They were both good looking male specimens, but she had done her duty.

As she maneuvered her way to say goodnight to Nadine, hoping her friend would let her go without a fight, Jackie remembered the spring of her freshman year at college. She'd had a job at the library and worked the 7-10 shift at the desk three or four nights a week. Like now, the last hour of every shift had seemed endless, her eyes moving over and over to the large wall clock, waiting for the moment she could walk out the door.

All that had changed when she met Leo. It had begun gradually, her eyes following his handsome frame when he walked by the checkout counter, his backpack on his shoulder and a coffee cup in his hand. Their eyes would meet, and at first they just exchanged shy smiles. Then he started to say hello, and one day he stopped with a book, saying there was an error message when he tried to check it out.

Part of the barcode sticker had come off, so once she manually checked the title and entered the code properly, she handed it to him, along with his I.D.

"Now you know my name, so it's only fair you tell me yours." He smiled at her, and the skin around his blue-gray eyes had crinkled, and she'd been gone. Utterly gone.

After a while he'd taken to studying on a stool next to hers behind the desk, and after that she hadn't cared how long a shift lasted.

Now, feeling decades older, she was back to waiting for her shift to end. So much for growing up. She was as miserable and as desperate now to get out of where she didn't want to be as she had been as a lonely freshman. But she was leaving, no matter what cheerleader enthusiasm Nadine might throw her way.

She was close enough for Nadine to hear her, or at least she hoped so. "I'm heading out. It was really great." *Keep your voice loud enough to be heard but keep the tone peppy and self-assured.*

"No! You can't go yet."

Nadine shook her head vehemently at Jackie while putting her hand on the arm of the guy they had seen by the bathrooms. He must be Jake, the tech phenom Nadine couldn't stop talking about. She said something Jackie couldn't hear and moved towards her. Jackie noticed the friendly bearded face of the one who must be Danny. He smiled at her before turning to a group of people to his right. She saw Jake glance her way before he quickly turned around completely to face the bar.

The noise was raucous, lively, and upbeat, so Jackie saw the blood spurting from the man next to Danny before she registered the sounds that didn't fit. But those sounds continued—not musical, not conversational—but a rapid *pk, pk, pk,* interspersed with screams and chaos.

She would later remember the look of horror on Nadine's face and the jolt to the back of her own head against an arm, and most oddly, a wristwatch, as she was thrown to the ground, a man's body on top of her.

"Jackie. My God, Jackie, are you all right?"

She stared into the brown eyes of the man crying out to her. Who was he? Why did his voice sound familiar? Pain burned through her left arm, pinned to her side between the floor and this stranger's chest.

"Jackie, please. You've got to be all right."

Her eyes had closed, but they opened again, confused. What was happening? How could it be Leo's voice speaking to her from this unknown man? She tried to focus. There was so much noise, and he was bleeding, or she was bleeding, or everyone was bleeding. The eyes gazing so ferociously into her own were brown, but they shouldn't be. Leo's eyes were blue.

More pain: sudden, blindingly fierce, exploding in her head. She couldn't open her eyes, felt nothing but pain, but knew joy, nonetheless. She had seen Leo's crinkled skin surrounding her unknown savior's brown eyes. He had come for her. Her Leo had come back for her.

CHAPTER FOUR

S am checked his watch. The plane should land in less than a half hour. Jake hadn't responded to any of his attempts to reach him, and the "medics" Sam had sent to the hospital hadn't reported back yet. It was lucky that technology had evolved to the point where he could track Jake's whereabouts even without his active response.

He glared at the notification on his screen. For the fourth time in as many months alerts had come in about messages that mentioned finding the "Man and the boy" or "the Lady and the boy."

What had happened to Jake tonight, and was there any connection between it and these bizarre alerts? How in the world, after so many years, could anyone out there still be looking for him? No official intelligence reports showed any interest whatsoever from the top. If it was the guy in charge trying to hunt down an old nemesis or the offspring of him or one of his cronies, he was doing a good job of delegating far outside the normal rank-and-file apparatchiks and hiding it from the Americans' normal surveillance methods.

He checked his phone again, even though he would have

caught any ring or vibration. God, he hoped Jake was okay. The kid had gone through so much already. Sam would do all he could to get him back on his feet once more, assuming he was still alive. He sent a silent prayer to the universe and vowed that if the poor guy lived, he'd make sure this time to obliterate any trace Jake had ever survived.

CHAPTER FIVE

"Austin police continue to comb the wreckage left behind in the wake of the horrific downtown shooting last night at the Texas Tango nightclub."

"Turn the volume down. I don't want that to be the first thing she hears when she wakes up."

Was that her mother? What was her mother doing here in Austin?

"Mom?" Her voice was raspy, and she had to blink a few times to make her eyes focus properly.

"Oh, sweetheart. Thank God. You're awake."

"What are you doing here?"

"You got shot, honey. The hospital called when they found our number in your phone. But you're going to be fine. Everything's going to be all right."

Jackie tried to think, tried to remember. *"You've got to be all right."* Someone else had said those words. The bar, the music, the noise, the shots—it all came back to her in odd flashes, like one of those Cubist paintings she had never learned to appreciate.

"What are you doing here?" Wait, had she just asked that?

The scent of her mother's perfume wrapped her in a blanket of comfort, and the cool touch of fingers pushing hair back from her forehead made Jackie turn towards that beloved hand.

"It's all going to be okay, sweetheart. It's all going to be fine."

She opened her eyes again, confused. Was her mother here, or had that been a dream?

"Mom?" Again, her voice sounded raspy, but this time her dad's face appeared in front of her.

"Hey, sleepy head. Your mom just went down for coffee."

"What are you doing here?" But it all started coming back to her again just as he began to speak.

"I keep telling you girls to be more careful with your phones and your private information, but in this case, your silliness paid off. The police said they always try 1-2-3-4 to open up phones because, lo and behold, it often works. They called us last night about midnight, and we were able to fly in this morning. We're just so grateful you're alive and are going to be fine."

"What happened?"

Her dad scrunched up his face, and she could tell he was trying to work out what to say. He seemed to have used up all his energy in that last burst of information.

"Whatever I say, your mom will tell me I said the wrong thing."

Jackie's lips moved into a tired smile as his words confirmed her suspicions.

"It's okay, Dad. I won't rat you out. I need to know."

Her father shook his head. They all tended towards the liberal end of politics, and she'd heard his diatribes about the need for stricter gun controls countless times growing up.

"Some idiot waltzed into the nightclub you were at and started shooting his semi-automatic. We worry about you girls all the time, but I never expected you would be out at a place like that on a Thursday night." His voice broke, and he looked away.

It all came roaring back to her: the noise, the blood, the pain, and that man.

"It's not a bad place, Dad. But you're right—it's not where you'd normally find me on a work night."

She stopped and focused briefly on trying to make her breath go in and out at something close to a normal rate. It hurt—taking a stupid breath hurt, but she had to understand. She wanted to grab hold of him, to demand answers, to ask if her Leo had been found alive. But even in her drug-induced stupor, she knew she could do none of those things. If she wanted answers, she couldn't let them think her brain was addled.

"Dad, do you know what happened to the people I was with? The guy who saved me?" *Leo,* her mind was screaming, but she wouldn't say something so obviously wrong out loud.

"Not really. But we have no idea who you were with. We've heard there were over a hundred people there alto-gether. We do know you were one of the 'lucky' ones." His fingers made quotation marks in the air. "Your left arm was hit near your wrist by a bullet, but they think you'll get full use back fairly quickly. Then you were apparently hit from falling debris which cut into your temple and left you mildly concussed. Or you were concussed from hitting the ground. Whatever it was, they put about 10 stitches in your head."

Jackie's right hand moved to her head at his words, and she felt the pull of an IV needle in her arm. Sure enough, there was a bandage on the left side of her forehead that went back to where hair should be. An irrational panic surged through her, and she went to move both hands up and over her head, wanting to make sure all her hair wasn't gone, but her left hand and most of her forearm were encased in a thick, firm bandage.

Of course. He had just said she had been shot in the wrist. She remembered the pain that had burned through her fingers and arm.

Leo had knocked her down, protecting her body with his own. He had shielded her and spoken to her. But Leo was dead. He had died more than nine years ago.

Her dad was still speaking, and Jackie realized he was crying.

"So many people. You could have been killed."

"It's okay, Dad. I'm fine. Really. I'll be fine."

She wasn't fine. She felt heavy everywhere and wanted badly to close her eyes. But her dad looked so old and defeated.

"I'm sorry they had to call you. It must have been terrifying."

He took in a deep breath and visibly pulled himself together.

"You don't need to worry about us. You have to rest and heal. That's all that matters. It's been too long since we've seen you, anyway."

"I was home at Christmas."

She was so tired. Her dad was saying something about only seeing her at holidays not being enough, but she had to close her eyes for a minute.

He had called her Jackie. It had been his voice. She could still hear him singing to her, his blue-gray eyes moving from her to the guitar strings and back again. His voice smooth and clear—not too deep, but perfect.

My love will never leave you. Hold me tight and say the same.

He had sung to her, always to her, whether next to her on their bed or from a stage looking out into a crowded student auditorium. She would know his voice anywhere. But Leo's eyes were blue-gray, and the man who had saved her had brown eyes. How had Leo's eyes changed color?

WHEN SHE OPENED her eyes again, Nadine was standing talking to her mother.

"Hey."

At her croak, both women turned.

"Oh sweet Jesus, Jackie. I am so sorry. The one night I finally talk you into going out with us."

"Don't worry about it. I won't hold the date against you."

Nadine looked different, and it took Jackie a moment to figure out what was off. Her normally colorful attire and lavish make-up were missing. Today her face looked pale and tired, she was dressed in jeans and a UT sweatshirt, and her lustrous black mane was pulled back into a simple ponytail.

"Are you okay? You weren't hit?" Her throat hurt as she spoke, and she wondered if a tube had been in her at some point.

"I'm fine." Nadine gave a shaky laugh. "I guess the St. Christopher medal my godmother insists I wear paid off." Her hand went to the chain that hung midway down her chest. Even toned down, her outfit included bracelets that moved on her arm as she gestured, and her fingers sought out the one medallion among several others adorning the necklace.

"What about everybody else?"

Nadine's eyes looked away before coming back to meet Jackie's. "It was . . ." She stopped and took a few breaths.

"A lot of people were shot." She stopped again, obviously struggling with what to say.

"I think they're saying now that eight people died. And

Danny . . ." Her voice broke. "Danny is one of them. And Gloria."

Jackie could see Nadine's pain, and she forced herself to try and remember. The smiling man with the beard. The bar owner. The man who had been standing next to Leo, who had saved her, who couldn't be Leo because Leo was dead and looked nothing like that man. And who was Gloria?

"Gloria?" she asked softly.

"From purchasing. She came to the bar with me to get refills. She was only twenty-seven, and her fiancé was on his way to meet us there, and it's my fault she's dead."

Jackie heard it all again: the noise, the screams, the shots. And then that jolt of being pushed back and down, away from the exploding chaos at the bar. She closed her eyes and fought to keep her breathing quiet and minimize the pounding in her head.

"The guy who helped me—do you know what happened to him?"

"That was Jake, remember?" Nadine's voice was thick with emotion. "I thought you said you didn't know him, but he definitely acted like he knew you. I think he's dead, too." Her voice broke and she turned away, fumbling in her pocket.

"Here, sweetheart." Jackie's mother held the small hospital tissue box out to Nadine. Jackie saw, as if from afar, her friend blowing her nose. But time had somehow slowed down, an icy chill was creeping up her body, and the words Nadine continued to speak seemed to come from far away.

"There were two of them. At least that's what they're saying. One came in and started shooting at everyone close to the bar, while the other one sprayed the people outside. They're saying it was a miracle more people aren't dead. But three people I know are, and you're here, and a bunch of people I kind of know are in other beds in other rooms."

29

As though trying to see through a dense fog, Jackie saw Nadine's tears become more intense, and Jackie's mom took her in her arms. Nadine let herself be held for a few minutes and then struggled to pull herself together.

"I'm just really glad you're going to be okay, and I'm so sorry I let this happen to you."

A truck was sitting on her chest, but Jackie forced herself to focus on her friend and reassure her. "It wasn't your fault. None of it was your fault. But that guy, Jake." She tried to breathe normally, tried to make her question seem reasonable. "He died? Are you sure?"

"I think so." Nadine was wiping her eyes. "It's hard to get exact information. Everything happened so fast, and I couldn't see who was where. There was broken glass everywhere, and so much blood . . ." Her voice broke off, and Jackie's mother reached out again to hold the now sobbing young woman.

Maybe it had all been her imagination. Maybe she had been close to death, and her brain had played tricks on her, creating links to the familiar in the midst of chaos. Or maybe she had been so close to death that Leo's ghost had come for her.

She looked away from Nadine, now once again blowing her nose and wiping away tears, and felt tears roll down her own cheeks.

Leo was dead. He hadn't been there at the bar, and if his ghost had come for her, she had missed the chance to reunite with him by living. She squeezed her eyes shut, trying to contain the storm of emotions. She was alive. Her best friend was alive, her parents were with her, and she would get up soon and walk out of the hospital. She *was* lucky, her father's air quotes notwithstanding.

But by surviving, she had lost him again. Would he continue to wait for her? His song had promised that his love would never leave her, but *he* had left her. *Damn him.* Damn him forever for doing this to her. Again.

Nadine seemed to have her distress under control, at least for the moment, and she gave Jackie a watery smile.

"Your mom told me they say you're going to be fine. I'm so glad." She inhaled forcefully a few times and then spoke with an attempt at lightness.

"So you and Jake did know each other, after all? It was kind of weird how in the middle of all that craziness, he dove straight for you when the shooting started. You acted like you didn't know him when we saw him and Danny near the bathroom." Her voice choked up and she looked away for a few seconds.

When she resumed speaking, it was obvious that tears were still winning. "He told me when I picked up my laptop that he had a girlfriend. Please tell me that wasn't you. If you two had a secret thing going on, and I ruined that as well . . ."

Jackie's mom took the crying girl into her arms once more, giving Jackie a puzzled look.

"Did you have a boyfriend, honey?"

Jackie looked down and absently noticed a tingling sensation in her right hand. Her fingers had balled a section of the sheet up and were holding it tightly, no doubt interfering somehow with the steady operation of the I.V. Why had a perfect stranger tried to protect her? Had Leo's ghost inhabited Jake's body before he was killed? If Nadine had seen him move to help her, it couldn't just be Jackie's imagination. She tried to force her fingers to relax, but they squeezed even more tightly as thoughts darted through her mind. *What if Leo had really been there, but now was dead again?* She shook her head and became aware of throbbing pain everywhere: her head, both her arms, and her entire body.

"No. No," she whispered, unable to understand everything that had happened and the crazy thoughts that kept reverberating through her mind. Her head continued to move back and forth of its own accord, trying to negate all the confusion and horror.

"It's okay, sweetie. Don't get upset. You need to rest and let your body heal."

Her mother's gentle voice reached her, but from far away. She closed her overwhelmingly heavy eyelids. If Leo hadn't died all those years ago, she never would have been at that bar last night. *Why had he left her behind?*

CHAPTER SIX

Jackie was released late the next morning. She had instructions to see the hand surgeon the following week when she would receive a plaster cast that would stay on for a month or so. She was advised to stay moderately active, but not to spend much time in front of a screen for several weeks—concussion protocol to allow her brain to heal.

"You guys should go home. I'll be fine. Really."

Her parents had both insisted they wanted to stay, but by the second day of watching them try to perch nonchalantly in her studio apartment, she knew she had to put her foot down.

"You can't leave the dog with the neighbors any longer. You know he's got to be driving them crazy."

She saw the guilty look they exchanged and pounced.

"He is, isn't he? I'm fine. Home Pantry's giving me all the time I need, and I have lots of friends I can call if I need help with anything. But who are the Johnsons going to call to help them with Smokey? You know he's probably not eating or sleeping."

The family dog had always been anxious, but at thirteen, his distress was palpable when his routine was upset.

"I can't lose him, too. Not right now. Go home and take care of him, so I'll be able to play with him at Christmas."

"Why don't you come with us and rest at home for a few weeks? We can get the name of a hand doctor in our area, and you won't have to struggle on your own."

Her father's voice was persuasive, and Jackie realized immediately that they had been waiting to try this tactic on her.

"Thank you. But I'm fine. I've got everything I need right in the neighborhood, and I like it here." She didn't want to tell them that she was determined to learn more about the mysterious Jake and had been anxious for them to leave for that very reason.

"But honey, at home you don't have to worry about food or laundry, and you know Smokey would be in heaven."

"I know, Mom. But I'd have to get a jacket on over this." She held up her thickly bandaged arm. "I probably won't need a jacket here for months."

Her mother made an inarticulate noise and pursed her lips. "You don't have to prove anything to us. We know you're a grown-up. But that doesn't mean you have to deal with this all by yourself. You went through so much last time."

Last time. The last time death had touched her so intimately. Her parents had been supportive and loving when Leo died, but they hadn't known him well, and she had never shared just how very close she and Leo had been.

Jackie moved to the sink in her tiny kitchen and busied herself washing the teacup she had just used.

"You're proving my point, darling. You don't need to be by yourself, struggling to wash dishes with one hand."

Damn. She had just been trying to avoid looking at them.

She turned. They were trying to help, and she loved them for it, but they couldn't help her figure out what had really happened Thursday night. And if they knew her thoughts, they'd definitely think she was crazy and try even harder to take her with them.

"I love you both so much, and you were so wonderful to jump on a plane and fly out here the way you did. But I'll be fine. The sooner I get back to a routine, the quicker things will seem normal again. I've got everything I need here and good friends. And this kind of thing is part of life now, as horrible as that reality is. It can happen as easily in Virginia as it did here."

She didn't have much of a life here, and not that many good friends, but all that was her own fault and would probably be true anywhere. Her definition of life had changed nine years ago. Her parents needed to believe she was okay. That was all that mattered.

She pushed to make the reassuring smile reach her eyes.

"Mom, you saw what a mess Nadine is. I need to be here for her. I got hurt physically, but she might be more messed up for having walked away." It was true, she realized. In many ways Nadine was where she had been all those years ago. "We need to take care of each other. You didn't raise me to desert my friends."

She saw the resignation pass over her mother's face and knew she had won. Her father might take longer, but her mother could handle him. She walked the few steps necessary to touch them both and felt their arms encircle her. She *was* grateful. They had always been there for her. She was certainly not going to repay them by letting them think their daughter was now irrationally searching for a twice dead man.

"Go home and take care of Smokey. If you don't, you

know Britney's going to think she has to rescue him, and that will just turn her life upside down."

Her younger sister lived in Maryland and had a full-time teaching job as well as two-year-old twins. She most certainly didn't need a geriatric, needy dog added to the mix.

The furtive look passed between her parents told her she was right again.

Jackie laughed. "Gotcha. I'll be fine. The hand and arm will take a little while, but it's my left hand, and I can manage. I want to get back to work and back to normal."

Her mother's eyes looked up as if seeking divine guidance, but she had always been good at understanding when to back down.

"If you're sure that's what you want . . ."

"I'm sure."

Her mother called up a defeated smile, and Jackie saw her father's eyebrows lower as he squinted at her mother.

"We're going home? Without her? Is that a good idea?"

"Yes."

"No, but . . ."

Jackie and her mother spoke simultaneously, and all three of them laughed.

"You guys go home, take care of Smokey, and let me try to get back to normal. It's September something or other, so I'll be home for Christmas in no time."

IT WAS the next day by the time they were actually gone. They had made trips to the grocery store to stock up her refrigerator, and then her mother had gone through all the already opened jars and made sure the lids were loosened. She'd changed Jackie's sheets and washed every even slightly worn garment in the apartment. By the time Jackie gave them one last wave as she drove away from the departure area at the airport, she wanted nothing more than to go home and curl up in her freshly made bed.

Once there, though, the clips of the two almost contradictory memories ran ceaselessly through her head. The first was horrific, and its images of blood, noise, and chaos made her literally curl into herself, a pillow tucked tightly against her midriff with her bandaged arm resting on top.

The second was so much more perplexing. At that last moment, before everything had gone black, she had known, KNOWN, that it was Leo's body thrown over her own, Leo's voice calling to her with love and concern.

But Leo had died nine years ago. She had seen the ruins of his house, had been told by the fire and police officers she had sought out that there were no survivors. That horrible woman on the street where Leo's mother had lived had confirmed that Leo had been there when the explosion occurred. Leo was dead. Jackie had spoken, with tremendous difficulty, at the memorial service organized on campus after his death.

Leo was dead.

So how could he have thrown her to the ground in a bar during a mass shooting in Austin, Texas?

Jackie had had to read *Atlas Shrugged* in an American lit course at college. The class had enjoyed mocking the easily argued principles espoused ad nauseam by the author in the endless book, but one phrase had stuck with Jackie over the years: "Contradictions do not exist. . . Check your premises."

Her mind was handing her numerous stark contradictions: Leo was dead, and Leo had saved her life during a shooting just a few days ago. Leo's eyes were blue-gray; the person who had saved her was bigger and stronger than Leo had been and had brown eyes. On top of that impossible conundrum was the equally devastating thought that a somehow still-alive Leo had been killed during the blood-bath. Which would mean that he was dead. Again.

Jackie rubbed her head back and forth against the pillows, a moan of anguish escaping her. Her eyes caught on the dusty guitar case standing in the corner between her narrow bookcase and her chair, two sweatshirts tossed casually atop it. She had taken it out of her car three times before shaking her head in frustration and propping it on the passenger seat floor when she moved to Austin years back. She hadn't wanted the constant reminder but had been viscerally unable to leave that last tie to Leo behind. Why the hell was she putting herself through all this? *Again!* Leo was dead. He had either died more than nine years ago, or he had somehow died four nights ago after leaving her alone and heartbroken for almost ten years. Either way, he was dead, and she, Jackie, was alive. And still so very much alone.

CHAPTER SEVEN

E very inch of his body hurt. Forget the agonizing ride in what he was pretty sure had been a hearse that they had used to bring him here—it felt like they had run him over with the damn thing instead. Between the pain and the godawful memories of that horrible night, he wanted nothing more than dark oblivion.

But the words spoken in the next room were becoming more distinct in his muddled brain, and he knew that sinking back into sleep was not going to be an option, especially as the voices drew closer.

"Jake. Jake, you've been asleep for a while. How 'bout waking up. You need to eat something."

So he was still Jake, at least for the time being. He struggled to turn over, and a wave of nausea hit him along with excruciating pain across his back, neck, and shoulders.

"Fuck." The word came out involuntarily. He was lying on his stomach, obviously positioned that way to avoid pressure on his back.

Strong hands reached out to assist him, and their touch on his skin was bad, but not insupportable. He tried to focus on the face that accompanied the hands and found he had to squint to counter the pounding in his head.

"Is that you, Sam?"

"It's me. Older, grayer, but still me. And I'm really glad you're still with us. We're lucky you got the alarm off before you went unconscious. Otherwise we might never have been able to get you out."

And Jackie? He wanted to ask. Wanted so badly to ask. But even in his miserable condition, he knew it wasn't smart. He could only hope he hadn't said anything while unconscious.

"Tell me what happened." It hurt to speak, and his voice sounded hoarse and weak, even to his own ears.

"You were shot. But by some miracle, nothing major got hit. A bullet went through your back and out your chest without destroying anything important, and you were hit hard on the head from some debris. But from everything we've been able to learn, the incident had absolutely nothing to do with you. You were just in the wrong place at the wrong time: a mass shooting at a crowded nightclub—something that's unfortunately happening all too frequently these days. The timing worked out well for us, though, since we were thinking it might be a good idea to move you soon, anyway. There's been increased chatter lately. And we thought a more remote location might be better."

"Chatter?"

"Yeah. Nothing specific, and nothing you need to focus on right now. Just increased activity overall, and Texas itself has drawn too much attention recently—again, nothing specifically to do with you, but there's no harm in being cautious."

"My mom's okay?"

"She's fine. And it looks like she's won her battle and is going to marry that guy she's with. He's been checked and triple checked, and his anonymity will probably keep her safe in the long run. She'll be Frau Anna Müller now, and hopefully for good, of Winterthur, Switzerland—just about as obscure as you can get."

Jake gave a weak laugh. "She gets to be Anna again. Good for her. Where am I going?"

"Just outside Albany, New York. It's a good middle-of-the-road area. No fierce political goings on that would attract outside attention. New York City and the surrounding area are deep blue, upstate is more and more red, but the Albany area is a nice boring purple and relatively quiet. You'll stay Jake, if you like, which will be your middle name, but your full name is now David Jacob Hilderman. Your birthday is June 26, 1992."

"I just got younger. Can we market this?"

His croak was met by a tired smile from his handler. He had no idea if Sam's name was Sam. It was how the American man had been introduced to him when the young boy trying to get used to the name "Leo" was just turning eleven. A guardian angel from the country that had taken them in and saved their lives—an "Uncle Sam" who represented truth, justice, and the American way.

"I'm just glad you're okay. You were close enough to death there that it was relatively easy to get you out of the hospital in a body bag."

"How bad was it?" *Jackie?* His brain kept screaming the question.

"Eight people died, including Jake Carpentero and one of the shooters. Two people are still in critical condition, and several more were hurt but are expected to recover."

"I think I knocked a woman down when I was hit. Do you know what happened to her?"

Sam looked at his phone. "Three women and five men were listed as killed, which included one of the gunmen, and you, of course. The other perp was shot but will recover to stand trial. Say what you will about Texas, there were apparently enough good guys with guns in that place going after the shooters to take down the fucking Alamo. So in terms of victims, three women and three men in total, not counting you, which I suppose is relatively light, all things considered. One of the bartenders was able to hit the inside shooter, and the police got the guy outside—the one who's still alive."

"Who were the six that got killed?"

Sam studied his face, and Jake saw compassion there.

"I hope they weren't friends of yours. You were just living your life, exactly the way we keep telling you to. The owner of the place died, and the rest were customers. I don't have their names, but I can get them."

"Oh, God. Danny?" Despair, frustration, and anger fought for supremacy in Jake's heart. "I know the owner. I rent—rented—my apartment in his father's house. The old man will be destroyed."

Sam blew out a tired breath.

"Yeah. It sucks. I'm sorry."

"People from my office were there that night. I'd really like to know the names, if you can get them."

"Will do. I'm pretty sure at least one of the women who died worked at Home Pantry, but I'll get all the names for you."

Jackie could not be among the dead. *She could not.* If she were gone from the world, there truly would be no point. He had knocked her down, determined to keep her from harm. Everything alive left in him prayed that he had succeeded.

Sam's hand touching his shoulder was strong and comforting. "I'm sorry, Jake. Truly."

He meant it; Jake could tell. Sam was the closest thing to a father figure he had known since he and his mother had been transferred from one unmarked car to another on a cold winter night many years ago after crossing the border from Canada.

Sam had greeted them warmly and had handed a small American flag on a stick to the frightened young boy. "Welcome to America," he had said. "Your name is Leo Jorgensson, and my name is Uncle Sam."

And Sam he had been to him ever since—the only real constant in his disjointed life.

"I heard you talking with someone before. Where are we now, and what's the plan?"

"We're in a safe house outside of Austin. We had to make sure you'd be strong enough to handle the trip. We're tentatively scheduled to fly out tomorrow morning."

"Who's with you?" Sam had been a constant, but the others Jake had seen over the years had come and gone without leaving so much as a shadow.

"Just a couple of people from my office on hand to help out. They're working their magic to make sure your death is well-documented."

So he was dead again. Another life snuffed out. He had learned after Leo's death to keep things superficial, not to make attachments. Leaving Jackie a decade ago had been the hardest thing he'd ever had to do, and for a time, he'd wished he *had* died in that explosion. Part of him still did. But he'd been told at the time he had no choice—both to save himself and his mother and to protect her, as well.

And now, improbably, unbelievably, he was doing it again. She didn't know, thank God, but he was leaving her once more. All this time at Home Pantry, she had been right there, and he'd been too chicken to find out. He'd told himself it couldn't be his Jackie, but it had been. She'd been just a floor or two away from him. The thought was like a stake in his heart.

It was, of course, just as well he hadn't checked. Had he realized it was the Jacqueline he had once known, he would have had to leave. As soon as he recognized her outside the bathrooms, he knew he had to cut and run. The catastrophe had given him an easy out.

But to actually see her up close once more—to look into her deep brown eyes and to feel her soft body under his, even in such appalling circumstances—and then to have to leave her again, was close to unbearable.

No other woman had ever broken through his barriers the way Jackie had. Every other experience had been an act, a charade perpetrated to maintain his cover or try to fool himself into thinking he was real, even as far back as high school. With Jackie he *had* been himself, regardless of his name or his story. With her the world made sense, and ever since he'd left her, he'd felt like he was in permanent jet lag— not quite in step with the world or people around him, a 2D figure in a 3D puppet show.

Except he really hadn't become the cold cyborg he had wanted to be. He had let himself get closer to Danny and his friends than was wise, and he had developed a sense of attachment to Danny's father. The poor man would be utterly lost now, and Jake felt an irrational longing to tell Sam NO, to tell him he had a responsibility to an old man who needed him. And maybe to a young woman who might not need him, but whom *he* desperately needed.

But it wouldn't happen. He was walking away again. Or in this case, being carried away. *Fucking hell.* Thank God she hadn't seen him, would never know he was alive, would never know what a spineless coward he was. He couldn't even begin to imagine what confusion and hurt learning of his deception might cause.

Please, please, please let her not have recognized me. He prayed to deities he normally forswore, knowing that Jackie Bourne could not have recognized Leo Jorgensson in Jake Carpentero. Yet in that split second before the world went black, their eyes had met. He had stupidly said her name, had spoken directly to her. And her eyes had looked into his, and they had been together again. And he had known a nanosecond of joy.

No. It wasn't possible, and it had not happened. Leo Jorgensson was dead. Jake Carpentero was dead. Jackie Bourne was never meant to meet Jake Carpentero, and now she never would. He was dead once more. It was time to move on. Again.

CHAPTER EIGHT

A memorial service was going to be held at Texas Tango, one week to the day after the shooting. Jackie couldn't decide how she felt about it. Part of her wanted to stay cocooned in her own bundle of misery and confusion, but the other part was determined not to let things get awkward with Nadine. The conscientious side won, and she listened as Nadine talked endlessly about all the victims and their families and agreed to attend, if not participate in the service.

Danny hadn't owned the place outright, of course, so the future of the nightclub was up in the air, but the staff who worked there was a tight group. Everyone said Danny had been a friendly, kind, and sympathetic boss, always willing to scramble if someone needed to take time off. The odd assortment of young and old staffers had loved him and were doing all they could to care for each other in their grief.

They were taking turns trying to look out for Danny's dad, Mr. Riga, as well. In a horrible twist, his tenant had been at the bar that night, so he had lost two major figures in his life.

Nadine had heard from one of the waitresses she knew

about how Mr. Riga had appeared at the bar on Friday morning. He stood in the middle of the wreckage as police and staff moved around him, a look of utter devastation on his face.

"Sylvie said that watching him was almost as bad as the shooting had been."

Nadine was sitting on one of the two chairs in Jackie's apartment. Neither woman had returned to work yet but were intending to do so the following Monday.

"She said she's sure he'll fall to pieces completely at the memorial. You're not the only one who doesn't want to go." Nadine's voice was quiet, and Jackie could hear the fatigue in it. They were all exhausted and lethargic, apt to sit for hours staring unseeing at nothing or gnawing at already chewed fingernails. "But we have to go. We can't let the bad guys win."

"Bad guys. Good guys. What does it even mean? Why did those two people think shooting a bunch of random strangers was a good idea?"

Nadine gave a bitter snort. "If I had the answer to that one, I'd probably be a top official at the FBI instead of a lowly marketing associate. My brother says neither of those guys had even so much as a parking ticket."

Nadine's brother, Russo, was a cop. Nadine had unsuccessfully tried to match Jackie with him a few times. Two years younger, he was undeniably gorgeous, fit, and funny, but Jackie felt like he was from a different species. Despite his job, Russo came across as young and carefree, while Jackie felt old and indifferent. She was someone not meant for happiness.

Her dreams the last few nights had been a bizarre mixture of terror and fantasy. Sometimes she was back in even more horrifying versions of the shooting, unable to move or make a sound as cries of terror surrounded her. Other times she was once more in her apartment as a student, with Leo singing to her. Everything would be perfect, until Leo's face would start to change before her eyes, morphing into a stranger whose eyes kept changing colors. Waking from those dreams somehow tormented her the most, as she was now afraid she no longer even clearly remembered Leo's face.

"Some of the staff have been taking turns visiting him to make sure he's okay. Since I knew both Danny and Jake, I told Sylvie I'd drive over there this afternoon. My mom's making empanadas for me to bring, and I thought maybe you'd like to come."

Shaking her head to try to dispel the fog that surrounded her, Jackie knitted her brows. What was Nadine saying?

"I'm sorry. Who are you talking about? And are you asking me to go with you?"

"Yes. Come with me to see poor Mr. Riga. He's Danny's father—was Danny's father, I guess, and Jake rented an apartment in his house. He lives only about ten minutes away. We could even walk if you wanted to. Well, no. I have to go to my mom's first, to get the food, so that won't work."

Jackie's instinct was to say no. Nadine was always trying to get her to go here or there, do this or that, but there had been something in her babble that had broken through the murkiness of her brain.

"You—or we—are driving to your mother's house to pick up empanadas and take them to Danny's father's house. Is that what you said?"

"Yes." Nadine's eyes drew together as she frowned at Jackie. "Listen, sweetie. We both were messed up the other night, you far more than me, obviously. But we're alive and able to return to our normal lives. Poor Mr. Riga lost both his son and his tenant. From what people are saying, he really depended on Jake and is totally lost now with them both gone."

Jackie's consciousness finally kicked back into gear.

"Jake lived with Danny's dad?"

Nadine tilted her head and glared at her.

"That's kinda what I've been telling you, yes."

Jackie reached up her good arm. "Help me up. I feel like I've been sitting or lying in this bed for weeks."

"It feels like that for me, too, but it's only been six days." Nadine grasped Jackie's arm and helped her up off the bed. "Six days that feel like a hundred years and five minutes all at the same time. Patrice got out of the hospital yesterday, but Eddie is still there. I'm going over to Texas Tango tomorrow morning to help set up for the service."

Jackie studied her friend. Nadine had no physical wounds from the attack—no cast or scar that would awaken sympathy from friends and strangers alike. But she had taken a beating as well, perhaps even more so because of her extraordinary empathy and her unnecessary sense of guilt.

"I'm sorry I've been so preoccupied. I'll go with you now, and then you should go home and take a nap. You look like you're ready to fall over."

Seemingly unable to hold still, Nadine redid the ponytail in her hair and started to straighten the bedding as Jackie moved towards the bathroom.

Jackie stopped and reached out to catch Nadine's arm.

"Nadine. Look at me. None of this was your fault. We were there to have fun, and two assholes were there to kill people. It just happened."

"Yeah, but you wouldn't have been there if I hadn't dragged you, and Danny and Jake might not have been standing exactly where they were if I hadn't been pestering Jake."

"You went to get drink refills. That's what people do in

bars. You have to stop tormenting yourself like this. It's not your fault."

The two women moved instinctively to each other and embraced, tears coming yet again to the eyes of both of them.

Should she tell Nadine her crazy thoughts about Jake? Would it help distract her or make her worry even more? She had never shared any real details about Leo—only admitting when pressed that a serious boyfriend had died when they were in college to wave away attempts by Nadine and others to match her up with this or that perfect guy.

But what could she say? That she thought a man she had insisted she didn't know was her long-dead boyfriend? Nadine would assume the concussion had rattled her brain.

It probably had. She had seen the devastation of Leo's house with her own eyes. Had smelled the smoke and understood that no one could have survived such an explosion. And if, by some remote chance, Leo had survived, he would have come to her. He had loved her. She had been sure of that. If he had somehow survived but had total amnesia— Jackie rolled her eyes at the many paths her tormented imagination had explored—then the person in the bar Thursday night would not have known her name.

Nope. Nothing to tell Nadine that would even resemble sanity. The man who had knocked her down, who had undoubtedly saved her life, probably hadn't even said her name. She had been shot and knocked unconscious. Anyone's brain might invent fairytale scenarios under such duress. For the millionth time, Jackie told herself she was imagining something that had never happened. Experts claimed that near-death experiences were simply the brain's way of trying to supply false explanations for unfamiliar sensations and occurrences.

People *had* died at Texas Tango. Other people were hurt and still suffering. She had a bandage on her arm and a few months of rehab in front of her but was otherwise fine. Time to put nonsense behind her. But the idea of seeing the house where the mysterious Jake had lived was nonetheless intriguing. He had, after all, apparently saved her life.

IT WAS ALREADY mid-afternoon by the time they drove up to the well-kept house where Mr. Riga lived. The path on the right side that led to a second story entrance was clearly visible, but Jackie forced herself to pay attention to Nadine and not go down her own cuckoo path.

"Have you met him before?" she asked as they waited at the door.

"I think he was around last Christmas, and I said hello to him, but I doubt he remembers me. But Sylvie told him someone would be coming by."

They rang the bell a second time and waited.

Finally Nadine knocked hard on the door. "Mr. Riga? Mr. Riga, it's Nadine from Texas Tango. I brought you some food."

A minute later the door opened a few inches, and they could see a pair of eyes behind thick glasses staring at them suspiciously. Jackie's heart spasmed with sympathy.

She held up her thickly bandaged arm. "I was there, too, Mr. Riga. I'm so very, very sorry for your loss. Could we come in for a minute?"

An indecipherable utterance and then the door swung open. An old man stood before them, pants that appeared too big sagging at his waist, a faded white t-shirt his only other attire. His feet were bare and the look on his face was of someone with no life left in him at all.

"Yes?" he asked, looking like he didn't care if they answered or not.

"Could we come in?" Nadine asked. She held up the plate wrapped in foil. "My mom made some empanadas. They're really good."

Mr. Riga looked from the girls to the plate and then back again. "I'm not hungry," he said. "But if you want to come in, go ahead." He turned his back on them and walked away from the front door.

The two young women looked at each other and shrugged.

"You were right," Jackie whispered. "I guess we got off easy."

They entered the house and pushed the door shut behind them. The house was neat but looked almost as if no one lived there. The television in the tidy living room was off, blinds were closed, and the desktop computer on a small table set up near the bigger kitchen table was dark. There was no sign of dirty dishes or pots and pans. An empty mug on the table where a chair was pushed back was the only sign any life had been present.

"How are you, Mr. Riga?" Nadine asked gently.

The man looked at them, and they watched his shoulders rise and fall in an almost silent sigh.

"I'm alive. My wife died three years ago, and now my Danny is gone, and even the nice young man who lived upstairs is gone. If crazy people want to shoot other people, they should look for people like me. I don't want to be here anymore."

Another stab of pain shot through Jackie, and she closed her eyes briefly. She remembered the sense of utter loss—had felt echoes of it again this very week—and how long it had taken her, a young, healthy woman, to climb out of the pit of darkness. *Who're you kidding?* she thought. *You never really made it out.*

She moved towards Mr. Riga and took one of his pale, dry, cold hands in her good right one.

"We know this must be incredibly hard for you. I can't even imagine the pain you're going through. But those of us who are left need to help each other. Nadine and I were there on Thursday night. We know that Danny was doing what he loved. He shouldn't have died, but it happened where he was most happy."

Mr. Riga closed his eyes, his attention obviously leaving them for a moment. When he opened them, Jackie could see only despair.

"I know Danny loved that place. He knew that life is crazy and that bad stuff happens with no reason. He grew up hearing about the slaughter at U.T., and his whole adult life has been filled with news stories about one horror story after another."

His eyes moved back and forth between Jackie and Nadine, a fierceness now enlivening his words as he pulled his hand from Jackie's.

"When my Sophie died, he told me he'd always be there for me. He was such a good boy . . ." His voice cracked and his eyes closed again.

"He even found Jake to live in the apartment, knowing that he'd be around to help when Danny was busy. But I sent Jake back to the bar that night. He was here—safe—and I climbed those damn stairs and knocked on his door and told him he had to go back because he'd left his phone. It's my fault that Jake died. And maybe if Jake hadn't been exactly where he was, then Danny might have been somewhere else in the bar. Maybe they'd both still be alive."

He turned away from them, walking over to the kitchen sink and staring out the window behind it.

Jackie and Nadine looked at each other again, and there were tears in both their eyes.

Jackie wiped at her eyes angrily. She was so damn tired of tears.

"Mr. Riga, come sit down and try one of the empanadas Nadine's mother made. They're really good, and you have to eat."

He didn't answer for a moment, but then he, too, seemed to pull himself together. He turned and gave them a polite smile.

"I'm sorry. Forgive my outburst. It was kind of you to come. Did you tell me your names? I guess one of you is Nadine?"

Nadine walked over and gave him an awkward hug. "I'm Nadine and this is Jackie. We were both at Texas Tango on Thursday night. My mom says everything is easier when you have good food you don't have to cook yourself. I can't promise that's true, but I can promise you they'll taste terrific. Do you have some plates and napkins I can put out?"

Unlikely as it seemed, the next several minutes passed tolerably well. An innate sense of manners and hospitality appeared to kick in, and Mr. Riga made an obvious effort to appear tolerant of their presence.

"You were right. These are delicious," he said, after a few bites. "And thank you. I'm not sure when I last ate anything."

Nadine nodded. "My mom's gone through a lot herself. Even after my dad died, she concentrated on making food to help other people."

"She must be a strong woman." He spoke quietly, but his words were sincere. He looked at Jackie. "Were you hurt badly?" He gestured toward her arm.

She looked down at the thick bandage. "No. I was one of the lucky ones." She smiled briefly, remembering her father's words in the hospital.

"A bullet went through some tendons and bone near my wrist, but they were able to repair most of it and put a metal plate in. I might need some more surgery down the road, but it'll all be okay in the long run."

"Did you girls both know Danny and Jake?"

Jackie fought to quell the insistent paradox that kept poking at her imagination as Nadine answered.

"I knew them better than Jackie did, but we both loved the friendly atmosphere Danny created for everyone at Texas Tango. No one there will ever forget him."

"They've asked me if I'd like to say a few words at the service tomorrow. I probably will." He gave a deep, tired sigh. "Apparently Jake had no family, so I'm supposed to feel free to talk about him, too."

He shook his head. "Two vibrant young men. Gone. Just like that." He looked towards Nadine. "Maybe you can say something about Jake?"

Nadine made a distressed grimace. "I actually only met him a few times. He was very quiet."

"He was. But he was a real gentleman. The polar opposite of Danny in many ways except that they were both incredibly responsible and decent human beings. My Danny was always the life of the party, but Jake was, as you said, quiet. This house was well built—" he gestured towards the ceiling — "so I seldom even heard him moving up there. But after we got to know each other, he always stopped to say hello and ask if I needed anything. I told him he needed to find a nice young lady . . ." He paused and looked down, folding and refolding the napkin at the side of his plate.

"They were both such decent men. You seem like wonderful and beautiful women. What's the matter with all you young people that you don't find each other? Danny always said he had a million girlfriends, which is utter rot, of course. And Jake said he thought he was meant to go through life alone, which is also utter rot. And now they're both gone."

He stared off into space for a moment and then turned and looked at Jackie, his eyes coming together as if trying to remember something.

"You said your name was Jackie? Life is full of crazy coincidences, I guess. Jake had the strangest tattoo, and I'm remembering now that I'm almost certain it said Jackie."

All the air was suddenly gone from the room. Jackie couldn't breathe.

"A tattoo?"

"Yeah. So unusual. I would never have seen it except that I got this thingamajig to attach to my toilet that was supposed to help with . . . well, not important. It was supposed to be easy to install, and I thought I could do it, but it absolutely did not work the way the instructions said it would. Every time I turned the water valve back on, water sprayed everywhere. I thought I'd need to call a plumber, but Jake stopped by and said he'd be happy to look at it."

Mr. Riga chuckled softly, shaking his head and briefly closing his eyes. "He worked on it for about 45 minutes and made it work in the end, but he was completely drenched."

His smile broadened in memory. "This was last February, when it was still cold, so I told him he wasn't going outside in wet clothes. I made him take everything off and gave him sweatpants and a shirt to put on and told him the least I could do was wash his clothes. He said it wasn't necessary, but I didn't want him getting sick on my account, and he eventually gave in. So he stripped right there in the hall" — Mr. Riga pointed to the small hallway off the kitchen where a door, presumably to a bedroom or bathroom was partly ajar — "and I saw it low on his belly. I was afraid it was a bruise and that he had hurt himself with the wrench or something, so I asked about it."

Mr. Riga sighed again, and a look of complete exhaustion passed over his face. "He was such a sweet but serious young man. Not the type you'd expect to have a tattoo, especially there." He looked slightly embarrassed but went on to finish his story.

"Anyway, he said it was the name of the girl he'd loved and lost, and he'd put it in a spot where only he would ever see it."

For a man sunken in grief, he'd been able to tell an animated story. Through her mesmerized attention, Jackie could see a resemblance to the gregarious and effervescent Danny she had never really known but heard so much about. It was his words, however, that had her biting her lip hard enough that she only stopped in surprise when she tasted blood.

She and Leo had joked frequently about getting tattoos. Several of their friends had them, and Jackie had teased Leo about going together one day and getting them in places only the two of them would ever see. But like so many other plans, that one had vanished when Leo had died.

"What kind of tattoo was it?" She had to know, despite the odd look shot her by Nadine.

"I didn't get up close to see, since I'd only meant to make sure he wasn't hurt." Mr. Riga reddened slightly, the spots oddly sweet on his otherwise pale face. "But he was a nice guy and saw I was curious. He drew a picture of it on a piece of paper. He knew I understood music because I'd told him I played the violin. He said it was something he'd doodled long ago and only had made into a tattoo one night after he got stupid drunk."

He smiled at Jackie and Nadine. "Whoever that Jackie was, she must have been pretty special. When he talked about the tattoo, he was almost like a different person. But after that night, neither one of us ever mentioned it again."

"What was special about it?" Nadine asked, and Jackie was

grateful for her friend's curiosity. There was no way she could have forced her voice to work.

"Well, he'd drawn a small musical staff." He looked at them. "Do you ladies know what that is?" When they nodded, he continued. "And you know what a G clef sign is?"

Jackie nodded, not breathing, while Nadine just shrugged. "He made the core of the clef sign stand out as the letter J and then had the rest of the letters of the name Jackie going up the staff like small notes. It was quite beautiful and unlike anything I'd ever seen."

But Jackie had seen it. Years ago. Years ago, miles away, and in an entirely different life, the young man she had been in love with had sketched just such a design when they had joked about getting tattoos. They had never gotten them because Leo had died.

Except apparently, he hadn't.

———

JACKIE DIDN'T REMEMBER SAYING goodbye or leaving Mr. Riga's house. She became aware of her surroundings a few minutes—hours? years? who knew what was real anymore? —later.

"Do you think you could pull over?"

Nadine shot her a confused look.

"Here?" They were on Lamar Blvd., not a superhighway, but not a side street, either.

"Wherever you can. I need to get out and walk."

"Are you okay? Are you going to be sick?"

"No. I just need to get out."

Nadine pulled into a post office parking lot and turned off the car.

"What's going on?"

"Do you want to walk with me for a few minutes?"

Still looking confused, Nadine peered around the lot, a frown creasing her forehead.

Jackie tried to keep her voice steady. "Yeah, I know it's after five. But there are a couple other cars here, and if you get a ticket, I'll pay for it."

Nodding slowly as if not wanting to disturb a deranged person, Nadine unbuckled and got out of the car, swinging her small purse over her shoulder.

"I think there are a couple coffee shops near here. We can start walking and get a cup, if you'd like."

Jackie choked on a tired laugh. "Where aren't there a few coffee shops in this city? But I think what I'm going to tell you will make you want more than coffee."

They started walking, and Jackie spilled out her inconceivable suspicions. She told Nadine about Leo's death and how no other person she had met since had awakened anything more than tepid interest. She recounted how she had been sure at that horrible moment when chaos erupted and shots were everywhere, that Leo, somehow completely different but still Leo, had thrown her to the ground and said her name.

"Except that person, the one who saved me and said my name, was the man you've been calling Jake."

Nadine stopped and stared at Jackie, her brows drawing together in confusion.

"What? You told me you didn't know Jake. And that doesn't make any sense, anyway."

"I know it doesn't. That's what I've been telling myself for the past week. That Leo was dead and that I had imagined him—his actions, his expression, his voice—because I was traumatized and concussed. It's why I didn't say a word about it to you or my parents. I knew it was wrong, crazy, impossible, and that you'd think I was suffering brain damage or something."

59

"But Nadine . . ." Jackie closed her eyes for a moment. There was no logical way to proceed other than the truth.

"The tattoo Mr. Riga just described—I've seen that image. I saw the exact design he described years ago when Leo drew it for me. Leo Jorgensson sketched a G major clef sign on a staff with the J part in a different color and wrote my name going up the staff. Leo Jorgensson, who died in a horrible gas explosion, drew the picture that Jake Carpentero apparently had on his belly—but not really his belly, if you know what I mean—in the exact spot Leo said he would put it. He said he wanted it where his hard-on would rub up against it in his jeans because his hard-on belonged only to me."

"Holy fucking shit."

CHAPTER NINE

David "Jake" Hilderman was able to walk, albeit slowly, from the nondescript white Malibu towards his new apartment building. A bitter wind blew across his unzipped jacket, and he shivered, the movement causing ripples of pain through his entire upper torso. There was no cold wind in Austin right now; he was damn sure of that.

His "uncle" was with him, pushing the elevator button that took them to the third-floor apartment.

"This is the top floor, and there's an emergency exit to the roof at the other end of the hall if you ever need it. You won't, but just in case."

David/Jake shut his eyes. His job was to do what he was told. No more, no less. Nothing even resembling choice had brought him to this safe location just outside downtown Albany, New York.

He had never really thought of Austin as home. Virginia *had* been home for a wonderfully idyllic period. Middle and high school in an obscure suburban area followed by three glorious years at the University of Virginia. Three years of choosing his own courses, making friends based on shared interests and pursuits, and falling in love with a girl with whom he had imagined building a life.

It had all been ripped away in one short phone call.

"I'm so sorry, my love," his mother had said. "You need to come. The furnace is broken." All code for *"We've been discovered. We have to die."*

Sam had warned them there were signs that trouble might be brewing, and different scenarios had been tentatively discussed. Leo had tried to object, had even suggested he be left out of plans to keep his mother safe, but their reaction had been adamant refusal, and in the end, there had been no time. No time to come up with alternate solutions, and no time to find a way to spare Jackie pain.

And so Leo Jorgensson had died.

Sam had been compassionate but thorough during the painful months following their Virginia deaths: his mother would go in one direction and he in another. She would be a mature, unattached woman pursuing a new career path in nursing in the Pacific Northwest. He would be an orphaned Mexican-American young man who had triumphed through the beneficent wonders of good public education and strong ambition.

Several weeks of visits to a plastic surgeon operating out of a boring strip mall in Chevy Chase, Maryland, resulted in two, shiny new individuals ready to make their way in the world.

Allison Cameron was a green-eyed, middle-aged woman with a pixie haircut dyed a bright red and a cute turned-up nose. The almost undetectable accent in her American English could easily be ascribed to her prolonged childhood stay in Ireland.

The new "Jake" passed easily as a Mexican-American.

Leo had inherited his mother's linguistic skills and always excelled at languages. When he was growing up in Virginia, the two of them always spoke Swedish in front of anyone who might hear them and Russian when they were alone. He had finished the AP track in Spanish in high school, continued Spanish in college, and had been scheduled to spend two months in Latin America during the now aborted time-off between his junior and senior year. Now, as Jake, his facial features had been altered slightly, and he, too, had been fitted with colored contacts: his a dark brown to match his newly darkened hair. He had been rigorously worked to the point of exhaustion in the gym to harden his physique. He would blend into the multi-racial community of Austin with little difficulty.

Their transformation period included tutoring to hone his already good computer science skills into job-readiness. Two years of good performance evaluations plus an impressive BS with honors from a reputable college in the Southwest had been added to his well-rounded and mostly fraudulent résumé. No one asked him if he minded the three years added to his age.

But Leo, then Jake, now David, had hardened himself to inconsequential details like age or interests and erected a wall of indifference. He didn't try to follow Jackie from afar and abandoned music. He stopped following politics and social issues. He existed, but his life was over.

And somehow, more than nine years had passed. His mother had thrived, and Jake was truly happy for her. Improbably, she and a Swiss tourist injured in a car crash had fallen in love while she nursed him in a Seattle hospital. With Sam's hesitant approval, she had relocated to Switzerland last year, and Allison had even begun using her "middle name," Anna.

Jake was happy for his mother. Their contact over the years had been sporadic, made more difficult by the almost complete disappearance of pay phones. Envelopes would

63

arrive occasionally with a burner phone and a number programmed into it. They would talk for an hour or two, trying to catch each other up on details big and small. But over the years they inevitably grew apart.

His mother had never been happy in Virginia. The life of a Swedish-American writer and translator hadn't inspired her, but for whatever inexplicable reason, nursing had. She had embraced her new career, her new identity, and now, her new husband and a completely new life in Switzerland.

"If my mother's safe, and I've died twice, why do we have to continue this charade?"

Sam studied him without speaking, and Jake wondered how many sentences he was mentally auditioning and discarding. Finally he spoke.

"It's a good question. You're past thirty now, and the information and experiences your mother had—has—is even older than that."

"What do you mean by experiences?"

Another prolonged regard.

"Do you remember your father?"

That was a shot from nowhere. *Did he?* Not really. There had been a few snapshots in the house in Virginia that he could bring to mind with effort, but they had all been lost in the explosion. He suspected his mother might have secreted one or two in her pockets that long ago hateful day, but if so, they had gone to Seattle and probably now to Switzerland.

He had a distant memory of riding high on his father's shoulders and laughing as snowflakes fell on them. His mittens had been red, and he'd clapped them in delight.

But the memory of the mittens was more vivid than any clear memory of his father's face. All other images blurred into a vague impression of someone tall, with light hair, and loving eyes. Someone he had loved completely and lost.

"Not really, no."

"What did your mother tell you about him?"

Now it was Jake's turn to ponder a reply. When he finally spoke, his words were quiet.

"My first day of school in Virginia was hard. Even the name of the town, Ruckersville, sounded incomprehensible to me. I was scared. I was going into something called fourth grade, in the middle of the year, and I didn't even really understand what the words fourth grade meant. Class levels had different names in Russia. But everything had been hard and strange for so long that one more thing hardly made a difference. My memories of life at home were that everything there was always dark and unnerving. I had two parents, but all I really remember from the time before we left is how frightened they would both be whenever the phone rang or the door buzzer sounded."

He stopped a moment, surprised at the memory of the door buzzer that had come to him from out of the blue. It was a sound he had not heard in this new country, this new continent. Doorbells here sounded normal, not scary. He was briefly overcome by a slideshow of images: a narrow corridor, shoes and boots lined up by the door, and tapachky, or slippers, nearby, to be put on by anyone entering.

"And then Papa was gone, and Mama was crying. I kept asking where he was, and she would only say he couldn't come back and that we had to leave. It wasn't until we were on a plane—I don't even remember which one—that she told me he was dead and that I could never see my friends or family again."

He paused again and blew out a breath.

"Every day was bad. Bad, frightening . . ." He looked at Sam and sent him a rueful smile.

"You were kind. I don't mean to imply otherwise. But you said to call you Uncle Sam, and I had no idea what you were talking about. Do you know . . ." He paused again and laughed, but there was no humor behind it.

"It wasn't until I was in AP history and learned about the War of 1812 that I finally got the joke. That's how long it took me to try and figure things out. And part of me has wanted ever since then to ask you your real name, but a bigger part of me just said, 'Why bother?' My life has been nothing but lies and secrets anyway."

Sam moved into the small but fully equipped kitchen. He went to the sink and began filling a stainless-steel teakettle, a fixture he had equipped Jake's Austin apartment with as well. He raised his brows in silent question, and Jake nodded.

"Most American kitchens don't have a teakettle like that on the stove, yet my apartments always do. You've been a good friend, Sam. Do you even like tea?"

Now Sam gave a smothered chuckle. "Your mother is one of the most gracious women I've ever met. That first night in Ruckersville, I hadn't thought to get a kettle, and she immediately set to filling a saucepan with water and boiling it for tea. I hadn't arranged for tea, either, only coffee, but she took a little bag from her assortment of tightly packed items and insisted I have a cup of tea with you both. I've been a convert ever since."

When Jake didn't respond, Sam repeated his earlier question. "But your father? What did your mother tell you about him?"

A wave of exhaustion swept over Jake, and he sank into a comfortable looking armchair that conveniently provided a line of sight to anyone in the kitchen. Sam was a genius. Jake was pretty sure interior design was nowhere on his job description, but it was one of the infinite number of services he so aptly performed.

"That's what I've been trying to explain. We very seldom talked about anything from our past. Those first years . . . I was so overwhelmed, trying to communicate in English and understand the world around me, and of course I had to master basic Swedish, as well."

He shook his head in remembered bemusement. "That was one of the few things that didn't change; my mother had been teaching me Swedish and English for years before we left home, but I always thought it was some kind of game. In Virginia, though, by the time I was truly comfortable, I was a teenager. I had a life of my own and friends of my own. What teenage boy hangs around chatting with his mother when there's basketball practice, soccer practice, or cool video games to play?"

"My mother was proud of me, and she always said Papa would have been proud. She told me he had loved football, which she refused to call soccer, and she said he had been an excellent student who got top grades and made it into a good university. And that was pretty much the extent of our lengthy discussions. Those little things were inspirations for me, though. I wanted to be a good athlete and a good student, as he had. I always wanted him to be proud of me."

Jake stopped speaking and stared hard at the plain beige carpet. He realized his right knee was jiggling up and down and he forced himself to relax. When he thought he could continue without his voice cracking, he raised his eyes to meet Sam's.

"Until those last days, the only time my mother cried after we came to this country was when I sang. I was in chorus all through school and made it into the all-county and all-state choirs. Whenever I had a solo, she would go to pieces. She said my voice was exactly like my father's."

He stopped while various scenes from years past flitted across his consciousness: his mother, with flowers in her arms at a school musical, tears streaming down her face but a brave, encouraging smile there as well. Of her standing at his bedroom door, gazing at him wistfully as he strummed his guitar and sang songs he had composed.

Finally he continued. "It probably sounds crazy to you, but the first serious conversation we had about anything was over Christmas break that last year."

Another pause, but this time he was trying to ignore the images of Jackie that screamed for his attention. He had to be careful not to reveal his current torment to Sam.

"I brought my girlfriend home for a few days. Her family was in Northern Virginia, so it wasn't that far for either of us, and I had been to her house a few times. My mother seemed to really like her, and I was glad they got along. But when she left to go back home, Mama said we had to talk."

He tilted his head and looked at Sam, who had carried over two cups of tea and pulled a chair over from the seating area to face him. "I just told you that I didn't even get the joke about your name until high school. But I still never thought all that much about why I needed an Uncle Sam in my life. It wasn't until that moment, just a few days before the spring semester of my third year, that my mother told me my father had been murdered and that we, too, might still be in danger." Jake closed his eyes briefly and then gave Sam a rueful smile.

"You guys did a good job—you and my mother together. You gave me almost ten years of blissful ignorance. By that time I thought I was a normal American boy living a normal American life. I played sports, I sang, wrote songs, played the guitar, and was a genius at Minecraft. And, oh yeah, I had a girlfriend I loved. Really loved." He stopped, unable to go on. *Slow breaths in and out. Don't open your eyes. Sam sees everything. Do not let him see Jackie.*

Jake steeled his features. "Yes, I knew things about my past were murky, but they were just that: the past. Then all of a sudden, they weren't."

Sam's eyes met his own, and those of the older man were filled with compassion.

"I wish it all could have remained that way. We thought for a while—for those ten or so golden years—that you were both free, that we had achieved the near impossible. But the person responsible for your father's death and your mother's need to disappear is known for his inability or . . . unwillingness to forget."

Sam stopped speaking, and Jake could see he was choosing his words carefully. His eyes, when they returned to Jake, were searing.

"This apartment has been carefully checked and rechecked. What we say here and now can never be spoken of anywhere else. You understand?"

Jake nodded, holding Sam's gaze.

"Do you know your name, your father's name?"

Jake cocked his head, trying to understand where the conversation was going.

"I know I am Nikolai Gregorievich Polivanov. My father was Gregoryi Vasilievich Polivanov. I knew my grandparents as Dedya and Baba." A dull pain tugged at him. He had not allowed himself to think of his grandparents for years.

Sam was kneading the bridge of his nose, obviously still trying to choose his words. Jake had never known him to be so hesitant.

"We are trying—carefully—to make contact with surviving members of your father's family. We are hoping at some point to get DNA samples from them, so that your father's identity can be verified and documented."

"My father's identity?" His voice was sharp. "What the fuck, Sam?"

"Yes." Sam looked down. His knees were spread slightly, and he shifted, moving his now interlocked fingers back and forth between them. He appeared almost as a man deep in prayer.

When he raised his head, his gaze was steady but compassionate.

"A group of men raped your mother sometime near the time of your conception."

Waves of nausea sweep over him, and Jake struggled to breathe, but Sam's voice continued, relentlessly.

"Then there was a concerted attempt to destroy your parents' lives that continued for years. Unfortunately, I mean that literally, and they succeeded by imprisoning your father and . . ." Sam tilted his head in disgust and his lips pursed, "allowing him to die there."

Sam paused and stared hard at his tightly interlocked fingers.

"That left you and your mother. She was still a problem they wanted to get rid of, but you were a different sort of problem. You might be the son of an inconsequential bug, in their eyes, or . . ." Sam paused again and shook his head slowly as he looked at Jake. "Or you might be the offspring of someone important. Your mother knew secrets that could implicate many in the upper echelons of power, and neither she nor the Americans trying to help her knew what that might entail for you. We got you out, thought we had made you anonymous, and left you to establish a new life. But then messages started appearing that suggested you'd been found, and we decided you had to be killed. Hence the explosion in Ruckersville. We killed you before they could. But there have been inquiries recently regarding the explosion that have led us to believe there may be suspicions regarding your death. That's part of the reason we were glad to have you die again in Austin."

What the fuck was Sam talking about? Cold fury and horror

creeped over him. *What the hell had happened to his poor mother?*

She had explained to him during that long ago college winter break conversation that her earlier work in Russia had left her vulnerable, and that she needed to avoid people who insisted she return. She said the U.S. had given them safe haven, and they had assumed the identities of a Swedish-American mother and son as part of their cover. All of that he had more or less already known. Her next words had been the land mine. Due to recent developments, and in order to conceal the extent of the protection they had received, it might be necessary—at some not too distant point—to stage their deaths.

But now Sam was blowing up what little remained of his sense of identity. It hurt to breathe—the recent injuries to his chest and back compounding the pain. He stood up, staring wildly around the still unfamiliar apartment. There were no windows in the colorless living room, only bland, off-white walls with equally bland framed artwork. Just another goddamn fucking prison. He was thirty-one years old, had lived his entire life as a marionette controlled by distant puppet masters, and now he was being told that even his secret, hidden identity might not be his and that his mother had survived nightmares he never imagined.

He paced a few steps, but there was nowhere to run. He was both trapped with no escape and overflowing with impotent rage. Desperately hoping he could find a hole in Sam's devastating revelation, he glared at the man he had alternately loved and resented for so many years.

"I just told you five minutes ago that my mother said I had my father's voice. Who are these sons-of-bitches you say may be my father instead?"

Sam did not answer, at least not in words. He simply

looked at Jake, the lines around his eyes revealing boundless sadness and fatigue. The silence in the room grew ominous.

Jake backed away.

"You don't know, or you won't say?"

Another long pause, and then Sam's soft words sent shards of horror through Jake's already aching chest.

"They're all still around, and they're all still dangerous. Maybe we should leave it at that." Sam's eyes closed, and his face looked old and worn.

Jake finally understood. The lock on his jail cell could never be broken.

CHAPTER TEN

Organizers tried to put a "Remembering with Joy" spin on the memorial, but a service to honor seven young people senselessly gunned down while out socializing with friends failed utterly at being anything beyond gut-wrenching.

Speakers strove to celebrate the achievements and positive attributes of Danny, Gloria, Jake, Antonio, Frank, Karina, and Rosa. They spoke of their kindness, their love of life, and their friendships. Various family members, some with tears streaming down their cheeks, mentioned how much their loved ones had enjoyed spending time at Texas Tango.

Mr. Riga spoke quietly, and Jackie, standing in the back of the crowd, strained to catch his words. Danny had never been happier, he said, than when he signed the papers making Texas Tango his own—his and the bank's, of course. The crowd laughed, and Mr. Riga joined them with a tired smile. He then turned them all into bawling baskets of mush when he recounted how he and his beloved Sophie had tried for so many years to have a baby, and how Danny had surprised them when they had just about given up hope.

"He was the best son anyone could ever have. He took care of us both, and when his mother passed . . ." He stopped, and the effort his next words took was palpable.

"When he moved into his own place, closer to the bar and the hub of things, he thought having tenants would make us less isolated. He set up the apartment upstairs, and a nice young couple moved in. That didn't last, but then Danny found Jake for us. Jake checked in on us, lent out with things around the house, was always happy to help Sophie, and listened to me blather on about how the world was going to hell. He's been . . ." He stopped and cleared his throat. "He was almost like a second son to me since the death of my Sophie. Two extraordinary young men, both now gone. I know Jake had no close family of his own. So I ask you to hold the memories of both these fine souls in your hearts. Maybe in your prayers, too, but I don't know if prayers mean anything anymore."

He moved away from the podium, and the room was silent, save for the sound of countless sniffles and quiet sobs.

The band began another soothing number, and Jackie stepped outside. She couldn't listen to any more stories. She didn't want to hear how wonderful all the dead people were. None of them should be dead.

Thoughts swirled around her mind incessantly: Danny had been a terrific person, and he was gone, his father now alone in the world. Leo had been the best person she had ever known, and he had been ripped away from her in a meaningless accident. *Or had he?* Had he been here, all along, mere feet away from her? Was it all some kind of cosmic joke, the gods of the universe pranking her? Or had Leo himself pranked her for some incomprehensible reason?

Had he ever loved her? Two weeks ago, she would have

answered that question with perfect certainty. Leo Jorgensson had loved her. Their bond had been absolute. They shared interests and encouraged each other's individual passions and pursuits. Their lovemaking had been joyful, fun, and glorious, and scorching memories of their hours in bed still haunted her dreams and left her doubtful that she might ever enjoy sex with another man. And he had sung to her, time and time again, of his love, sometimes playing popular songs they both knew and other times composing pieces that spoke directly to her.

She still had the troubling lyrics he had sung to her that last week. Just last night she had unfolded the worn and yellowed paper from Leo's guitar case and stared at them, anger rising where before she had only felt love. She had kept his guitar, unable to part with it, hauling it across the country when she moved to Austin even though she couldn't play. She had slept with his sweatshirt bunched up against her tear-stained face for months, only finally washing it and folding it carefully when she packed up to return to her parents' home for the summer, that first horrible year without him. It too, had come to Austin with her.

The words and notations on the paper were faded, and the areas where the paper had been folded and refolded were hardest to read. But she knew them by heart, having read them over and over these past nine years.

> *I look into your amber eyes and want no more*
>   *good-byes*
> *I want to walk the world with you and forever sing*
>   *my love to you*
> *But morning comes and sirens scream*
> *I fear the world where all this seems like just a long-*
>   *lost dream*

> *I wake up with your hair all round and your*
> *sleeping breath the sweetest sound*
> *I hold you tight and hate the morning's lies*
> *I want to walk the world with you and never fear*
> *good-byes*
> *My love will never leave you*
> *Hold me tight and say the same*
> *I'll forever sing my song for you and cry that*
> *morning came.*

They were words penned by an emotional 21-year-old, deeply in love with her and with life. Young people wrote songs, stories, painted pictures, all filled with melodrama—it was part of being young and sentimental. Or so she had believed until last week. But now the words took on an entirely different aspect. *Had he been warning her?*

There *had* been sirens in Ruckersville, or so she had been told. And there had definitely been sirens after the shooting at Texas Tango, though she had been unconscious and hadn't heard them herself.

But those words! All these years she had thought them at most sadly prescient. Young people always believed their love was the most passionate and intense the world had ever seen. The lyrics had been the romantic outpouring of a fervent young man to an equally enthralled young woman, each believing the world around them at once both precious and precarious. The older Jackie got, the more cynical and dispassionate she had become, and until this week, it had probably been at least a year since she had thought about that song.

But had Leo *known* he was leaving her?

"I hold you tight and hate the morning's lies."

If Leo hadn't died that day in Ruckersville, then he *had*

lied to her. Lied in his good-bye that last morning and most definitely lied in disappearing from her life.

But why? Goddammit, *WHY*?

She didn't know whom to ask or whom to trust. If Mr. Riga had not mentioned that freaking tattoo, she could have convinced herself that her illusions during the shooting had been just that: *delusions*. But no one else would have that same tattoo in just that spot. He had to have been Leo. He had also, apparently, been Jake Carpentero, who was now dead.

But Leo Jorgensson had had a memorial service, too, one that she had been forced to help plan and where she had needed help to leave the stage after speaking to a crowded auditorium.

One fact stood out: whether the struck-down man was Jake Carpentero or Leo Jorgensson, whoever it was had saved her life. Had that tackle not sent her to the floor, her family would doubtless be among those mourners currently trying to find meaning where none existed. If that fact, bizarre as it was, meant something, she was hopelessly confused as to what that something might be.

Questions, doubts, and suspicions all fought for dominance in Jackie's turbulent musings. But one niggling idea kept returning to the forefront.

If Leo hadn't been dead during his memorial service in Charlottesville, was it remotely possible that Jake Carpentero wasn't dead now, in Austin?

Somehow, she had to find out.

CHAPTER ELEVEN

He hid his cards from Sam, but David "Jake" Hilderman had gone from shocked and disconcerted to furious.

Nine years ago, Leo Jorgensson had done what he was told and become Jake Carpentero. He took as gospel the admonitions that his strict adherence to the plan laid out for him was all that would keep him, his mother, and his now former girlfriend alive.

Sam had seemed sympathetic when Jake mentioned Jackie after the "explosion" in Ruckersville. Sympathetic, but adamant. If she had any suspicion that he were alive, her life could be in danger. Foreign intelligence had been sniffing around his and his mother's covers and that's why definitive action had been required. Linnéa and Leo Jorgensson needed to die. As long as no one suspected otherwise, the search would end, and the threat of danger would be permanently removed.

And so Jake Carpentero had put Jackie Bourne and Leo Jorgensson out of his mind. Or at least he had tried to. Social media, 24-7 connectivity, and the ability to learn everything about anybody were all exploding on the world stage, but Jake did his best to ignore them all. He put his head down, mastered the IT skills needed to perform his work perfectly, and worked out endlessly. He ran, lifted weights, and studied martial arts. He learned rudimentary cooking skills and read Stephen King and Lee Child. He made friends but didn't get more than superficially close to anyone. He occasionally went to parties, and over the years had been invited to a few weddings.

It was the second wedding that almost did him in. The bride was a fellow Tai-Chi student, and she and her groom seemed so in love. She pestered him to dance with one of her friends at the reception where alcohol had flowed freely.

Watching the besotted couple, Jake allowed himself to drink more than his customary single beer. The tattoo experience the previous year had been a wake-up call, but the sentimental vibrations pulsing through the reception hall weakened his defenses.

He danced twice with the girl pushed his way by the bride. She was friendly, cute, and talkative. She had light brown eyes in a pretty face. Jake looked at her and felt nothing. Nothing beyond an unbearable pang of longing for the beautiful amber eyes he had loved so deeply. He mumbled a stilted apology, left the reception, and ended up at Texas Tango, where he ordered a Coke and gave himself a silent lecture.

The year before, on the fifth anniversary of his death, he had let himself go to pieces. He couldn't do so again. If his undying love for Jackie was just that—undying, then it was up to him to keep her safe, even if she never knew it.

Danny came over a few times, refilling the soda in Jake's glass and making small talk to show he was available for more.

"You seem down tonight, Jake. Anything I can help with?"

"No. Just remembering stuff that should stay in the past."

Danny raised his eyebrows inquisitively and then laughed. "My mother, before she got sick, was completely taken by this guy on PBS. He used to say things about a boat's momentum not being controlled by its wake that she found fascinating. Even now, whenever I complain about anything, she tosses out his handy-dandy advice: 'Don't let the wake steer your course!' I get mad at her sometimes, but it's advice that's stuck with me."

Jake pondered the words. They made sense, and since he had no real options, he might as well try to live by them. He doubled down on his resolve. He had to let memories of Jackie go and hope and pray that she was happy. When the name Jacqueline Bourne appeared on the company staff list, he forced himself to ignore it. *His Jackie* was in the past and on the other side of the country. Whoever this new person was meant nothing to him.

Where had all that resolve and discipline gotten him? The life he had painstakingly built for himself had been wiped out in an instant, and all that had been Jake Carpentero was now a footnote to a heinous crime.

Worse, Jackie's life had almost been snuffed out as well. She was alive, but it hadn't been foreign intelligence operators threatening her but rather everyday jerks with access to weapons of mass destruction. His disappearance from her life nine years ago hadn't guaranteed her safety; she was still as vulnerable as any other human being on the planet.

And now she was alone, grieving once more, and hurt.

Fuck cutting off all ties. Fuck cutting himself off emotionally from his past. And fuck taking Sam's words as law! Yes, he undoubtedly owed his continued existence to Sam thrice over now, but was that all he was entitled to: an existence?

Sam wore a wedding ring. He had a life. Privy as he was

to international secrets that Jake couldn't even imagine, he had a life of his own he could keep in its own compartment. Hell, even Jake's mother was now living a life—a real life, even using her own first name, for fuck's sake.

Angrily he stared at himself in the mirror. He was furious at it all, but what pierced him to the core was the devastating hint that Sam had left dangling unspoken. He was not the goddamn son of one of those fucking bastards. He was Nikolai Gregorievich Polivanov, son of Gregoryi Vasilievich Polivanov.

His confrontations with the mirror were now almost an hourly obsession. His newest contacts were a hazel-brown, but the eyes underneath were gray-blue. Meaningless. Lots of Russians had blue eyes, including his mother and—he was almost certain—his father. His nose and cheekbones had been subtly altered nine years ago, and he didn't even remember what they had looked like before. His own light-colored hair had grown out and now sported natural look-ing, artificially added, red highlights. How the fuck could he learn anything from the mirror when he himself hardly knew who he was?

But he continued to stare, searching the reflected image for clues. If the horrible suggestion Sam had dropped was true, then he was the biological offspring of some hateful monster. Jake was tall with a finely sculpted physique. The current head of Russia and his cronies, who appeared some-times on news broadcasts flanking him, tended to be shorter and quite literally called to mind the cartoon-like villains seen in animated movies.

If only he remembered more about his real father. Anger bubbled up anew—against Sam, against his mother, and against everything that had conspired to deny him a genuine identity. And for the first time in his life, he hated his father. Where had he been when his mother needed protection?

Why had he taken risks that cost him his life and left them alone?

They had made him give up Jackie, and she was still vulnerable. Hell, maybe the fucking shooter who had survived in Austin had buddies out there who would go after anyone who had walked away from the massacre. He was as useless protecting her as his father had been to his mother.

He paced his small, colorless apartment. He had to report to his new job on Monday and become a cog in a wheel at a "responsive and strategic" technology company.

The phone and laptop Sam had provided sat on the nondescript dining table. They were most likely bugged. Sam would contend it was to keep Jake safe. David Hilderman had two new credit cards and a debit card to accompany his New York driver's license, and all log-in and password information was in a document he could easily access.

Jake had never actively questioned Sam's instructions, but working in the tech world had kept him abreast of innovations, and a few years ago he had begun playing around, conservatively, with minor stock investments, some day trading, and even crypto currency. The small, inexpensive tablet he had used lay in his top desk drawer at Home Pantry.

JackSparrow451 was the name on all those accounts. JackSparrow had his own email, his own VPN account, and his own, now remarkably sizable, financial resources that Jake was fairly certain Sam knew nothing about.

It would take a few weeks, but once he'd ostensibly settled in his new, monotonous existence in Albany, he'd use cash withdrawn in small increments to buy himself another tablet and access his accounts.

Jake's fingers flexed and contracted. He wanted to be online now, searching for information about Jackie, about his mother's past, and finding out all he could to disprove Sam's loathsome suggestions. Most of all, he wanted out of this cage that was his life. Frustration roiled up inside him, but he willed himself to tamp it down. His lingering injuries and weakness precluded any strenuous exercise, but he could still fucking walk. He picked up his jacket and headed for the door. Time to learn all he could about his new surroundings.

CHAPTER TWELVE

Jackie's return to work was a distraction that helped fill hours in the day but did little to keep her attention. Though only late September, Home Pantry was already in the final wrap-up for the all-important holiday season. Jackie tried to care about whether organic truffles were going to be big that year, but her thoughts instead sifted and discarded one implausible idea after another. Was she crazy? Was Leo alive? Was he even now maybe still here somewhere in Austin? Or could some other random dude possibly have a tattoo similar to the one her dead boyfriend had drawn for her in a different lifetime? By Thursday, she was utterly exhausted, and her head jerked up guiltily when she realized her manager was standing by her desk.

"Jackie, do you remember I told you after the shooting to take as much time as you needed?"

Jackie nodded. Was she in trouble?

"I said it because I meant it. Our leave policies were designed to be comprehensive, so that when people are at work, they're able to give 100%."

Jackie winced. "I'm sorry, Chris. Have I messed something up?"

"Your last procurement proposal included shipments of 3000 units of organic cocoa gift baskets to our North-East stores. I'm assuming you meant 300, though even that seems a bit overly-optimistic."

Jackie's head drooped. How could she have done something so stupid?

"I'm sorry, Chris. I'll send out a revision immediately."

"That's twice you've said you're sorry, but that's not what I want from you. I want you to take the time you need to heal, physically and emotionally. The work you've done here for the past few years has been exceptional. Go home. Give that arm a rest." He gestured to her newly casted wrist area. "I had one of those when I was a teenager, and I remember. It gets tiring dragging it around all day.

"This isn't an order, but why don't you stop by the medical suite? They have a ton of resources available and can help you get in to see someone quickly. The shooting hit this whole office hard. We lost people we cared about. Our priority now is to help everyone still here feel whole again, and talking to a professional might do you a world of good."

He paused, and she realized he was waiting for her to meet his gaze. Reluctantly, she did.

"Whatever you decide to do, I want you away from this desk for a while. Understood?"

Jackie nodded. His words had most likely been passed down from higher-ups in the corporate channels, but she knew him to be a kind and supportive supervisor. And he was right. She had been screwing up, and her job deserved better. It paid well, and the benefit and leave packages were generous. Consumer enthusiasm for organic truffles and cocoa gift baskets allowed Home Pantry to staff a fully accessible medical unit.

Jackie bit her lip as she turned off her computer and gathered her things. Should she stop by medical? *Did* she need to talk to a mental health expert? Was she losing her marbles?

Memories of those words: "Jackie, please. You've got to be all right" continued to play over and over in her head. If she told anyone that her dead boyfriend from almost a decade past had died saving her from a random shooting ten days ago, they'd be right in thinking her off-balance. Worse yet, if she told them she was now wondering if that same twice-killed person might be alive, they'd probably have her committed.

Feeling Nadine's eyes on her, she looked toward her friend. Nadine's head was tilted as she tried to figure out what had been said and what was going on.

Jackie shook her head slightly and tried to imbue her strained smile with an "everything's fine" message. Nadine's eyebrows drew together, but Jackie gave a small wave and turned away. They'd talk after work.

Except that her phone was already vibrating.

"You ok?"

"Yeah. Chris just suggested I take some more time off. DON'T WORRY!"

"Of course I'm worried. Call me later."

Jackie shot her another forced smile and moved to the elevator. She stared at the buttons. All she wanted was to go home, crawl in bed, and wake up three weeks ago. Should she visit medical? No, but suddenly a different idea came to mind. She pressed two. She'd start with personnel and see if she could learn anything there.

Decision made, Jackie tried to simultaneously scratch the annoying itch just beyond her reach under her cast and come up with a logical, believable approach.

She wanted to talk more with Jake Carpentero's landlord. She could use the excuse of delivering any of Jake's personal effects, if there were any, as he was the closest thing to family. That sounded feasible. And she really would like to see the older man again. If anyone knew anything that might help her clear things up, it would be Mr. Riga. And he could probably use the company. He had seemed so lost the day she and Nadine had visited him. The poor man had now lost both his wife and his son, as well as the tenant he depended on. The tenant who had apparently had a tattoo designed by Jackie's long-dead boyfriend. Okay, so her motives *were* mostly selfish. But he still had to be pretty lonely.

She glanced in the elevator mirror. Normally she wore her hair tied back in a ponytail or barrette. With only one functional hand, though, she'd been forced to leave her shoulder-length hair loose, and she'd been washing it less frequently since covering the cast was such an enormous pain in the ass. The woman in the mirror struck her as old, drab, and exhausted.

The last few weeks had robbed her of anything resembling equilibrium, and she was now being sent home because her work was shoddy.

She'd been shot, and a person she loved had been ruthlessly torn from her life. Exactly how and when was now an ongoing and mind-boggling mystery, but she had loved him, and he was gone. She, however, was alive, dammit. She forced her shoulders back and straightened her spine. She would speak to people in HR as a poised and articulate professional. Her arm was in a cast, but she had *not* lost her marbles. She had a right to know what facts there were about the person who had undoubtedly saved her life, and she was going to find answers. The Leo she had loved so deeply would have done the same for her, wouldn't he? She didn't want to admit that she now had no clue whatsoever as to what Leo might have done.

AN HOUR later Jackie stood staring pensively at her car before finally clicking the unlock button. She would do it. She would go see Mr. Riga. He was a nice man whose life had been meaninglessly laid waste. He was also the only person who might shed light on who Jake Carpentero had been.

Personnel had been both helpful and obstructive, as she had expected. Privacy was such an easy shield for gatekeepers in all walks of life to put up without a second thought.

Anticipating roadblocks, Jackie had used her phone to check privacy rights of dead people before entering the HR department and had been surprised to learn there were few, aside from those concerning property.

On her side as well was the cast on her arm and the dubious renown of being one of the Home Pantry "survivors." People everywhere were treating her like a fragile piece of porcelain, so she might as well take advantage of their sympathy.

Jackie had embellished her relationship to Mr. Riga, and real tears had come yet again to her eyes when she said quietly that mementos of Jake and Danny were all the older man had left in the world.

The forty-something woman, Mrs. Rodriguez, stood up and gave Jackie a gentle, awkward hug.

"You poor dear. It's so kind of you to look out for him. He must be devastated. But you know, Mr. Carpentero's desk area was surprisingly clean. He wasn't like some of the young parents who have family pictures and kids' drawings everywhere around their workstations. Let me see where we put his things."

She moved out of sight for a few minutes and came back carrying a Home Pantry tote bag.

"This is all there was, believe it or not. John Riga was listed as his emergency contact, so it saves us the hassle of getting it to him if you're going to see him."

"Can you tell me where Jake worked before he came to Home Pantry?"

Mrs. Rodriguez puckered her face in thought. "I can't share his personnel records, of course, but I've been here about five years myself, and I know I didn't process his onboarding. I'm pretty sure the memorial notice they put out said he had been here for seven years, but I have no idea offhand where he was before that."

Feeling foolish, Jackie realized she had read the same notice herself. An official bio had been released with the company's circulated tribute in which Jake, Gloria, and Karina were memorialized. The details presented about administrative assistant Karina included the names of numerous siblings and other family ties, her participation in the Home Pantry welcoming association, and her work with local animal shelters. Gloria's mentioned her quick rise in the purchasing division, her family, her love of tennis, and her fiancé.

The paragraph on Jake had been sparse. It said he was thirty-four, had grown up in Central Texas, and had received outstanding evaluations throughout his time at Home Pantry. There had been no mention of family or outside activities.

If Jake were Leo, he should have been thirty-one. Jackie shook her head as she drove. Similar inconsistencies kept ricocheting around her thoughts, driving her crazy. But her mind persisted in mulling over one unrealistic idea after another. Leo had survived the explosion in Virginia but had permanent amnesia. Or he and his mother were part of the mob. *But who had ever heard of a Swedish mob?!* Or perhaps one or both of them had witnessed a crime and were in a witness protection program. Or maybe Leo had been kidnapped and brainwashed and was now part of some bizarre religious cult.

Each and every one of these ideas was preposterous. Yet the combination of her own instincts and Mr. Riga's account of the tattoo made her absolutely certain that Leo and Jake had been the same person.

Jackie snorted. She was absolutely certain of nothing. Except for the amnesia storyline, which would fit easily into a soap opera but had little likelihood of being real, all her other ideas involved deception of one kind or another. Perceptive Nadine, after all, would presumably have caught on if Jake had been a brainwashed zombie.

Yet one thought kept nagging her: the Leo she had known —the Leo she had loved and whose love in return she had been sure of—would not have deceived her.

She found a spot easily on the residential street and sat for a moment, considering. She had to at least offer Mr. Riga the tote bag, even though she was pretty sure he'd have no desire for it. She looked at the contents again. There was a folded navy-blue blazer, nice and generic looking. Something a man could slip on while casually dressed if called to interact in a more formal setting. A coffee mug that had the word Austin emblazoned on it.

A spurt of irritation shot up Jackie's spine. No one could be this bland without it being intentional. A small cardboard desk-top calendar, the same every Home Pantry office employee received, had September showing, but there were no marks on the page.

Mrs. Rodriguez had told her they had kept the miscellaneous office supplies. The only remaining items in the bag were a phone charger, a tablet of some kind in a sturdy protective case, and an additional charger that presumably went with the tablet.

Unless the tablet contained the secrets of the universe, which she highly doubted, it all amounted to nothing. Jake Carpentero had left almost no human footprints. Only someone living a lie would behave that way.

But why? The memories she had for years both clung to and tried to keep buried swept over her again. Lying in Leo's arms, tracing his light, curly chest hair and replete from toe-tingling ecstasy, had been the closest thing to bliss she had ever known.

Improbably, they had learned about sex from each other. They were both guilty of insinuating that they had prior experience, but the first night they had gone all the way, Leo stopped after pulling on a condom, took her face in his hands, and caressed her cheeks with his thumbs as he stared into her eyes.

"I don't have all the expertise I may have pretended to have. I want to make this good for you, but I'm scared I'll mess it up." He shut his eyes tightly for just a second before looking at her again. "I've never done this before with anyone."

Jackie bit her lip, nervousness and fierce joy competing for preeminence. Then she laughed, pulling his head to hers and trying to talk and kiss him at the same time.

"I'm so glad. You're my first, too. I never really wanted anyone the way I want you. We can figure it out together."

And had they ever. Their delight in each other's bodies, in finding the perfect ways to torment, tease, and thrill, had been unceasing.

But there had been joy in everything else, as well. In sleeping together, cocooned in a pocket of absolute contentment. In walking around the university, their hands interlinked. In the short but often subversive texts they sometimes sent each other during class.

My professor just mentioned Reagan's attempts to lick inflation, and it made me want to pull you out of class, drag you home, and lick you everywhere 🩶

How Jackie had struggled not to laugh, her insides filling with warmth and anticipation.

Could all that have been a charade? She had spent the last decade of her life half-dead inside, mourning the happiness that had been ripped away. The peculiarities bombarding her these last few weeks had been seismic, but a fiercely indignant ember inside refused to be doused. He *had* loved her. It had not been a delusion on her part.

As she sat in the car, staring at the meager possessions left behind by Jake Carpentero, Jackie felt a wave of determination sweep over her.

The man who had knocked her down at Texas Tango—whoever he had been—had cried out words that showed genuine concern, not indifference or deceit. She had to decide right now who she believed that man had been. If she was certain he was a sham or a criminal, then she'd hand over his possessions, say goodbye to Mr. Riga, and try to move on. If he was her Leo, then she needed to fight for him. She needed to find out why the man she had loved as Leo in Virginia had turned up as Jake in Texas. And then she had to find out if he was alive or dead.

CHAPTER THIRTEEN

S even fucking paces. That's all the space the sterile apartment allowed him to stride in exasperation from one corner of his main room to the other before crashing into utilitarian furniture. The incessant grayness of the Albany weather matched David's mood to a T. During the workday he feigned polite interest in his new coworkers and surroundings, but he refused all invitations to afterwork happy hours or other social gatherings. At Sam's suggestion, he dropped hints about the severe car accident he had been involved in that had left him physically recuperating. When pushed for other personal details, he deftly diverted the conversation. He'd been doing the same thing for years in Austin, so obfuscation was almost as instinctive as breathing.

At home he pushed himself relentlessly, walking up and down the apartment emergency staircases for thirty-minute stretches and slowly and painfully working himself up to full push-ups and planks. Some muscle tissue had been irreparably damaged, so teaching the surrounding tendons and muscles to compensate would take time and perseverance. Perseverance he could muster, but he chafed at how slowly time was passing.

As he paced, he kept a mental list of items he needed to attend to in order to do what he really wanted: find out how Jackie was. Kept tightly locked up for so many years, his emotions now exploded with fierce anger, indignation, and regret. Why had he allowed them to take from him the only thing, the only person, who gave meaning to his life? Why had he believed that thinking him dead was the only way she could be guaranteed safety? She wasn't safe. She had been shot, for fuck's sake.

Sam had finally found and read to him the names of the dead during the miserable journey to New York. The wave of relief—not hearing Jackie's name on that list—had been so great that he was happy he had been lying on his belly, his face hidden. He didn't want Sam to have any inkling of how important that information had been.

He had read the accounts of the shooting online and obsessively followed the news that quickly faded about the victims. The names of the dead had included a few he remembered from his work at Home Pantry, but he could find little about those who had been injured.

He burned with the need to know where she was, how she was recovering, whether her memories of him flamed as vividly as his of her. He cursed his own sheep-like behavior over the past decade and remembered a meme he had seen once: Keep your nose to the grindstone, and all you end up with is a flat nose.

That's what he had done: followed instructions and kept his nose to the grindstone. And what did he have to show for it? A dead soul, an empty life, and a fit body that had none-theless been knocked down by a psychopath's bullets.

Abutting his indignant anger, however, simmered an even hotter hatred and fear of the horrible insinuations Sam had finally let drop. If it were true—and, goddamn it all to hell, it was not true—that he was the progeny of an oligarch or worse, there was no way he could allow Jackie to know he was alive. She would, indeed, be in danger then, probably even more danger than she was in now merely living her life in a gun-crazed environment.

And so the hours he didn't spend trying to rehab his body or wear out the industrial carpet were spent scouring the internet. He would not do any checking on Jackie that might make its way back to Sam and company. That would have to wait until he had procured new devices on his own. He didn't give a shit, though, if they knew he was searching for information to contradict their absurd innuendo.

But he wasn't an idiot. Sam had protected him and his mother well these many years, so he couldn't jeopardize that care now by lighting a flare for the Russians to find. Sam might have his actual devices bugged, but Jake used the VPN account he had memorized from his time in Austin before any search session. It might tip off Sam that he was acting independently, but hopefully it would keep the Russians from paying a call.

He had been ten years old the last time he had been required to read and write in Russian with any regularity. He had read some literature online, often at his mother's urging, but a young, tech-savvy Mexican-American was not likely to have volumes of Dostoevsky or Pelevin lying about his home or office. So on top of the repulsive nature of his research, reading details about men he considered less than human, he had to scavenge through long-buried brain cells and actually resort to a dictionary at times, all of which left him even more exhausted and resentful.

How could he prove a negative? Prove it so conclusively that there could be no lingering doubts? He remembered little of his beloved Papa and even less of his grandparents.

They had all been part of his life when he was a young boy, and then they were gone. Blurred images slipped through his memory like a kaleidoscope: walking outside in snow with a grandfather on each side holding his hands, teasing him about *Dyed Moroz's* upcoming visit. One grandmother singing to him while the other baked mouth-watering *pechenye* in the kitchen.

Jake's head fell back as memory of those cookies flooded his senses. His tongue touched his teeth as he remembered the dual sensation of pain and delight when he gleefully "snuck" a cookie directly from the baking tray, his grand-mother laughing and kissing him. Were those memories all from the same occasion, or was he conflating them? Had they left those freshly baked cookies out for *Dyed Moroz*, or was he superimposing ideas from the American tradition of leaving cookies for Santa with his own recollections of the Soviet version, secularly renamed Grandfather Frost?

He gritted his teeth, trying to get hold of his anger. So much had been ripped away from him. His mother had given him love, security, and support, but her refusal to talk about the past—or even, he now realized, their present—had denied him memories and a foundation that most people took for granted.

What had become of those four wonderful people he had loved so dearly? Why had he allowed the door to be shut and been complicit in its shutting, countenancing his own trans-formation into a two-dimensional caricature?

He knew his name, and he knew his father's name. But he didn't know where his father had been born or the full names of any of his grandparents. His parents had met in Leningrad, before it became known once again as St. Peters-burg, but they had been living in Moscow before he and his mother had fled.

Fled. He had known his whole fucking life they had fled,

but he had never seriously questioned why or from what. Those first few years had been overwhelming, and his mother had always distracted him when he tried to ask questions. And then he had been caught up in the challenges and drama of teenage life as an American boy and had focused his attention on important things: sports, video games, and girls. Then had come college, he had met Jackie, and every part of his life had seemed perfect.

He remembered the night he saw her for the first time. Not sure if he was allowed to bring coffee into the library, he held the cup down by his side with his right hand, glancing at the girl working the desk. Though he was anxious to pass without being noticed, his feet and breath had stopped of their own accord, and he had stood, for just a moment, spellbound. She was so pretty, and at once both so different from other girls he had met and somehow strangely familiar. She was caught up in the book she had propped up to the side of the large library computer screen in front of her, and she was oblivious to the students moving past her.

Or so he had thought. He found out later that he was, indeed, allowed to bring in coffee, and that she had been amused by his attempts at subterfuge. Apparently he hadn't been the first to think he was getting away with something forbidden.

His visits to the library grew more frequent. His course work, always good, showed no obvious improvement since he spent so much time thinking of one reason or another to visit the front desk. When it finally entered his thick head that she was watching for him as much as he for her, he got up the nerve to ask her if she wanted to go for a walk after her shift was over.

He had optimistically brought a flashlight, and when she agreed, he led her up the hill behind the freshman dorms to an area shown him by a friend taking an astronomy course.

An old observatory stood tall and majestic, now seldom used and locked tight, but the land surrounding it was perfect. Lying on the ground, their backpacks as pillows, they watched the wonders of the night sky and began the enchanting journey of getting to know each other.

His life shifted from good to perfect. He enjoyed his classes, had time and opportunity to sing and compose, and was in love with the most wonderful girl on the planet. The iPhone had recently been released, there was a young and progressive president, and life held nothing but glorious opportunities.

And when he fell asleep at night, it was a sleep of profound joy, more likely than not following a round of toe-curling bliss. Jackie was on the pill, so there was no messy condom to deal with. She often fell asleep nestled perfectly on top of him, and more than once, she had shifted, still half-asleep, to take his morning erection inside her, a smile on her lips as they both woke up and delighted in each other's presence. He was the luckiest guy on earth.

Christmas of his third year had included Jackie staying a few days with him and his mother, him visiting Jackie's home in Northern Virginia for a few days, and then spending the rest of his break again with his mother in Ruckersville. And that's when reality had come crashing back.

"I don't know for sure. It might still be okay. But Sam says we have to be ready."

"Ready? There's no ready. I can't just up and leave school! I'm getting a degree. I have a life. I have Jackie. You have a life! Mama, come on. This is all crazy."

She had looked at him then, tired blue eyes that had so seldom showed tears now brimming with them.

"You're right. We both have lives. But it's only thanks to the grace of God, the integrity of the U.S. government, and Sam's constant vigilance."

"What are you talking about? We left Russia years ago. This is our home now. This is our house, our street, our world. Nobody cares about us here. We're not in any danger."

His mother bit her lip and turned away, looking wrung out, and for the first time in his memory, like she was truly getting older.

"It's complicated, *golubchik*. More complicated than you would ever want to understand. But you have to trust me."

She took his face in her hands and spoke to him gently, in Russian, something she rarely did anymore.

"This is truly important and could literally mean the difference between life and death. Yours, mine, and even Jackie's. If I say you have to come, you have to come, instantly. Do you understand?"

He stared back at her, confused and frightened. Was she delusional? Paranoid? Could she be ill?

"My sweet Kolya."

More warning bells. She almost never called him by his real name, Nikolai, or its diminutive, Kolya.

"I see what you are thinking. I am not crazy, my love. Someday, when the danger is truly past, I will explain everything to you. But until then, we must trust Sam. It's what your father would have wanted."

She turned away, tears once again welling up in her eyes, and he had surrendered, resigned. He had come to suspect over the years that his foggy past was strewn with landmines, and at age twenty, almost twenty-one, he could admit that cowardice had prevented him from digging for answers.

Exposed to people and ideas his small-town adolescent years had spared him, he had spent only a short time as a scholar at a competitive university before he grudgingly acknowledged to himself that brilliant, multi-lingual translators didn't live in his small hometown. Nor did the other residents of Ruckersville, Virginia receive regular visits from

Uncle Sam, in person, and driving a Ford. And yet he had deliberately shut his eyes and his thoughts, and looked away, not wanting to know.

But when faced with his mother's palpable fear, he nodded, finally, and promised that he would stay ready. He would come if she called. He just hoped to hell whatever was scaring her at the moment would blow over and she would never call.

Those last few months at UVA had been both heaven and hell. Heaven, to have his life and his nights so closely interwoven with Jackie's, to sing with two classmates in the tiny band they had formed, and to truly enjoy the computer science, politics, and Spanish literature courses he was taking. Hell, fearing that the ground could give way at any moment, and he could lose it all. Wanting desperately to confide in Jackie but keeping silent, as he had promised his mother and Sam.

Because Sam had called him directly not long after his mother's bombshell.

"Leo, I need to be able to trust you. Your silence matters. If you care for your girlfriend, you need to make concern for her safety your highest priority."

And so he had tried to keep everything normal, crossing his fingers that his luck would last and holding Jackie tightly in his arms long after she fell asleep.

Luck. To this day the word made him snort derisively. He wasn't really Swedish, certainly wasn't Mexican, and had not even a drop of Irish blood. Which was maybe why the luck of the Irish was indifferent to his pleas when his mother called on that horrible St. Patrick's Day morning.

"You need to come. The furnace is broken."

Eight simple words, and life, as he had known and loved it, was over.

THE FUCKING Russian genealogical sites were a joke. There were no indexes, and months or even years were missing from some archives, both historical and contemporary, with no explanation. It probably didn't help that his childhood had occurred during a time of political and social upheaval. He was born in Moscow, the capital of both the Russian Republic and the Soviet Union. Before he was out of diapers, the Soviet Union was history, the configuration of Europe and Central Asia had been drastically changed, and the bedrock of millions of people had shifted.

He knew he hadn't lived a normal life, even aside from his chaotic childhood. Whenever documentation was required: for a driver's license, for his school enrollment, or for medical records, Sam was always there, handing over whatever was required. He knew that Leo Jorgensson's birthdate was slightly different from Nikolai Polivanov's, and that Jake Carpentero's and David Hilderman's varied still more widely. So why was he even bothering to think that online records might be a source of valid information?

He scowled at his screen, angry at his years of complacency. He was no better than a stupid marionette, mindlessly manipulated by all-knowing puppeteers.

Trawling the internet was proving to be useless, as he had both feared and expected. Jewish researchers were taking pains to unravel family histories in historic Russia, the Soviet Union, and now Russia again, but Jake was pretty certain he had no Jewish ancestry.

His head turned partly away in disgust, he squinted at pictures of the head villain's children. Three of them, supposedly, with hints of perhaps others, though there were few public records. All nondescript looking, with no remarkably unique features. Couldn't the same be said of him, whoever he was?

Fuming, he stared at an ad for DNA research. Should he submit a sample to 23andMe or AncestryDNA? His two-minute perusal showed they offered optional relative-finding services.

Sam would kill him.

Did he give a shit anymore?

Was it possible that stray ancestors generations back had emigrated to the West and now had descendants that might be his distant cousins? If he remembered correctly, random Russians had arrived in the colonies and the new country in the 1700s and many more in the 1800s. Alternatively, might distant stray ancestors of the monsters currently in charge have emigrated, leaving their DNA available for comparison?

Sam would kill him.

If he submitted anything, he would have to use a fake identity, a fake email, a fake IP address. He doubled over in humorless mirth, the sudden movement evoking a hoarse cry at the lingering pain in his chest. When he finally did die, how in the world would anyone be able to identify him? And if he ever, EVER found Jackie again, would there be any possible way to regain her trust?

CHAPTER FOURTEEN

"Thank you for letting me take these things. We're going to try to find any distant family members and see if they want them."

The lie sprang easily from her lips, but she felt no guilt. It was obvious that Mr. Riga had no desire to keep Jake Carpentero's belongings. The burden of losing his own son was his primary preoccupation.

"If no one turns up, donate everything to charity. He was a genuinely kind person. I'm sure that's what he would want."

"Is there anything I can help you with? I know this has been so hard." She should just leave, but he seemed so alone.

Mr. Riga's eyes, as they passed distractedly over her, were sunken deep in his face. He looked thinner and more stooped than he had just a week ago at the service.

Jackie's stomach rumbled, and she took a step back, startled and a little embarrassed. When had she last eaten? She'd been too tired lately to bother with a real breakfast, sometimes grabbing a bar on her way out, and sometimes not. Today had evidently been a "not."

If she had been eating poorly of late, Mr. Riga had probably fared far worse.

"Mr. Riga, I don't mean to be rude, but I'm starving. How about you come with me to get something to eat? I saw a taco place that looked good just a few blocks away."

His eyes focused on her, perhaps for the first time since she had rung his bell. Letting her in with barely a glance, he had said that not only could she hold on to whatever had been in the office, but that she could take anything left in Jake's apartment.

"The police came and took a couple boxes of stuff, but the rest is all just sitting there. Do whatever you think best with it."

That was odd. Why had the police taken stuff? The question flitted through her consciousness, but Mr. Riga seemed unbothered, so she let it go.

He gave Jackie the key, and she had spent almost half an hour in Jake's apartment, once again both surprised and not surprised by the spartan remains of the shadowy figure's occupancy. She put aside a small pile of items that might hold some interest but didn't bring them with her when she came down again, thinking perhaps Mr. Riga hadn't really intended her to take everything.

"Let's go get some lunch, and then I'll pack up the rest of what's left upstairs, if that's really all right with you."

He gave a tired half shrug and first shook his head and then nodded. "That's fine. But I don't need any lunch."

Jackie's eyes narrowed as she studied him. Yes, her motives for coming here were selfish, but the elderly man was really hurting. She had been without Leo, or Jake, or whoever the hell he was, for almost a decade. This poor man's grief was raw and inflamed. And it seemed he had no one.

"Come with me, Mr. Riga. If you don't like tacos, we can go somewhere else. Maybe ice cream?"

Where had that come from? *And oh, damn,* it seemed like she had somehow managed to upset him even more.

John Riga turned away from her and sat on the edge of an old, tired-looking sofa, tears rolling down his pale cheeks.

"Danny loved ice cream. He always said the best things about Austin were the music, the people, and the ice cream, and if Texas Tango didn't work, he'd open an ice cream shop."

Confused and overwhelmed, Jackie found tears welling up in her own eyes. She sat down next to him and reached for his hand.

"We can get through this, Mr. Riga. I know it's hard. It's not right, and it's not fair, but we can get through this. Danny wouldn't have wanted you to be so unhappy. If he loved ice cream, we should go get some. The person I loved most in the world adored music, and when I lost him, I stopped listening to music. That was stupid. We need to keep the people we love alive by honoring their memories."

His fingers were thin, cool, and dry in her own, his knuckles slightly swollen and small age spots visible on his hands and wrists. Looking at their two, so different, hands, she felt a surge of compassion. She would be his age soon enough, and she'd likely be alone, too.

Mr. Riga let out a long, quiet sigh and tightened his fingers around hers.

"Okay, my dear. Let's go get some ice cream. It'll be my treat, in honor of Danny."

THEY ENDED up spending more than two hours in the ice cream parlor. Mr. Riga turned out to have a wicked sense of humor, noticing small things about other customers that Jackie didn't see and regaling her with stories about old Austin.

"Once Willie Nelson came to town, the whole world started paying attention to all the great music that was here already: folk, Cajun, jazz, Mexican, and rock. Young people love music, so the tech companies first started having meetings here, then opening offices, and the rest is history. And of course, young people love ice cream. It goes down easily after a hard night of sex, drugs, and rock 'n' roll."

Jackie choked into her dish of salted caramel pecan.

"Is that what brought you here?"

"Nope. I was born here. Not many people in town can say that anymore. But it certainly helped encourage me to stay, especially after my Sophie arrived. She was a transplant from the east coast like you."

"How do you know where I'm from?"

"I don't. But I can tell you're not a native Texan. You also don't have a southern drawl or a mid-western lilt, and you're certainly not a crazy Californian. No New England affectedness, so I'd guess somewhere between New York and Maryland, though definitely not Baltimore."

Jackie burst out laughing. "Northern Virginia, actually."

"Close enough. My Sophie was from New Jersey, but the normal part, away from the cartoonish circle surrounding New York City."

"So what are you, Mr. Riga? A linguist, a sociologist, or maybe an historian?"

"You're a sweet child. I spent my entire career in food services at UT, believe it or not. I started right out of high school and worked my way up. I got to take classes over the years and eventually earned my BS, and that's how I met Sophie. But I never left food service until I retired five years ago. I retired, they found Sophie's cancer, and it's all been downhill since then."

He stopped speaking, but his fingers continued to tear tiny pieces off the top of his now empty paper ice cream dish.

"You must have met so many people over the years. No wonder you're an expert on accents."

His smile was lackluster, but at least he was meeting her eyes now.

"That I did. I used to keep a tally sheet, but I gave up after a while. I've met people from every state, of course, and from most foreign countries. Although I've been around so long, even the names of several countries changed during my career. But I was always fascinated by how people from different parts of the world were able to make English their means of communicating."

Feeling slightly guilty, Jackie grabbed the chance to do some digging.

"Jake was Mexican-American, right? How long did he live with you, and how was his English?"

Mr. Riga snorted. "His English was as good as yours or mine. Better, probably. He was a smart one, that boy. He didn't have a particularly Mexican accent, but I heard him speaking Spanish a few times, and he always sounded fluent."

He frowned a bit before continuing. "I speak Spanish, of course. I grew up here and worked among locals all my life, so my Spanish is conversational. I couldn't read a book in Spanish or anything like that. But Jake's Spanish always sounded more educated, somehow. If he didn't hear something, he would say 'Perdón' more often than 'Cómo,' and he'd never say 'Mande.'

"As to when he moved in . . ." His glance turned pensive as he mentally calculated. "Danny opened Texas Tango about eight years ago, and he brought Jake to see the apartment right after that first couple moved out. Danny did all the work to separate the upstairs from our section about the same time he was shopping around for where to establish his bar. He knew I was planning to retire sometime soon, and he thought renting the space, as long as it was to someone decent, would be a good way to bring in extra money. He was always looking out for us, Danny was. He was the best son we could ever have wanted."

She spoke quickly, hoping to keep him from becoming too emotional once more.

"How did Danny get to know Jake?"

Mr. Riga stared off into the distance.

"I'm not sure I remember. The bar, probably, although Jake was never a partier, and I know he didn't spend much time there after he moved in, aside from gaming nights now and then. But you're right about accents. He certainly didn't speak English like he grew up around here. His accent was probably more like yours or Sophie's, if anything."

"Did you ever hear him speaking other languages? Or did he ever talk about his family?"

"Nope. He told me when he moved in that his immediate family was all dead and that he had lost touch with everyone else. He seemed awfully young to be totally alone, but I didn't press him. Sophie loved him dearly, and he was very good with her at the end, helping me whenever he was around. Before she got sick, she used to tease him about spending too much time in front of screens, but he said that computer work was what kept his mind occupied and out of trouble."

He chuckled. "He wasn't the type to get in trouble, so that was just nonsense."

Jackie was struck by a sudden thought.

"You said he was into computer gaming?"

"Yeah, he was, but he was never crazy like the warped young men you hear about on the news. Most young men these days waste time on that sort of thing, though, don't they? Danny doesn't."

He stopped, and it took a few seconds before he continued. "He didn't. But that's maybe because he was always so busy. I know there was a group of them that met at the bar on Mondays, when crowds were low, and I'm pretty sure Jake went to those fairly often."

"But you never heard him speaking other languages?" *Like Swedish?*

Mr. Riga blew an almost silent raspberry while shaking his head. "I don't think so. Did he need to, for work?"

"No, no. I just wondered. He didn't seem to have a lot of things in his apartment. I didn't even see a computer."

Mr. Riga stared into the distance, obviously thinking. "He had at least two computers up there, if I recall. They were probably in the boxes of stuff the police took."

"Why would the police want his computers? He was a victim at the shooting, not one of the suspects."

"I have no idea. Two men came, showed me their badges, and said they had to examine Jake's apartment. I was so upset at the time, I didn't really pay any attention. And what does it matter? The poor boy is dead, and I certainly have no use for his computers or any of the rest of his things."

It was Jackie's turn to methodically tear apart her ice cream dish. Why in the world would the police have wanted Jake's computers? Should she press Mr. Riga further about the men who had come to his house or mention any of her other thoughts? Would involving him make things easier or harder for him? And what if he just came to the conclusion that she was a raving lunatic?

She certainly wasn't going to get anywhere staring at her apartment walls or crying into her pillow at night. She had unloaded onto Nadine, and so far, no men in white coats had come to collect her.

"Mr. Riga, I can't even imagine how awful it's been for you to have lost Danny. I was there, and the horror of that night will never leave me. So many young and innocent people lost their lives for no reason."

She looked up and found he was meeting her eyes again, still sad, but in control.

"I hope you don't think I'm on a wild goose chase, but I'm convinced there was something odd about Jake. A lot of details about him don't really add up, and I'm trying to figure out . . ."

He studied her, obviously uncertain where she was going.

"Figure out what? If he wasn't who he said he was, what does it matter? He was a good man, and now he's gone."

Jackie took a deep, slow breath. If she continued, it would now be two people who knew her perhaps insane thoughts. Would that drive them away, or might it lead to new ideas for finding the truth?

"Remember when you mentioned the tattoo that Jake had?"

Mr. Riga looked momentarily confused.

"Oh, right. That day you and that other pretty girl came by. I probably shouldn't have talked about that. It was none of my business."

She reached over and took his hand once more.

"Mr. Riga, I think I might be the Jackie that Jake said he lost. I think maybe his name wasn't Jake, and that maybe, just maybe, he might not even be dead."

CHAPTER FIFTEEN

You're acting like a two-year-old.

The internal rebuke was merited, but Jake couldn't help the delight he felt carrying his new iPad out of the store. He had bought it with cash, calmly shaking his head at offers for extended service plans or registration. Waiting to get access to his funds had been frustrating, surreptitiously signing into different accounts from various workstations at his new job whenever the people assigned to them were away from their desks, or on the rare occasions he needed to physically work on their devices as part of his job. His job, to which he was devoting probably less than ten percent of his conscious attention.

Thank God his new position at Today and Tomorrow Tech was less challenging than the work he had done at Home Pantry, since he was certainly short-shrifting it. For all its impressive moniker, the company handled relatively simple accounts, and he could do most of what was asked of him on autopilot.

Now that he had his own device, untouched by Sam and his well-meaning associates, Jake hoped to follow whatever ideas came to him down whatever online rabbit holes he found. He would find out all he could about Jacqueline Bourne.

Don't get carried away.

He voiced the warning to himself innumerable times per day. She was not *his* Jackie. He had abandoned her, broken her heart, and ignored her very existence for more than nine years. And there was no point in finding out any more about Jackie until he had resolved the problem of the other elephant in the room.

His attempts at self-discipline were more challenged at night. His bedroom was as nondescript as the rest of his apartment, and the double bed, with its oh-so-exciting, scratchy beige sheets did little to invite restful slumber. Instead, he lay awake, night after night, senselessly trying to think of ways he could have circumvented Sam's instructions those many years ago.

Should he have told Jackie his true identity? Could he have found a way to warn her when Sam and his mother first hinted that trouble was brewing?

The circle of questions kept leading him back to the basic premise he had incomprehensibly left unexamined these many years: *why were he and his mother a threat so terrible that they were safer dead than alive? Even supposing the unspeakable idea hinted at by Sam were true, that he was the by-blow of some powerful autocrat, why did that mean he and his mom had to die?*

He had gotten involved with a few online games during his years in Austin and even participated in game nights at Texas Tango. He used the name PantryTech—a bland enough designation that had served him in his position and locale. Now, during the long sleepless nights far from anyone he knew, his thoughts coalesced on what he wanted most desperately: to put his new HarryAlfred online-Avatar-self on a plane in two directions at once: one to Switzerland to interrogate his mother, and the other back to Austin to find Jackie. Yes, he had managed, more or less successfully, to put Jackie out of his mind for years. But in those terrifying seconds after the shooting had started, his love and core-deep connection to her had come roaring back. He had felt her body under his for the briefest of moments and had looked into her warm, beautiful eyes. He had held her in his arms, and now his arms physically ached with the need to touch her again.

Instead, he did push-ups, paced, climbed stairs, and trawled the Internet. And now he had a device that he knew Sam hadn't touched. He had VPNs to obscure his IP address and fake identities online.

When his thoughts grew too tortuous and his research fruitless, he turned to online chess, something he had always loved, or the game, *Battle Realms*, a role-playing game he had been playing for years.

His father had taught him chess as a little boy, and his first school in Virginia had a chess club. The timeless game had been a way for him to feel less conspicuous amongst other children and the monitoring teachers when he was still struggling to feel comfortable with English.

As an adult, he had played online, sometimes against the computer, but more often with opponents around the world. PantryTech, Jake Carpentero's username, was obviously no longer a viable presence, and David "Jake" Hilderman was careful about where he kept JackSparrow451 active. Harry-Alfred was his new, online persona. He and Jackie had both loved the Harry Potter books, and Tennyson had been one of her favorite poets. HarryAlfred was beginning to establish a reputation, both in the chess arena and in *Battle Realms*.

He had seen himself as solitary and untethered throughout most of the last decade, so he was now surprised at how much he missed the people and habits that had infiltrated his supposedly introverted existence in Austin. He realized now that he had spent more time chatting with his landlord, John Riga, than he would have consciously admitted, especially as he sometimes found himself imagining telling him one silly detail or another from his new position at Today and Tomorrow Tech. How the old guy was surviving without his son, Jake didn't even want to think about. Jackie, thank God, didn't know he had been near-at-hand, but Mr. Riga had depended on him and was now alone in the world, and Jake wished he could reach out to him.

And Home Pantry had been a good place to work—the job itself challenging and the corporate atmosphere supportive and friendly. Plus he had enjoyed the workouts and camaraderie at the martial arts dojo and his semi-regular nights with the gaming group at Texas Tango.

There were dojos in Albany, he was fairly certain, but he hesitated to immerse himself into the life and culture of the New York state capital. Sam had presented this new life as another "permanent" solution, but Jake had no intention of putting down roots.

He missed Austin, and that one simple fact astonished him. If one could stand the heat, which he could, the climate was fine, the city was progressive, and despite the increasingly visible signs of poverty and homelessness, Austin itself was like a young person in their early twenties, with limitless possibilities. Albany felt more like a tired bureaucrat counting the days to retirement and hoping that nothing much would be asked of him or her.

Even the coffee shops seemed listless. Unwilling to spend time in the office break room, Jake had taken to prowling the streets nearby after finishing whatever food he had brought for lunch and eaten at his desk. There was a Starbucks within walking distance, of course, and two other shops in the general area. They served coffee, yes, but they didn't seem to offer anything else visually or musically, and even the community bulletin boards were empty. Perhaps it was the cold, which even in late October seemed to loom like an approaching maelstrom. Or maybe it was just him, projecting his own sense of impotence onto the innocent city around him.

Today, however, he spared no thought for his surroundings and ignored his cooling coffee. Instead, he stared at his screen, trying to decide if he was imagining things.

A new player had showed up on *Battle Realms*. The username was JackieNotO. Normally tags meant little, except to whoever created them and perhaps their immediate friends. But the reference to Jackie "O" rang a distant bell. When they were first getting to know each other, Jackie had mentioned her mother's fascination with Jackie O, someone completely unknown to Leo.

Long time Democrats, Jackie's grandparents had been ardent Kennedy supporters, and Jackie's mom had grown up enchanted with the Camelot legend. She had named her first daughter Jacqueline, partly in homage to that shattered dream, and partly because—or so she claimed—she just liked the name.

Jackie maintained that she was nothing like the glamorous former first lady. After looking her up, Leo disagreed, but his Jackie joked she was most definitely Jackie B, not Jackie O.

It could not be his Jackie. Not that there was a *his* Jackie, he reminded himself for the thousandth time. She hadn't played games of any sort, in person or virtually, preferring to curl up with a good book. But the coincidence was odd. And Nikolai/Leo/Jake/David/JackSparrow / PantryTech/Harry-Alfred had learned not to disregard coincidences.

CHAPTER SIXTEEN

The internal debate raging in Jackie's mind—which of her wild suspicions to share, in whom to confide, whether or not she should have herself committed to a looney bin—had not really subsided, but taking the plunge and voicing her suspicions to Mr. Riga had paid off almost instantly. The first words out of his mouth after she stuttered out her Swiss cheese-like theory were practical.

"You should check with the people he played games with. Those guys are all addicts. My guess is, if any one of them was beamed up onto another planet, he'd find a way to connect online before building an outhouse. If Jake's alive, he'll have an online presence somewhere, and his fellow gamers are the ones who could most likely identify him."

Jackie had stared at the older man, realizing after a second or two that her mouth was literally hanging open.

"You don't think I'm crazy?"

He emitted a soft, prolonged sigh as his gaze moved up again to the ice cream shop's ceiling and stayed there for a few seconds before returning to her.

"What's crazy is that two people thought it was okay to

116

waltz into a crowded bar and start shooting. What's crazy is that I had a beautiful family, and I'm the only one left. That's not the way life is supposed to work."

His eyes widened as he tried to hold in the suddenly brimming tears. He picked up a used napkin from the table and pressed it in turn to the thin, pale skin beneath each eye.

"Jake was a good boy. He was a good, decent human being. If he had secrets, there were probably good reasons for them. If he's someone you love, I understand why you'd want to find him. But don't forget about those good reasons. Jake talked about the woman on the tattoo with something like worship in his voice. If he walked away from her, and if that someone was you, there was a reason."

JACKIE KEPT his admonition in mind when she first relayed the conversation to Nadine. Her friend still voiced gentle doubts about Jackie's suspicions, but she tilted her head and considered her before speaking decisively.

"We need to talk to Russo. My brother's online whenever he's not on duty. We all tell him it's why he can't find a nice girl. If there's anyone who can say whether what Mr. Riga said makes sense, it's him. And I'm pretty sure he used to play with the group at Texas Tango, too."

Jackie sat back, stunned. That last particular detail somehow made the whole idea seem logistically possible.

"He played there? That means he probably knew Jake. Oh, Nadine, this is the chance I've been hoping for."

It had taken a few days to find a time when the three of them could sit down in person, and at first, Russo had assumed Jackie wanted to learn more about the investigation.

"I don't know any more than what's been on TV. The last

I heard, they don't even know if the shooter in the hospital is going to be able to talk again. Those guys defending the bar took care of him pretty damn good, just like he deserved."

Jackie and Nadine shared a wordless glance. They had both been there, both suffered in different ways from the horror of the shooting, but neither one of them was completely at ease with community vigilantism. Nadine had confided in Jackie that Russo was pushing her and her younger sister, Ana, to get a gun and let him teach them how to use it.

"I know, Russo. And honestly, I don't want to know any more about him. I'm just happy he's not going to walk away and shoot anyone else. I wanted to talk to you about Jake Carpentero. I heard recently that he used to play computer games at Texas Tango."

Taking a deep breath, she proceeded to give him an abridged account of her history, her speculations, and her idea for trying to find Jake online.

Hardly surprising, Russo's initial reaction had been incredulous.

"He's dead, guys. I'm sorry. You were both at the service. And dead people don't get to keep playing online."

He looked back and forth between Jackie and Nadine, his expression sympathetic.

Nadine held up her hand and gave her brother a warning look.

"We are not delusional, *hermano mío*. Listen to what Jackie has to say. Listen with an open mind and stop trying to see everything in black and white."

Jackie picked her words carefully, repeating some of what she had said a few minutes earlier, and saying it was just a hunch that kept bothering her. She had no reason to think there was anything sinister going on. She even threw in some pop psychology, hoping to make her ideas sound both reasonable and light-hearted at the same time.

"They told me at work to take time off in order to get my head together. I know this all sounds silly, but once I check it out and convince myself I'm just trying to avoid facing reality, I'll be able to get back on track."

Russo looked at her. He was cute, in terrific shape, and had probably never sat through a complete episode of Jeopardy in his life. But he wasn't dumb.

"You really think there's a chance this guy is alive?"

Jackie bit her lip, her eyes meeting Russo's. They wordlessly assessed each other for a few seconds. Finally she spoke, again choosing her words carefully.

"If it is at all possible that Jake Carpentero was the same person I once knew as Leo Jorgensson, then yes, I think there's a remote chance that Jake Carpentero didn't die in the shooting."

Russo scrunched up his face, processing all he had just heard.

"This should be easy enough to settle. I'll find out what happened to his body and get back to you."

Three days passed with excruciating slowness. Jackie and Nadine talked and texted, but Jackie forced herself not to ask if her friend had heard anything. Finally, Nadine called and said Russo wanted to meet them again.

He named a burger shop not far from the central library and said he'd meet them as soon as Nadine got off work. Having time on her hands, Jackie arrived early and ordered burgers for all of them with an extra-large serving of fries. Nadine arrived and smiled at the spread, but Russo grunted appreciably and swallowed several fries before wiping his mouth and giving them both an enigmatic look.

"I have to say, I thought you were both going off the deep end. But I've spent the last three days trying to check things out informally, and I've come to the conclusion that there's something. I don't know what that something may be, but you're right to at least have questions. Cause I'm finding nothing. Jake Carpentero was taken by ambulance to Seton. That's where you ended up, right, Jackie?"

Jackie nodded, and Russo continued.

"He's listed on the police report as a fatality, but when I finally found a death certificate, it lists his time of death as 11:15 p.m., and almost everything else is illegible or blank. When I looked at the other records for the night, it showed the first ambulance didn't even arrive until 11:32. I checked with a friend who works at the hospital, and he couldn't find a record of the disposition of the body or anything on file regarding treatment. He didn't do an extensive search, of course, which I wasn't asking him to do, cause I didn't want him to get into any trouble. But we both concluded that it was a little odd.

"So I'm definitely not saying you're right, but I can't say for sure that you're wrong. I haven't been able to find any kind of open and shut answers to your questions. Then there's this: you mentioned that the police had been to his apartment to collect some of his things. That's not normal, unless there's some suspicion of a tie between a perpetrator and a victim, and you'd still need a warrant. I haven't seen any evidence of one, but again, I'm trying to be careful about how many questions I ask."

He stopped speaking and mimed an exaggerated imitation of the shoulder-shrugging emoji. "I suppose there could be a logical explanation, but on the surface, it makes no sense. For any more digging, you'd need a court order, and I wouldn't be the one to help you."

"No, no, no." Jackie's objections came out instantly. "I don't want any kind of official investigation."

She looked down at her untouched burger and then back up at Russo.

"Thank you for checking on the police side. It really means a lot to me. Do you think you'd be willing to put your policeman self aside and look at it from a gaming perspective?"

Russo made another face. "You two are determined to play Nancy Drew, aren't you? I still think you're crazy, but I'll take a look."

Days later, Jackie had now spent more hours than she ever would have thought possible watching a young man do incomprehensible things on a computer screen. Russo claimed the game he, Jake, and the others from Texas Tango had played, most often involved world-building, strategy, diplomacy, and yes, a fair bit of violence, but it seemed like a complete waste of time to her. Russo seemed to be having a blast.

"As far as MMORPGs go, *Battle Realms* is one of the best."

Jackie and Nadine both stared at him as if he were speaking another language.

"It's a massive multiplayer online role-playing game."

At their continued look of bewilderment, he just shrugged and smiled. "This is what you wanted me to do, so you might as well try to enjoy it."

Nadine gave Jackie an exaggerated look of disgust but then poked her with her elbow and laughed. They were in an upstairs bedroom of the Perrera house where the family had all grown up and where everyone, except Rudi, the oldest and only married child, still lived. Russo had been "playing" —whatever that all entailed—for about two hours with both his and Jackie's laptops open in front of him. Nature had called, and he had stepped out just as Nadine stepped in.

"I cannot believe how you've got my brother helping you.

I've never known Russo to exert so much effort with a girl he wasn't hoping to score with."

Jackie winced. "Am I taking advantage of him? He said he liked playing and was having fun keeping two roles going at once."

Nadine shrugged. "Whatever. But you've got to admit, it's all kind of weird. Trying to find a dead man on a gaming platform is a little too *Twilight Zone* for me. When I suggested we talk to Russo, I would never have guessed he would take it all so seriously."

"He's still mocking me, but he did say that he's sworn an oath to serve, safeguard, and protect, and if it starts to look like there's any real funny business, he'll have to stop treating it like a game."

"So at what point do we call it 'funny business?' When one of the avatars shows up with a name tag saying 'hey, look at me! I've died twice IRL and am still here!'?"

Jackie closed her eyes, straining to identify the terms. Almost all the jargon was foreign to her, but she was trying hard to catch up.

"IRL?"

Nadine laughed. "Come on, girl. Join the 21st century. In real life."

Jackie grimaced. "Damn. Of course. I know that one from social media. I've heard so many crazy terms thrown around the last couple days that I lose track of what makes sense and what doesn't."

"Are you getting the hang of any of what Russo's doing? Any chance you'll start playing on your own, instead of him playing for you? Just trying to gauge whether I'm losing a friend to the dark side. And by the way, cute username."

"You think so? I couldn't decide whether it was better to go for subtle or obvious. If—and Jesus, a part of me still can't believe we're all acting like this is really possible—but if Leo is out there, I think there's a slight chance he might notice and recognize the name."

"Has Russo seen anything interesting so far?"

"He says players change all the time—new ones joining, others disappearing for long stretches, and some just popping in occasionally. He's keeping a list of new user-names—when he remembers, that is, or I keep it if I'm around. He's really into whatever's going on out there and gets pretty immersed when he's moving back and forth between laptops so quickly."

"So what, or who, has he found when he's aware enough to pay attention?"

Jackie held up the handwritten list she had started. Russo would call out names to her, and she would see if she had them already and jot down anything new.

"MustardGas, ToySoldier, Ebola, Pro-gram3d . . . these guys all sound a little twisted, don't you think? Makes Russo look outrageously normal. Did you know what he calls himself?"

Nadine shook her head.

"He's BlueLineBobby94. Apparently there are a lot of BlueLineBobbies out there, probably all cops, so he needed to add a number, and he chose his birth year."

Nadine rolled her eyes and then took over reading the list of names aloud. "MeatCleaver, ChopSuey, KingArthur, Atti-laTheHun, HarryAlfred . . . huh. I like the sound of King Arthur, but that last one's kind of boring, in comparison."

"Yes, I know. That one caught my eye, too. Gamers are making a statement with their gamertags. Russo's a cop, and he's not afraid to say so. And obviously a lot of these guys are harboring a love of violence. Russo says not many people use their actual names, so he really pressed me about using Jack-ieNotO. I originally put JackieBNotO, but he said absolutely no way to that one."

Nadine rolled her hand, signaling boredom, and Jackie took the hint.

"What it means is that HarryAlfred is probably some kind of statement of sorts as well. He—and who knows if it's a he, or a she, or a they—showed up last week and has been on regularly ever since."

"Is he any good? Does Russo assess their skills while trying to outmaneuver them as two different people? And is JackieNotO as good a player as BlueBoyWhatever, or is she an amateur?"

Jackie shrugged her shoulders and rolled her eyes. "Blue-LineBobby94! Keep up girl! Your brother has been incredibly sweet, buying into all this insanity and helping me out. He gets really wrapped up in everything and kind of barks out short answers if I ask questions, so I try not to bother him too much."

"Okay, let's look at this from an investigative perspective. Would Leo have any connection to MeatCleaver? Was he perhaps from a line of butchers? Or did he secretly want to join the military, like maybe ToySoldier does? Perhaps he loved Chinese food and he's ChopSuey? Or he's King Arthur, allowed to stay alive, despite having died twice, by the grace of Merlin?"

Jackie bent over laughing just as Russo re-entered the bedroom and took up his position at the desk.

"Quiet, you two. If you're going to babble, go somewhere else. And ChopSuey's an idiot. I hope he's not your elusive dead man."

"How's the posh HarryAlfred?"

Russo shot a condescending raised eyebrow at his sister. "That guy knows what he's doing. Things have notched up a good amount since he started playing."

Nadine shook her head at her brother's intensity and pulled Jackie out into the hall.

Jackie stared at the carpet, momentarily lost in thought. Nadine's questions made sense. People choose usernames based on their personal likes/dislikes/fascinations. What would the name HarryAlfred be expressing besides someone's actual name?

There was Prince Harry. She did a quick search on her phone of his full name: Henry Charles Albert David Duke of Sussex. *Holy shit. What a mouthful.* But no Alfred there. She put in just Harry, and the first populations were Harry Styles, Prince Harry, Harry Potter, and Harry and David.

"Alfred" brought her fettuccine Alfredo, Alfred Street Baptist Church, and Alfred Molina. Images for Alfred brought up Batman's butler.

She didn't realize how deep she was in her ruminations until Nadine tapped her on the head.

"Hello! You've been staring at your phone like it holds the secrets of the universe. What are you searching for?"

"HarryAlfred."

"What about him? It's probably some rich kid's name."

"Have you ever heard of Alfred, Lord Tennyson?"

"Is he some fancy royal?"

"No. He's a poet. Was a poet. He's dead. Been dead for more than a hundred years, I'm pretty sure."

"I'm not much for poetry. 'Roses are red, violets are blue, puppies are cute, and so are you' is about my speed. What's so special about this Lord guy?"

"He wrote some beautiful poetry. Kennedy liked him, and my mother's side of the family was all caught up in the whole Kennedy mystique. My mom had a poster with one of his poems on it, which she let me take, and I had up in my room at school. I remember it had the word *lees* in it, and Leo didn't know the word. He was Swedish, and though he spoke English perfectly, every once in a while there was a word he didn't know."

125

Nadine was looking at her like she was crazy.

"Listen, Miss Snootypants. I speak English perfectly, and I have no idea what a *lees* is, unless you're just pronouncing the word lease in some kind of snob accent. But more importantly, what the fuck do you mean Leo was Swedish? Jake Carpentero was not Swedish, of that much I'm absolutely certain."

Jackie let go of her bottom lip, realizing she was in actual pain from how much time she'd spent recently biting it.

"Yeah, I know. That's part of this whole mystery. The boy I met in college said his name was Leo Jorgensson, and that he and his mom had moved to the U.S. from Sweden. I know I've said his last name before, so it can't be that surprising."

"Listen, sweetie. I love you dearly, but I never paid any attention to his last name, even if you did mention it. Why should I? Besides, Leo is a perfectly good Hispanic name. I'm sorry, but if I had known you were imagining a Swede that had somehow magically turned into a Mexican, I would have told you that you were insane and stopped this silly search right from the start."

Jackie held up her hands, defensively.

"I know, but just wait. What if he wasn't Swedish? Or Jake wasn't Mexican? I never had any reason to question it until I started wondering about everything recently. Why would a smart, educated translator be living in rural Virginia? That's who Leo's mom supposedly was. There's nothing wrong with rural Virginia, but shouldn't she have lived in New York, or at least in a university town?

"And then Mr. Riga mentioned that Jake spoke very educated Spanish." Seeing Nadine's eyes narrow, she hastened to clarify.

"He made it sound like it was the kind of Spanish someone might have learned from a book, rather than a family. Did you ever speak Spanish with him?"

Nadine glared at her, lips pursed. Was she trying to remember or just seething, insulted by something Jackie had perhaps poorly verbalized?

"No." Her tone was clipped. "And I don't think I ever heard him speaking Spanish with anyone else. But his name was Jake Carpentero, for God's sake. He wasn't Swedish."

"But maybe he wasn't Mexican, either."

The two shot daggers at each other for a few moments, both internally processing Jackie's words. Finally Nadine shook her head.

"Okay, putting aside Mystery Man's ethnicity, what about your la-de-da word from your la-de-da poem that he didn't know?"

Jackie reached out and pulled her close, hugging her tightly.

"Please don't be mad at me. I'm so lucky I have you here, helping, instead of calling the men in white coats to come get me. There's no reason anyone should know that word, but Leo didn't realize that. It's archaic, I think, or at least not used very much. It means the sediment at the bottom of a wine glass, or maybe a teacup; I can't remember exactly. I only knew it because I loved the poster and looked it up. I had to tell Leo it was a word nobody knew, but then he started reading more of Tennyson's poetry."

She chewed on her sore lip, remembering.

"He actually checked a book of his work out of the library, and he read a few poems out loud while we were lying in bed."

She closed her eyes, memories coming back to her that had been buried for years.

"He even used a line or two in one of his pieces. Remember I told you he wrote songs? Hang on, let me think."

Another moment passed, and then the words were

somehow freed from their catacombs, and she sang a simple melody.

*'They made us love, like souls in Heaven, and now I fly from Hell.
And you with me; and we shall light upon some lonely shore.'*

"I remember kidding him that it sounded like something Meat Loaf would sing, and he said that maybe Meat Loaf had been inspired by Tennyson."

Nadine was staring at her, her face screwed up in a look of utter bafflement.

"Those sound like some pretty heavy lyrics. Was he one of those dark, moody types, this Mexican Swede of yours?"

Jackie shook herself, trying to come back to the present.

"No. Not really. He was serious, though. I mean he certainly knew how to have fun and we had a lot of fun together . . ." Another short silence, while memories pelted at her from unknown recesses: snowball fights on the Lawn, lying on the hill by the old observatory looking at stars, and trying to add as many ingredients as possible to the top of the soft serve in the cafeteria without spilling over on to the tray.

She exhaled slowly and focused on Nadine.

"I'm sorry. I got lost there for a minute. All these memories I haven't thought of in years are coming back to me. No, he wasn't dark and moody, but maybe he did have a way of looking at the world that was a little different from the rest of us. We didn't know each other during the 2008 elections, but he was crazy-interested in the midterms in 2010, more so than the rest of us. He said it mattered who was in charge, from the student councils at high schools all the way up to the presidency."

"Well, that doesn't sound like the Jake Carpentero who worked at Home Pantry. He seemed like a regular guy to me."

"But what if he had changed? Or been changed? Or been afraid for some reason to be the person he used to be?"

They continued to stare at each other, both contemplating Jackie's words.

"Okay, so let's pretend this HarryAlfred is your Leo, and he's sending a message only you would recognize about this dead poet person. Then where does the Harry come from?"

"Harry Potter, of course. We both loved him. Leo said they were the first real books he read in English all on his own. And I loved imagining myself as Hermione."

Nadine was rolling her eyes and mimicking gagging.

"Oh my God. What a pair of dweebs. You two sound like you deserved each other. But again, I've got to say that none of this sounds anything like Jake Carpentero."

"Okay, so tell me everything you know about Jake Carpentero."

The silence stretched, Nadine's eyes moving around unfocused as she tried to come up with details.

Finally she glared at Jackie.

"Fine. You win this round. I can't think of any specific details except the glaringly obvious fact that Mexican-Americans aren't usually mistaken for Swedes. But everything else: he was thorough, polite, we know he was kind to Mr. Riga . . . all of that fits in with your dead Leo. And he certainly kept to himself, most of the time. Remember how annoyed I was when we saw him the first time that night when we were waiting for the bathroom? He took off like hanging around with friends at a bar was some kind of horror. Come to think of it, it's pretty strange he was still there when the shooting started."

Jackie tilted her head, trying to sift through Nadine's words.

"That's right. I keep forgetting about that. Some things from that night seem crystal clear, and other memories are all blurry. We did see him, or at least you did. You wanted to go after him, and I was tired of waiting to pee."

She stopped and grabbed Nadine's arm. "Nadine, what if he recognized me, and that's why he took off?"

Nadine stared back, her own eyes narrowing as she considered.

"It *was* strange that he didn't respond when I called out to him. I remember that now. I remember saying something like I'd check with Danny, but by the time we finally got out of the bathroom, I forgot all about it. I just two seconds ago told you that Jake Carpentero was polite, but now that you've reminded me, I remember I was surprised when he didn't answer me that night."

Her eyes narrowed suspiciously as she looked Jackie up and down. "You're sure you never ran in to him at Home Pantry?"

"I'm pretty sure. I knew his name from tech messages, but I don't remember ever meeting him."

"Then maybe, just maybe, he did recognize you. I can't believe I'm even considering this, but if everything else you've come up with is even remotely possible, then it makes sense that he wouldn't have wanted to talk with you."

They were both silent, considering.

Jackie shook her head to clear out the *what ifs* and stood up straighter.

"You guys have been incredibly patient. You agreed to play along with this crazy idea of trying to find him online, and I'll never be able to thank you enough for putting up with me. But if there's any chance of it actually working, I have to pay better attention and be more proactive. Think about it. If it *is* Leo, and he's using the name HarryAlfred, he'd have to know there's a chance I'd recognize it."

"Because he'd assume you were playing an online game?" The skepticism in Nadine's voice was spot-on.

Jackie's teeth were back at her lip. "No, but maybe he's unconsciously putting out a beacon hoping someone will find him? Or maybe he's just trying to express a part of himself he's been hiding for too long."

Nadine continued to look at her doubtfully. "You might just be clutching at straws, sweetie."

"Maybe. And this whole thing may just be a colossal waste of time. But maybe JackieNotO needs to reach out to this HarryAlfred."

She scrunched her face and looked guiltily at Nadine. "Want to take bets on what your brother's gonna say about that idea?"

CHAPTER SEVENTEEN

The appearance of JackieNotO continued to poke at him. He had returned to the two sites he loved most: *Battle Realms* and online chess, mainly as a form of stress relief, and he recognized many of the *Battle Realms* avatars he knew from playing in Austin. New players turned up all the time, sometimes staying and becoming regulars, sometimes just existing as a presence for an hour or two and then disappearing. As HarryAlfred, he was a newcomer who had stayed and now had opponents in the chess games that he had run into before while playing as PantryTech in his earlier incarnations.

The group that had met at Texas Tango was a disparate bunch. Mostly young men, there were also an odd, married couple in their 60s, a high school girl, who was probably labeled neuro-diverse but who had a wicked sense of humor and drank colas by the gallon, and two friends in their 40s who both had spouses and kids at home and seemed to depend on their Monday nights out as their version of religious observance.

Jake knew all their usernames and encountered some of them at other odd times when he logged on. But they were all in place on Monday nights. It gave him some solace to know that they were still getting together, maybe even at Texas Tango. BlueLineBobby94 was there, as he had frequently been in person. Jake remembered him as a friendly young cop who would come in, have a few beers, play for a couple hours, chat with Danny, and leave.

But now JackieNotO seemed to be on whenever Blue-LineBobby94 was. A girlfriend? The idea shot daggers of unease zinging through him. He knew, as he had not known before, that his—*NOT HIS*—Jackie was in Austin and that she not only knew Texas Tango but had been there that night.

The thought of all the days, weeks, months, maybe even years, when she had been so close and he had been oblivious, drove him mad. Yes, the first thought he had upon seeing her that fateful Thursday night had been to flee—to leave town without a trace and start over.

But the ensuing weeks of pain, enforced relocation, and worry over Jackie's well-being had changed his perspective. He wanted desperately now to be able to see her, maybe overhear her speaking with friends, and learn more about the woman she had become.

Instead he was almost two thousand miles away and confined to stalking strangers through a fucking game platform. He played, he watched, he fumed, and he tried to figure out what the hell was going on.

If this person—this JackieNotO—was playing with the Texas Tango group, it had to be his Jackie. But Jackie didn't play games. He knew people changed, but he could not believe the Jackie he had known and loved so intimately now enjoyed playing online games in front of a screen.

So if she wasn't there for the pleasure of playing . . . that left only two possibilities. She was there as a girlfriend, participating as a partner, or she was looking for him.

He rewound the seconds surrounding the shooting over and over in his mind. Cycling back to the bar after receiving the message about his phone, the prospect of flight had reigned paramount. By the time he entered the nightclub, the noise level was mind-numbing. Relief swept over him as he looked towards the bar and caught sight of Danny. He could get in and out in less than a minute and decide on a course of action.

He got up to the bar, and Danny handed his phone over with a laugh. He said something to the effect that now he was back, Jake needed to stay and have a drink after all. Jake shook his head, smiling politely, but not bothering to try and make himself heard over the din.

That bubbly woman from work had been at the bar, and before Jake could escape, she reached out and put her hand on his arm, leaning in to say something and pointing to a far corner of the room. He looked, and there she was, heading their way.

He remembered feeling shock, joy, fear, and momentary paralysis. One part of him screamed *run,* while the other part wanted to stand there forever, taking in the sight of her. And then the first shot registered, and conscious thought fled. He acted only on instinct, throwing himself towards her, wanting more than anything to protect her.

What had happened to the bubbly one? The idle thought hit him as he went over those seconds again and again. He hadn't tried to save her, but he was pretty sure her name—Nadine, he thought he remembered—hadn't been on the casualty list. No, instead he had launched himself at Jackie, knocking her to the ground while protecting her head with his arm. He had cried out her name, and for that brief nanosecond, they had looked at each other. Seen each other.

And now, a JackieNotO was playing the same online game that Jake Carpentero as PantryTech had been known to play. She was either there with one of the regular players, most probably BlueLineBobby94, or she was looking for him. Jackie had been among the smartest people he had ever known. He'd put his money on the latter.

He was dead. He knew he was dead. He had read all the accounts of the shooting he could find, and Jake Carpentero was listed among the fatalities. Home Pantry had memorialized him on their website, and there had been a memorial service. Sam and his men were smart. They took care of details. If they wanted someone to be known as dead, they knew how to make it happen.

Yet Sam had hinted there might have been a problem brewing in Austin, anyway. If Leo Jorgensson had been successfully and definitively killed, then a connection to Jake Carpentero should never have surfaced on anyone's radar. No chatter should have come to Sam's attention necessitating possible action. But apparently it had. So not only was he not, in fact, dead, but whatever goons were out there determined to eradicate him were still searching, or at least had been, until recently.

His Jackie didn't play games. JackieNotO had to be his Jackie. The chance that an unknown Jackie had turned up at this precise moment, with that username, was close to impossible. Which meant that his Jackie was most likely playing games with the express intent of looking for him. And he had been stupid enough to sentimentally choose a username that might catch her attention. *What the fuck had he been thinking?*

His pacing grew maniacal. He had done everything he had done, acquiesced to leaving a life he loved in Virginia and going further into exile, in the belief that he was keeping her safe. Now it was clear she was not particularly safe, and he was less confident than he had ever been in the wisdom of Sam's all-knowing guidance. And he had left a trail of bread-crumbs like a stupid, love-sick amateur. HarryAlfred. Eleven self-pitying, wishing for something that could no longer be, keystrokes.

Fuck.

CHAPTER EIGHTEEN

J ackie's attention wandered absently as she did the annoyingly awkward and somewhat painful exercises needed to get her hand, wrist, and fingers back to something resembling normal.

Her physical therapist was wonderful. Kind, patient, and friendly, she gently massaged Jackie's wrist and forearm, paying particular—and painful—attention to the scar areas. She smiled with experienced understanding at Jackie's frustration with the simple but challenging exercises: gently swinging a hammer from side to side, kneading a clump of neon orange, Silly-Putty-like clay over and over, and lifting and moving little balls of fuzz with ridiculously large pincers. She patiently reminded Jackie of the link to her personal online exercise portal and reminded her how important it was to practice at home.

Which Jackie did. Sometimes. When she both remembered and then summoned up the discipline to do so. Because her days were overwhelmingly filled with doing . . . almost nothing.

She had checked in with Chris, her manager, who had

somehow guessed simply from the tone of her voice that she needed more time.

"Let's shoot for the last week of October, although we can touch base the week before and see how you're doing. Halloween's always a blast, as you well know."

Jackie felt suffused with guilt at his kind words. Halloween was, indeed, always fun at Home Pantry. The planning/ordering/advertising campaigns for the holiday season were done, and the entire building was populated with Marvel characters, ghosts, cowboys, and extrater-restrials.

She had good health benefits, an adequate salary, and generous and understanding supervisors. But she had been surprised to learn from her early morning walks following nights of restless sleep that homeless people encamped in her own neighborhood. They evidently disappeared later in the day when more people were around. She moved past them gingerly in the pre-dawn shadows but forced herself to remember that they were human beings, economically less fortunate than she was, struggling with their own unique demons. She was simply lucky to have comfortable surroundings in which to battle hers.

She had come almost to dread the rare occasions when she fell into a deep sleep. The dreams her unconscious mind crafted would no doubt fill volumes of horror novels or psychological dramas. Masked men shooting, characters from all stages of her life spurting wounds that felled them, and so very often, a figure she tried desperately to reach, but who kept moving further away. Sometimes he was Leo, but other times he was a dark-haired, dark-eyed stranger. Some-times he called her name, but often she would wake, strug-gling to call out to him, but unable to make a sound.

Jackie looked at the orange putty in her left hand and realized she had been kneading it for so long that it was becoming limp from the heat generated. She put it into its round, plastic case and stared at it, thinking.

Why *not* write a novel? She had written numerous short stories when she was young, even winning Scholastics competitions in both middle school and high school. She signed up as an English major immediately upon starting college, blithely assuming she'd embark on a long, fulfilling, literary career.

By the time Leo died, she had completed most of the requirements for her major. In the days, weeks, and months that followed his death, however, she had found herself unable to write. Unable and uninterested. Words were pointless. Stories were meaningless. Life dangled lollipops in front of innocent children and then snatched them away. So she had added business courses to her schedule and stayed an extra year, putting aside all fantasies about publishing fame.

But now she was not working, not sleeping, and not learning anything particularly useful from her many hours of searching the internet. She had mentioned trying to contact HarryAlfred to Russo, and he had pursed his lips, considering.

"Let's give it a few more days. See if he sticks around. And we'll have to think real carefully about what we say."

He had said "we," and she was struck anew by how kind and generous her friends were being. She had been coasting before—going about her life as a secondary or tertiary character in a quickly forgotten black and white film.

The shooting had knocked her out of that decade-old fog. Life was most definitely not black and white but an entire spectrum of changing hues. Russo was a cop, whom she had gently put off when they dated a few years back, but he had now proved to be an incredibly kind and generous friend. Nadine was a gregarious social butterfly, but she had turned out to be the best friend Jackie could imagine: perceptive, caring, and always ready to step in.

None of the men she had half-heartedly dated over the years had succeeded in lighting more than the smallest spark of interest. Each time a man had touched her—held her hand, put an arm around her, or kissed her—part of her had drifted away from the scene like a disinterested third-party ghost who stood back and shrugged at the play-acting before her.

"You need therapy," Nadine had said, when Jackie confided in her a year or so ago after her friend clamored for details on the latest guy.

To which Jackie could only silently reply: *Why?* She didn't care. The only man's touch she craved was dead, so what did it matter?

But now she was seeing people more clearly for the first time in years. Even Mr. Riga was proving to have surprising contours she never would have looked for in a grieving senior citizen. She had taken to dropping in on him regularly, and he was funny, thoughtful, and keenly observant of the world around them with its many nuances.

And then there was Leo. Or Jake. Or, perhaps, HarryAlfred. Someone both dead and not dead. And suddenly the possibility of being an active, engaged participant in life was gripping Jackie with an intensity she had not felt in years.

She had loved Leo, and then he was gone. She had suffered a near unbearable loss, and she had taken that loss and locked it away along with any real engagement in the on-going life around her. Why had she not let part of Leo live on? Why had she stopped listening to music, stopped writing, stopped being the person he had fallen in love with? If Leo were somehow returned to her this instant, would she even interest him anymore? Or had she become as insubstantial as her digital persona, JackieNotO?

She and Leo had shared passion, excitement, and joy. He had helped her look up and see the wonders of the night sky. She had let all that joy and wonder die with him. Had that been any way to honor his memory?

Her nighttime unconscious was offering up choose-your-own-adventure versions of horror, but what if she could channel her conscious imagination into creating stories of real people with real lives and real choices? What had brought Jake Carpentero, or whoever he was, to Home Pantry? Had he been a Mexican-American with a tale of family struggle and loss? Maybe that story needed to be told. Or maybe there were unfathomable intrigues that had led someone named Leo to assume that name and story. Every person on the planet probably had depths not visible or not seen by people around them. Who knew what experiences were tucked into the backpack of the older woman she now said hello to during her frequent early morning walks?

Jackie was getting nothing new out of her continued search for information on either Jake Carpentero or Leo Jorgensson. Wasn't doing the same thing over and over, expecting different results, the definition of insanity? Time to try living. She didn't know if Leo or Jake was alive, but she, Jackie, was. With an intake of breathless uncertainty and tentative determination, she opened a new document and began typing.

CHAPTER NINETEEN

Jackienoto had not been on in three days, at least not during the hours he was online. Was that tag's appearance perhaps a coincidence after all? Jake supposed it was even conceivable that JackieNotO wasn't female. Had his panic been for nothing? BlueLineBobby94 had been on briefly one of those nights, further evidence that perhaps Jake had been imagining things.

Should he change his username to something less obvious? His brain said yes, but his wayward fingers somehow refused to comply. His choice had been a silent homage to a love dead and buried, as was his foolish tattoo, and his use of Jackie's birthday on many of his passcodes.

He was wasting far too much time on games, anyway. His real task was to deal with the fucking dilemma suggested by Sam's thinly veiled insinuations.

Sam had given him his mother's address along with his normal, completely unnecessary admonitions regarding security. David Hilderman had a post office box in Norman-skill, a near-by suburb, as well as one downtown, and he chose that ominous sounding address to use when writing his mother.

He wrote in English, not trusting his very rudimentary German and not even caring enough to verify which language predominated in Winterthur, Switzerland. He took a moment to clarify for her that the "kill" in Normanskill apparently came from the old Dutch word for creek and was not indicative of an epicenter of violence.

> *Congratulations on your wedding! I wish you and your husband many years of happiness.*
>
> *I am now living in upstate New York and have a good job and a nice apartment.*
>
> *I have been helping a friend who is trying to learn more about his family's background in Europe. Perhaps you can help. This search is important to him as he is angry to have allowed so many years to pass without investigating. He is especially interested in his Eastern European roots and hopes to learn details about both sides of his family, but particularly his father's side. He has one uncle who is here in the States whom he is anxious not to offend by his search.*
>
> *Affectionately yours,*
>
> *David*

HE SAT BACK and regarded the letter. Would she answer, or should he expect more disappointment? Would she feel safe to reply with concrete information or decide on his behalf that it was better to let sleeping dogs lie? He and his mother had once been extremely close, but their long physical separation had led to inevitable emotional distance. Her attempts to divert his attention when he had asked questions as a youth had always been accompanied by a fierce hug and assurances that she loved him more than any missing family ever could. But now he was all grown up, and she wasn't at hand to distract him with hugs and kisses. Why the hell had he never pressed her for more facts?

He made the twenty-minute trip to Normanskill pondering his gilded imprisonment. The world, and even the U.S., was full of intelligent, hard-working people who never caught a break. Here he was, driving a good, if boring car, living in a comfortable enough apartment, and sliding right into a not-overly demanding job. All his creature comforts were seen to. Yet more than ever, he could relate to the beasts confined in seemingly humane zoo cages.

What was his value that he was so cosseted and protected? Why was his existence—or his demise—worth securing by some or pursuing by others?

Pulling back into his numbered spot outside his apartment building, Jake got out and stood, thinking. He absently wondered when the first snow would come. Naturally, Sam had put a window scraper and small shovel in the car trunk. Jake hadn't had to deal with extended winter misery in years. The deep freezes in Texas were newsworthy but normally short lived.

He pulled the zip higher on his jacket and began to walk, seeing not the urban landscape in the blocks near his apartment building but the snowy darkness on the night he and his mother had first met Sam.

His memories of their stay in Canada were murky, and he wasn't sure which ones overlapped with those of his final days in Moscow. Had they flown directly to Canada or gone somewhere else first? He remembered being on different flights and delighting in the unfamiliar meals that were handed to him on white, rectangular trays. There were small sweets wrapped in plastic, and his mother had let him eat hers as well as his. Why did he remember the fucking desserts but not the hows and whys of their travel?

He recalled a seemingly endless car drive with his new "uncle" and hurried trips to restrooms in the cold, his mother telling him not to leave the men's bathroom without "Uncle Sam." By the time they finally arrived at the house in Virginia he would come to think of as home, the snow was gone. A damp cold persisted for what felt like forever, but in fact must only have been a month or two.

He had memories of his mother coming into school with him not too long after they had arrived, carrying cupcakes— small little cakes he had never heard of or seen before—to celebrate his "new" birthday: February 22. When he had tried to argue, reminding her that they had celebrated his eleventh birthday in Canada, just a month ago, she had told him that he was now an American boy with an American birthday. It had taken several years for him to fully understand the dubious honor of being given a day to match George Washington's own birthdate, but by then he just shook his teenage head cynically at his mother's and Sam's sentimentality.

Who the fuck were they to receive such white glove care? Supposing the impossible were true, and his father was not his biological father—that still shouldn't earn him any kind of international protection. Why should anyone care if another Russian or two died under mysterious circumstances? It was a regular occurrence in that confused, backward country, whether ruled by tsars, commissars, or oligarchs.

No, there had to be something else about him and/or his mother that he didn't know.

He had searched for information concerning his father almost immediately upon getting his new tablet, but as he trudged aimlessly through the streets near his apartment, he vowed to begin again. There had to be something there. He and his mother had left Russia in early 2002. If nothing else, he could try to find out what had been going on in the world and what his parents had been doing in the months and years before his life had been split in two.

Even if more intensive deep-dive searching didn't require establishing accounts, he'd still be lighting a beacon for intelligence services. He'd have to trust his VPNs and no doubt establish yet another alias. God help him if he had to immerse himself in Russian social media. He wasn't sure he could keep up with modern slang in any language at this point, let alone one he had neglected for so long.

And so as he searched for hints at who he might be, he wondered yet again why anyone might bother searching for him.

CHAPTER TWENTY

The words flew across the screen faster than she would ever have imagined possible. Even taking frequent breaks to ease the pressure on the sensitive scar tissue around her left wrist and forearm did not distract Jackie from her newly rediscovered passion.

Without significant forethought, outline, or overall plan, she had begun a tender fictionalized account of a young John Riga, renamed Paul. Paul Tallinn worked long, thankless hours, saved every cent, and paid rapt attention to the people and world around him.

When not working on her new novel, Jackie wrote and rewrote the few words she was struggling to combine into a message she had persuaded Russo to try to relay.

"Can't you just DM them on a game like you do on social media?"

He had frowned at her, seeming to consider his words.

"Yes and no."

"What does that mean?"

"Every game is different."

"That's fine. I don't care about the others. What about

Battle Realms? Can you DM HarryAlfred? And D means direct, so no one else would see it, right? And it would appear only when he was actually online, playing, not in his email or texts, right?"

Russo continued to frown. Another moment passed.

"Yes. Pretty much, to all of it."

He looked uncomfortable, and Jackie peered at him, trying to understand.

"I'm in a weird position here. I play these games because I enjoy them. Everyone at Texas Tango is there for the same reason, at least I think so, and I would have said the same about Jake if you had asked me six weeks ago.

"But everyone in law enforcement knows that a hell of a lot of below-board communication goes on under the guise of online gaming. Terrorist plots have been planned in the middle of seemingly innocuous games. Supply lists, personnel assignments, targets . . . they've all been hidden under the cover of both the players' actions and the message platforms."

Jackie's brows drew together as she struggled to under-stand both his exact words and what he wasn't explicitly saying.

"So . . . you're saying that nothing is completely private? That people . . . law enforcement people . . . monitor these games, and that other not-so-good people monitor them, too?"

"Yes."

"But sometimes a cigar is just a cigar, right?"

Russo looked confused.

"Never mind. But if I'm understanding you right, I think you're saying it could be simultaneously safe and not safe to send a message. And the more I make it sound like code, perhaps the more likely it is to draw attention?"

Her inflection rose at that last point, and Russo nodded slowly.

"I honestly don't know what to tell you. A very large part of me thinks I'm in way over my head, and that if I were doing my duty, I would have alerted my supervisors and probably the FBI by now. On the other hand, there's still a large part of me that thinks you suffered a real loss once, then went through a horribly traumatic experience recently, and you're trying to work through your grief by pretending someone you thought you had lost might still be alive."

They stared at each other for several seconds. Finally Jackie shook her head and gave Russo a weak smile.

"I'm sorry. Maybe you're right. But I'm so grateful to you for putting up with me."

Russo's look turned to one of mild exasperation.

"See? You've said maybe I'm right, but I was distinctly hinting that there are two different scenarios here, and honestly, Jackie, neither one of them is ideal."

Jackie closed her eyes and worked at finding a convincing compromise.

"What if we set a time limit? Say two more weeks. I'll work on a message, and you get final approval over the wording, obviously. We'll send it and see what happens. And at the end of two weeks, if you think something illegal or just not right is going on, you go to whomever."

He put up his hand, halting her.

"Jackie, if I get a real sense that something illegal is going on, I have to report it instantly. There's no waiting two weeks."

"Yes. Of course, I understand that. What I meant is, if by the end of two weeks, we're no closer to a . . . resolution, then we'll drop it. You can go on playing like normal, and Jackie-NotO will just disappear, and I'll leave you alone."

She gave him a head-tilting 'please don't be mad at me' smile, and he laughed.

"Okay. Two weeks. Work on your message, and we'll see what happens."

It was amazing and gratifying to see how easily whole paragraphs and pages appeared on her screen when she was working on her novel. At the same time, the copy in her document named 'Dear HarryAlfred' had been started and deleted more times than she could count.

She had wasted two days, which meant her allotment of Russo's cooperation was running out.

Dear HarryAlfred,

The words stared back at her. Was this insane, or was there any chance at all that she was actually sending a message to Leo?

Fuck it. Maybe she just had to be blunt.

Dear HarryAlfred,

Hold on. People didn't use "Dear" in DMs, did they? No, they just typed. She hissed out her breath and made circles with her wrists, trying to ease the cramping in her left hand and fingers.

I had a friend named Leo who used to play online games. Do you know him by any chance? I have his guitar.

That was blunt and to the point. Either HarryAlfred would think she was crazy, or Leo would know she had recognized him.

She stared at the screen, frowning. Was there anything in

those twenty-three words that could be mistaken for an undercover terrorist message? Dear God, she couldn't see how, but Russo would have final approval. The last thing she wanted was for JackieNotO to create even deeper levels of confusion. Was she casting a fishing line or throwing a grenade?

CHAPTER TWENTY-ONE

oly shit. She knew. *And she had his guitar.* Any doubt he had held on to was now gone.

The same fight or flight response that had kicked in upon seeing her outside the bathrooms at Texas Tango arose again, lifting him forcibly from his chair and compelling him to move. He half ran into his bedroom and looked around frantically, unable to focus.

She knew.

He had to breathe. Had to think. What the fucking hell had he been thinking to pick a username that would stand out like a flare to the Jackie who had known and loved him so well?

But how in hell had Jackie thought to look for him on a gaming platform? Was he discovered? How many people now suspected that HarryAlfred was Jake Carpentero and perhaps even Leo Jorgensson?

He forced himself to stop moving. He was standing in front of his bedroom window, staring sightlessly at the street below. He had to figure this out. *She had kept his guitar.* Was there any chance in hell she might still love the boy he had been?

Why was Jackie online? She was always on when Blue-LineBobby94 was on. His real name had been Robby? Ryan? Russo? Jake couldn't remember. His own attendance on Monday nights had been sporadic, and he knew BlueLine-Bobby94 to be a nice young cop, who was sometimes there when Jake was and sometimes not. He certainly had never had a girl with him, let alone Jackie.

Was he only an Austin cop, or was he FBI or from some other intelligence agency? Was there a broader hunt for him going on? Maybe JackieNotO wasn't even a person, but a persona created to trap him.

But if that were so, Jackie would still have had to be involved. No one else would have created such a username. No, that tag had been chosen specifically to attract his attention. And Jackie, herself, must have chosen, or at least, suggested it.

And holy shit. It had succeeded. And she still had his guitar.

Scenario after scenario ran through his brain. She and the cop were working together to find him. They were both undercover . . . undercover what? Why should the FBI or any other U.S. agency be looking for him? He hadn't done anything wrong, at least not of his own volition. He had been under Sam's—*UNCLE SAM'S*—Svengali-like control for almost all his life.

Were they foreign intelligence? Even in his hyper-anxious state, the idea seemed preposterous. His Jackie could *not* be Russian intelligence. A person could simply not change that drastically.

He called up all his memories of BlueLineBobby94. Nice. Young. Had a beer or two. Chatted superficially with everyone. Danny always said hello when he came in, and *yes*, his name was Russo. Could he be Russian intelligence?

Jake knew next to nothing about any kind of intelligence. He had spent the last decade of his life doing everything possible not to think about anything important. But drawing from the little he had read in thrillers and crime novels, he thought it highly unlikely Russo fit the profile.

So that meant Jackie and BlueLineBobby94 were working together as . . . what? If they were romantically involved, then why were they wasting their time searching for him? Not having a lot of experience himself, he still could not imagine any sort of contemporary relationship that would involve spending time searching for a long-lost love. It made no sense.

Back to square one. Jackie knew. She knew, and a): she had figured out that she was likely to find him on a gaming platform, b): she was somehow working together with a cop to find him, and c): she had kept his guitar.

Even while his heart soared, his intestines seized. *Fuck.* The very existence of her message meant at least two people knew, maybe more, and one of them was perhaps capable of doing some serious sleuthing. Who played *Battle Realms*, either online or from the group he played with at Texas Tango, who might have linked him to the long dead Leo Jorgensson?

Jackie must have recognized him that night. His eyes and hair were a different color, but somehow, in that brief second, she had recognized him.

He remembered the jolt of joy, despair, and fear that had shot through him. His arms wrapped unconsciously around himself and he bent over with the overwhelming weight of that memory bringing a catch to his breath.

To hold her, even for such a short moment, had been sublime. But the fear that she might be hurt, might be killed, had been equally powerful. No conscious calculation had preceded his movement towards her or given thought to the words that had been wrenched from his panicked throat.

She had known him.

He sank down to his bedroom floor and tried to think, elbows on his crossed knees and his forehead pressed hard into his palms.

Jackie had known *him.*

She had known him, and now, she was looking for him. She had no doubt believed that Leo Jorgensson had died in a gas explosion, but she obviously wasn't going to be fooled twice. She did not believe Jake Carpentero was dead, and she was looking for him.

Was it to catch him? Turn him in? Turn him in to whom? For what? Yes, he had been part of a deceit created to fake his death, now deaths, but none of it had been his choice. But how could Jackie know that? Did she assume him guilty of some crime or involved in some illegal activity? Was that why she was working with a cop?

Or was it possible that she still cared for him? Still missed him as much as he missed her? Still longed to hold him once more as he yearned so desperately to hold her?

Was JackieNotO seeking HarryAlfred to catch and punish, or was it remotely possible that her love for him had survived a decade of deception?

He returned to his laptop, his fingers hovering over the keys. If he answered, he would be committing himself—and maybe her—to a path that might involve danger he couldn't even imagine. But he had already inadvertently given her years of pain. Before he allowed himself to second think his actions, he typed out a one-word response.

Yes

CHAPTER TWENTY-TWO

Y*es*
Russo's index finger remained pointed on the corner of the screen as he watched Jackie's face.

She stood motionless. It was a Sunday afternoon, and she and Nadine had been chatting in Nadine's room while Russo played in the room next door. His call had been abrupt, and she had known, instantly.

He was alive.

Leo, Jake, HarryAlfred—whoever the hell he was—he was alive.

She felt Nadine's fingers grasp her own and took in a shaky breath.

The single word on the screen was proof, but she had known six weeks ago. When the man saving her life had cried her name, she had known.

She squeezed Nadine's fingers tightly as her teeth began to chatter. Nadine pulled her close, and Jackie buried her head into her friend's shoulder, quiet sobs wracking her body.

Russo stood up and moved to hold her from behind, wrapping both girls in his arms.

"Hey," he said softly. "It'll be all right. We'll figure this out."

Jackie finally pulled herself upright. Nadine darted away and was back a moment later, holding out a handful of tissues.

Jackie blew her nose and looked at them both, unsure what to say.

Russo had taken a step back and was looking at her intently, arms crossed over his chest.

"Before we jump to conclusions, I need you to consider another possibility. Is there anyone out there who might be trying to mess with you? To gaslight you? Or is it possible there's someone who knew you both well enough to be trying to catch your attention?"

Jackie shook her head vehemently but then stopped, forcing herself to consider. Could there be anyone? Teeth biting down on her bottom lip, she shook her head more slowly.

"No. It's Leo. I've known it was Leo since I woke up in the hospital, and this just confirms it, at last. I've never talked about him to anyone."

"I can attest to that." Nadine's words were matter of fact, but she didn't seem resentful. "Until the shooting, you'd never been one to talk about anything personal beyond whatever book you were reading that you insisted was more fun than going out. Getting personal information from you was like trying to squeeze water from a cactus."

"That's not the same thing. I'm talking about someone who might have known you both when he was still alive." Russo paused and waited for her to respond.

"Wait a sec." Jackie spoke quickly, trying to forestall any additional police-like response from Russo.

"You said you would have to take action if there was any sign or proof of illegal activity. We don't have that, so far, right? All we know is that someone who was supposedly dead . . ." She stopped and closed her eyes at the enormity of it all. "Supposedly dead twice, might, apparently, not be dead and might be actively playing *Battle Realms*. There's nothing illegal in that, right?"

Even to her own ears, the question sounded both ridiculous and pathetic.

"It is *absolutely* illegal to forge legal documents, like death certificates. It is also illegal to assume multiple identities, which would, again, include falsifying official records."

"But we don't know that Leo did any of that on his own."

Russo's look was incredulous. "We're talking about a grown man, here, not a child. A man who I witnessed hang out during gaming nights and who held an important, demanding job at Home Pantry. We're not talking about a special needs adult, not responsible for his actions."

Jackie reached out and grasped Russo's arm, desperate to reassure him.

"He's not a criminal, Russo. I don't know who or what else he is, but he's not a criminal. Jake Carpentero was a valued employee who was respected at work and loved and trusted by his landlord. Even Nadine liked him, right?" She looked beseechingly at Nadine, who nodded.

"Of course I did. He was great at what he did at work, and he was a decent guy. I obviously didn't know him well, but Danny would never have let him live with his parents if he didn't trust him."

Russo's expression had turned skeptical.

"Or, he was the world's greatest con man. You're both admitting you know nothing concrete about him, and all I know for sure . . ." He stopped himself. "Okay, none of this would hold up in court as 'for sure.' So far all we have is a one-word response on a game played by thousands of people around the world to a hypothetical question."

Jackie pounced.

"So there's nothing illegal you could prove at this point, anyway."

She stopped and held up her hand, as if physically trying to hold back Russo's objections.

"What would happen if you arrested someone who turned out to be in a witness protection program? Say you pulled someone over for speeding. Would their license be real or not real? And what if someone in a witness protection program died in a car accident or something? How would they be identified?"

She watched Russo's expression change from one of condescending impatience to thoughtfulness. He tilted his head back and finally blew out a long breath.

"I'm trying to remember. I think there was something about turning a case over to superiors if anyone ever said something about contacting the U.S. Marshall Service or the U.S. Attorney General's office."

He closed his eyes for another moment, obviously trying to call up details. "I'm pretty sure there was mention of some kind of official list that was shared with local police offices. But it's not something I'd normally be able to access."

He shook his head as if resurfacing from a swim and gave Jackie a scathingly doubtful look. "Even so, I cannot believe you're seriously trying to convince yourself, or me, that your dead-not-dead guy was in a witness protection program."

"I have no idea what I'm trying to do. All I know is that Leo, or Jake, if that's who he is now, was . . . is . . . not a bad guy. He's not a criminal."

"Jesus Christ." Russo threw up his hands. "So now I could get in trouble for trying to out someone federally protected, or else get in trouble for letting a con man stealing identities go free."

Still reeling from the shock of that one word, *yes*, on the computer screen, Jackie searched Russo's eyes, desperate to find a way both to continue her hunt and to allay her friend's legitimate concerns.

"One more message."

Russo made a sound far more akin to a growl than a word but eventually gave a curt nod.

"One more."

———

THIS SECOND ATTEMPT came far easier.

"Write 'Let's talk by email.' I'll go set up an email account as JackieNotO. If he's who I think he is, he'll figure it out. We won't need to use the game, and you won't be responsible for anything I do."

Russo looked like he was going to object, but no words came out. After a moment, he shrugged.

"Fine. That's probably best. I don't like it. Not as a cop and not as your friend, but it does make some sense. Let me know what happens. I'm not kidding, Jackie. I know you and my sister think this guy is Mr. Innocent, but I'm still not sure. And I don't want you to get hurt. Or me to get fired." The last part was muttered under his breath as he turned back to the game to relay Jackie's short message.

CHAPTER TWENTY-THREE

The words sat on the upper right-hand corner of his page, oblivious to the non-stop action of *Battle Realms* that filled the rest of the screen.

    Let's talk by email

He had thought his last message had been his leap off the cliff, but replying to these words would really do it. If he reached out to Jackie by email, more than a decade of secrecy, lies, and precautions would be out the window.

He stared sightlessly at his keyboard, paralyzed with indecision. Contacting Jackie would be a violation of the trust Sam and his mother had in him. He had never signed anything even resembling a contract with Sam—what name would he even use to sign?—but his "cooperation" had been understood from his first days in the U.S. He followed Sam's instructions, and he and his mother were accorded a semblance of security and independence.

Allowing himself to be found by Jackie had happened too

fast. He hadn't figured out what the exact danger to him and his mother entailed. Still hadn't figured out why their very existence created such a threat.

His eyes closed as a storm of emotions and memories tore through him.

"I love you."

Those were the last words he had intentionally spoken to Jackie as he left their room all those years ago. He had loved her then, and he loved her still. The words that he had cried out at Texas Tango had been involuntary, wrenched from him when her life had been threatened. They, too, had been expressions of love, and now he longed more than anything to reach right through his computer screen. She was there, right there, at the other end of the cyberlink.

But he was here, in Nowheresville, New York. He had taken time away from research tonight by logging into *Battle Realms*, but the urgent need to return to his online digging for information hit him like a surge of Red Bull. He had to find answers, and he had to find them now.

But first, he had to answer Jackie. Had to create yet another email address and identity and then find hers, although he didn't think that would be a challenge. He'd stick with HarryAlfred but add a number that would only have meaning to Jackie. He didn't want anyone else from *Battle Realms* searching for him on email.

120210

He inhaled deeply and let himself sink into memories for one last moment. The Lighting of the Lawn, an annual UVA tradition since 9/11. It had been a cold evening but a stirring experience to be out among so many enthusiastic and jubilant students and faculty intent on celebrating music, dance, the beautiful lights, and the sheer joy of being alive on a crisp winter night. He and Jackie had kept their gloved fingers intertwined except for the moments when he had his arm around her, holding her tightly against him, her head nestled into the spot between his shoulder and his head that belonged only to her.

"I'll be out tonight," Jackie's roommate had yelled when they ran into her as the crowds dispersed. "You've got the place to yourself!"

Their eyes had met, and the heat that had simmered between them for months grew even hotter. December 2, 2010: The night he lost his virginity and what little was left of his heart that didn't already belong to Jacqueline Bourne.

His fingers were unsteady as he typed in the keystrokes to establish his new account: HarryAlfred120210. He hit "compose," and as the cursor blinked on the "to" line, he typed in JackieNotO and paused only for a second before typing the @. He'd start with the most popular email server. She had reached out to him because she wanted to find him, not because she wanted to hide.

Dearest Jackie,

He stopped. What was most important? He needed to tell her that he couldn't be found, at least not until he got to the bottom of this twisted maze that was his life. But she needed to know . . . God, how he wished for one of those Vulcan mind melds from *Star Trek*, so she could just know everything.

I love you. I always have, and I always will. I hate every moment of pain I have caused you. I am trying to find a way out of the constraints I live under, but I don't know if I will ever escape. And because even I still do not understand the extent of the threat, I have to ask you not to search for me and not to further involve BlueLineBobby94 or anyone else. I will keep this email account open, but it is best that we minimize communications. My username is obviously HarryAlfred, but I also now go by David.

Jake paused, and then he did perhaps the bravest and most foolish thing he had ever done.

Love always, Kolya.

CHAPTER TWENTY-FOUR

Jackie's eyes were fixed on her screen. She had been staring for who-knew how long, reading and re-reading the message. It was Leo. Any doubt that might have lingered was so far gone that it was laughable. 12/02/10. *December 2.* She remembered that night like it was yesterday.

The excitement and nervousness that she might disappoint had spiked the second her roommate had let them know she'd be gone. But then Leo had admitted that it was his first time, too, and all fear had vanished as they gave themselves over entirely to each other. She remembered how he had paused, once he was finally all the way in, and kissed every part of her face: her eyebrows, her cheeks, her chin . . . his breath raspy as he had asked, "Are you okay, my love?"

And she had trapped his head and held it so that his mouth was still, hovering just above her own, and whispered into his lips, "Always." He kissed her, then, so deeply that she lost all sense of self, and the stinging soreness between her legs had soon eased and then been subsumed by the sheer and unexpected joy of orgasming around him.

Her eyes closed and she almost stopped breathing, so

caught up in the sweet memory. With it came pain that shot straight down through her core, a yearning so intense that she rocked back and forth in anguish as she sat mesmerized before her laptop.

God, how she wanted him. Wanted him physically with every fiber of her being, but wanted to talk with him, to walk with him, to feel his arms around her after a long day, and to listen to him sing to her.

Did he still sing? Oh, dear God, how she longed to hear his voice once more.

Her Leo was gone. Jake Carpentero was gone. But at the other end of cyberspace, a man named David, but also Kolya, was alive, And whoever he was, he still loved her.

CHAPTER TWENTY-FIVE

K olya remained motionless, considering the possible consequences of the words he had just released. He had told her he was alive, told her he loved her, and told her his name. Until now only his mother and Sam knew his real name.

Except, of course, maybe his grandparents, if they still lived, at least a few of Sam's colleagues, and perhaps whatever fucking goons out there wanted him dead.

Those goons and whoever was giving orders were what he now needed to focus on. He had to put thoughts of Jackie aside and devote all his mental energy to unraveling this goddamn mystery.

He had picked December 2 to honor the first time they had slept together. The Lighting of the Lawn had been started after 9/11. He and his mother had left Russia in late 2001 or early 2002; he couldn't remember for sure. Either way, it was just a few months after 9/11. Could there be a connection?

Two hours later pressure in his bladder forced him to think about taking a break, and he glanced twice at the time

MEG NAPIER

to make sure he wasn't misreading. The information he had found was startling, some of it in English and some in Russian, and he had followed link after link in fascination.

He thought he knew contemporary history as well as any American Millennial, but he had known almost nothing about the period of U.S.-Russian cooperation in the early aughts. According to what he had read, Russian President Putin had actually called President Bush on September 9, 2001 to warn of intelligence suggesting a planned domestic attack. In the days and weeks that followed, Russia had seemingly cooperated in the international commitment to fight Islamic fundamentalism. Putin had traveled to the U.S. in November and even visited the Bush ranch in Crawford, Texas.

But a rift had grown, apparently, over the two countries' definition of terrorism and how/when/where it should be combatted. Russia saw its efforts at containment and subjugation of Chechnya as an anti-terrorist campaign, while the West saw them as evidence of human rights abuse.

Kolya's exhausted eyes squinted at the screen and finally zeroed in on words that jolted him upright. Two articles in a Russian daily started just months prior to 9/11 had the byline G. Polivanov. The articles concerned Russian vigilance against possible paramilitary training sites in Chechnya, but the gist of the article seemed to be questioning the necessity of Russian action. G. Polivanov. His father's name was Gregoryi Polivanov.

He read the articles several times, his mind gradually adjusting to the foreign vocabulary and subject matter, his online dictionary open and frequently consulted. The tone of the articles was skeptical, with phrases like "some villagers claimed" rather than direct reports of conspiracy.

Questioning the government's official stance on internal opposition was doubtless enough to get a Russian journalist in trouble, perhaps imprisoned, or even sentenced to an "accidental" fall from a window. But was it enough to pursue that journalist's family throughout year after year and thousands of miles?

Exhaustion finally won out. He still had to be at work by 9 a.m., now only a few hours away, and he wasn't even sure if the G. Polivanov he had found was his father.

But he *had* found Jackie. He had found her again after all these years and allowed her to know he was alive. He could go to sleep with that thought to comfort him and worry about the rest again tomorrow.

He had told her they should not communicate, so there was no point in checking his email again. He repeated that mantra over and over as he brushed his teeth and took off his clothes. His bed was only steps from his bathroom, yet he stood, exhausted but motionless, unable to look away from the tablet that lay in the living room on the table next to his laptop. He had not added the new email address to his phone, so the only way to see the account was to check the tablet one more time.

Go to bed.

He ignored the voice of common sense and walked over to open the account. The words were there, a response he had hoped not to see while hoping so desperately to find anyway.

I love you, too.

CHAPTER TWENTY-SIX

S he had to honor his request. Relief that she had not been wrong to trust him, despite her doubts, warred with a longing that had magnified a hundred-fold with the knowledge that he was out there.

What a simple, uncomplicated life she had led in her nine-plus years of walled-off hibernation. But if her life had been boring and empty, she could not even begin to imagine the difficulties Leo had surmounted in order to inhabit a completely new identity. *Kolya.* He had signed his email "Kolya," and she would try to think of him that way from now on. It fit, somehow, and as images of the fair-haired boy she had loved came to mind, layering the name Kolya upon them was surprisingly easy.

Her immediate challenge, however, was to create a foolproof impersonation of someone well and truly over the doubts, suspicions, and anxiety that had ruled her every waking moment since the incident and convince her friends that all was well.

She had confided in Nadine, Mr. Riga, and Russo. She couldn't erase everything she had said, but she could do her best to minimize it all. She needed somehow to reassure them that she had found sufficient answers to allay her suspicions. Had to convince them that she herself was persuaded by the information she had found and that she was now determined to look forward and not backwards.

This information had come from a relative? A friend? What might seem believable? *HarryAlfred.* An unusual combination, but what if some newly invented roommate of Leo's had been aware of their enthusiastic youthful passions? That roommate might now be an avid game player who had so many usernames that he had picked that combo out of the recesses of his memory banks. And her original message had said of Leo, "Do you know him by any chance?" Russo had suggested it might be a mutual acquaintance, and she had shaken her head. Now she had to tell him he had been right, and do so in a way that didn't make them further question her sanity.

What other clues had she voiced to persuade her friends to join her in her search? Her recognition of Leo's voice during the shooting was the easiest to explain away. There was ample scientific research of near-death experiences supposedly proving most of them to be hallucinations brought on by constricted oxygen to the brain.

And as for the tattoo . . . She'd deal with Mr. Riga privately, but she could tell Nadine and Russo that Danny's father had realized that the name Jackie had popped into his head because she and Nadine had just introduced themselves. Upon reflection, he had remembered that the name was Josie or Jeannie; he couldn't say for sure. And when she had asked him to sketch a picture of the tattoo for her, he had been embarrassed, saying that he had mixed things up because the discussion he had been having with Jake on the day of the water incident had turned to music. He wasn't even now sure if the picture had been musical in nature at all. Guilt rose inside her at the idea of making the quite rational older man seem more confused than outsiders might assume, but she'd figure out a way to make it up to him.

She sat at her small table, mentally preparing the conversation points that would best serve when she spoke to Nadine and Russo. She would need to be completely convincing while at the same time convey the genuine gratitude she owed them for all the help they had provided. She tried out numerous approaches in her head, and still nervous but hopeful, she leaned back and read Leo's—Kolya's—message one more time.

He was trying to understand the nature of the threat. What in the world could it be that continued to threaten him for more than a decade? *Who was he?* Had he committed some terrible crime as a child that he had run away from? Jackie's head shook back and forth in silent rejection of such an absurd idea.

Kolya. She did a quick search.

A 1996 Czech film. She peered at the synopsis and background information and dismissed it. If nothing else, Leo was her age, so he was older than the movie.

The name itself was listed as Russian: a diminutive of Nikolai.

Russian. She had a sudden flashback to scenes from the game show *Who Wants to Be a Millionaire?* Was that her final answer: Russian? Not Swedish or Mexican, but Russian?

She typed in Nikolai and found Nikola Tesla and Prince Nikolai of Denmark. Might he have been the prince, switched at birth? But no, the Danish prince was even younger than the Czech film. Other returns included names in a popular fandom, a *Call of Duty* character, a city in Alaska, and a brand of vodka.

Jackie frowned at the screen. What had she been expecting? That maybe something like *"Young boy named Kolya, with surgically implanted stolen Hope diamond, subject of world-wide manhunt"* would jump out at her from the search engine?

She cocked her head. It would make an interesting story. As would the idea that he was the missing heir to a vodka business empire or a kidnapping victim from Alaska who had never been found. But she sincerely doubted that any of these fanciful scenarios had anything to do with the boy she had loved and, God help her, the man she still loved.

Was a search for a Kolya even reasonable? Was the person at the other end of the email saying it was his real name or perhaps only his newest fake identity? But he had said he now went by David. She wanted to believe he was sharing something real, but she no longer knew whether her instincts could be trusted or how much of what he might put in an email could reasonably be construed as real.

Many long months after Leo died, she boxed up his clothing and his few random possessions and stored them in her parents' house, keeping only his guitar with her wherever she lived. She had stubbornly refused to wash a t-shirt that had been carelessly tossed on their apartment floor, choosing to sleep with it next to her pillow, instead. But by the time she graduated, she reluctantly put even that, now scent-less, memento away.

Now she willed herself to call up his face in her memory and then mentally kicked herself and opened the photo app on her laptop. Most of her photos from college had been taken with a digital camera and then uploaded on to her computer. There were only a few of her and Leo, a fact she had frequently berated herself over in the weeks and months following his death. She hadn't had a smartphone until her senior year when Leo was already gone, and how many college students in pre-smartphone days walked around with a camera in their backpack?

One photo stood out. Her mother had taken it of the two

of them when Leo had come to her house during Christmas break just a few months before he died. She had printed the picture and kept a framed copy near her bedside for years, reluctantly deciding to leave it with boxes at her parents' house when she moved to Texas. Looking at it had always brought more pain than pleasure, as had the guilt that swept over her each time her eyes focused on it, and she realized time had passed since she last thought of him.

She examined the digital image, enlarging and shrinking it multiple times. They had both been so young, and they looked so very happy, their arms around each other in front of her family's Christmas tree.

Jackie stared at the features of the young man standing next to her. Waves of yearning and sadness swept over her for all she had lost, but she forced herself to study him objectively.

A sudden idea struck her, and she opened her work email, searching back weeks for the memorial notices that followed the shooting. A mugshot-like photo of Jake Carpentero, most likely from the picture taken at personnel for his ID card when he was first hired, had accompanied the article. She put both images side by side on her screen and stared at them, gnawing on her lower lip. Hadn't there been a similar piece in her college magazine after Leo's death? A more drawn-out search finally brought up the obituary in the end-of-year edition of the school's magazine from those many years ago. The photo attached to that write-up was most likely the picture taken for his freshman ID.

Jackie screenshotted and copied it, placing the three images side-by-side on her screen.

Leo's hair was dark blonde/light brown and parted on the left side. It had been cut short in his freshman picture, but the Christmas picture of the two of them showed definite curls. The magazine photo was black and white, and the

Christmas photo wasn't well-lit enough to show his eyes, but Jackie remembered their beautiful blue-gray color.

Jake's hair was dark, cut very short, with a barely noticeable part on the right side. His eyes were dark, and he wore glasses.

Were they actually the same person? She was no forensic expert and generally didn't even pay attention to visual details. Her eyes moved back and forth, trying to assess similarities. The eyebrows. They stood out more in Jake Carpentero's picture, but the shape was the same. So were the ears. The nose was different, and while she couldn't articulate the specifics, the shape of the top part of his face seemed slightly different as well.

Leo was happy in the Christmas photo, and as Jackie stared at his image, she could see no hint of deception. His smile was wide, showing straight white teeth and a look of utter contentment. His head was tilted down as it rested against hers.

Her breath caught as she allowed the sensations to sweep over her: his arm around her waist, pulling her tightly against him. Her own around him, probably hooked into the waistband of his jeans. She could even remember the earthy, musky smell that was all Leo. However the scents of shampoo, deodorant, and his very own essence combined, they had always worked magic on her senses. Whenever they came together after being apart, she had always buried her nose into his chest, luxuriating in a deep inhalation of him before his lips claimed hers.

She sat upright. Leo's scent. Was that part of what she had recognized in the man who had saved her in the bar? She closed her eyes and allowed herself to return to those terrifying but agonizingly slow seconds. Pain, noise, and fear washed over her, but even in memory, it was only his words, calling out to her—in Leo's voice—that kept her from total panic. If she had been somehow aware of his scent, she didn't remember it now. Despite the warmth of her apartment, she shivered and forced her eyes back to the screen.

Her phone rang, jolting her out of her reverie. She saw it was Nadine and took a breath. Time to put her non-existent acting skills to work.

CHAPTER TWENTY-SEVEN

The hours at work felt like a different sort of prison sentence. Albany inmate "Jake" David Hilderman nonetheless did his best not to show his fierce desire to be out of his work-day cell and back to his home lock-up where his hours online demanded all his attention.

As far as he could tell, G. Polivanov had disappeared after November 2001. An article he (she?) had written in mid-November reported Russian cooperation with the U.S. concerning Afghani military enclaves but seemed to question the totality of the shared information. Whoever G. Polivanov had been, the journalist had skated a thin line by questioning his own government's motivations.

He searched for records of his mother, Anna Dimitrievna Polivanova, but could find nothing. That seemed particularly odd. He knew his mother had worked when he was young. Or at least he was pretty sure she had been at work since he dimly remembered spending a lot of time with his grandparents and even remembered it being one grandmother or the other who picked him up at the end of the school day. He cursed his own ignorance; he didn't know even his own mother's maiden name or any of his grandparents' full names!

When they had lived in Virginia, his mother had ostensibly worked as a Swedish writer and translator, and he was pretty sure some of her work had actually been published.

He began another frustrating search and finally found a few poems and two short stories from a literary magazine published in the aughts that included Linnéa Jorgensson as translator. He looked hard but couldn't find anything biographical about the translator in the archives.

Had she been a translator in Russia? He gave it a shot, but trying to search for unknown Russian titles with only the name of a possible translator left him growling in frustration and devoid of anything even resembling helpful information.

He needed answers. Real answers. He could not get on a plane and fly to Switzerland, though he absently wondered what might happen if he actually tried. But he could demand answers from Sam. He had been a sheep for far too long. It was time to start acting like a wolf.

He knew now that Jackie—alive, well, and still loving him —was waiting for him—*God, please let her be waiting for him*— on the other side of the country. He had to break through this cocoon of secrecy and find a way back to her. To *his Jackie*.

CHAPTER TWENTY-EIGHT

"I'm here to ask for your forgiveness. And maybe your help and advice, if you're not too mad at me."

Jackie had called Mr. Riga and asked if he minded her dropping by. She had reread Leo/Kolya's email countless times, weighed his words, and made an executive decision. She was going to keep Mr. Riga in the loop. Had he not described the tattoo and so fiercely defended Jake's character, she probably would have decided she was crazy and forced herself to forget about seeing—hearing—*knowing* Leo the night of the attack.

She stopped and picked up some cookies, and they brought forth a smile when he opened the door.

"Trying to fatten me up?"

"Not at all. But 'a spoonful of sugar helps the medicine go down,' so I'm hoping the cookies sweeten what I have to tell you."

Jackie recounted everything she had done and learned, leaving out only the tedious details of the long hours spent watching Russo play.

"So I'm a doddering old man now, who can't keep details straight?"

His words were blunt, but there was a gentle smile on his face.

"Yesss?" She drew out the syllable and gave him a "please forgive me" smile in return.

"And you really think it's Jake you've found, and that he is indeed, the boy you thought was dead?"

"I do. And based on the words he used, I'm trying hard to believe that there's a good reason for all of it, even though he, himself, might not completely understand the reason."

Mr. Riga took a bite of the cookie he had picked up. "What is this? It looks like a miniature pumpkin pie."

"That's exactly what it is. A pumpkin pie cookie."

He shook his head.

"I can't keep up with the world today. When I was young, we had maybe six different cookies: chocolate chip, oatmeal, sugar, peanut butter . . . see? I can't even get to six. So much has changed. Danny picked an unusual line of work given the current craziness. He wanted to create a space where people could relax, have fun, enjoy a drink and something good to eat. Probably not all that different in intention from an innkeeper a thousand years ago."

He blew out a sigh and put his gnarled fingers on top of Jackie's hand.

"My Danny's gone. I know that with absolute certainty, sadly. The world will go on changing, and he won't be here to see any of it. If there's a chance Jake is still out there, we should do everything we can to help him."

"I'm telling my friends that I was wrong. That I accept the fact that he's dead. Are you okay with going along with my lies?"

"Isn't that what I just said? The Jake who lived here was . .

. is, I hope, a good man. You can't fake common decency day in and day out."

He lowered his head and peered at her over the top of his glasses.

"What's your next move then? Are you going to do as he asked and wait? That's probably best."

"For now, yes. I'm going back to work on Monday morning. And I've started writing a novel."

She gave him a sheepish grin.

"I've dumped a lot on you today, but there's more. I'm kind of basing the hero of my story on you."

He snorted.

"Won't be much of a hero, then."

"I don't mean hero in the sense of Superman or Prince Charming. It just means my primary male character. He's a normal guy a lot like you." She smiled. "Which means, of course, that he's a lot like Superman and Prince Charming on the inside."

Mr. Riga laughed.

"Oh, my dear, flattery like that, especially when it comes with outrageous cookies, will get you anywhere."

Traces of a smile remained on his face, but Jackie could see the deep crevices of grief that never entirely faded.

"I'm glad you know the truth. I'll be able to talk to you about anything I learn, and I can show you bits of my story and get your feedback."

"I'd like that, my dear. I'd like that very much."

CHAPTER TWENTY-NINE

H e had to word the message carefully. Sam had always
provided Jake's cell phone and programmed an emergency contact number labeled "Uncle" as the top favorite.
Instructions had been repeated every time they met for as
long as he could remember: "If anything odd happens—
anything—hit that top favorite, even if you can't talk, and
we'll check things out."

The directive was so deeply ingrained that he had apparently followed it at Texas Tango without even thinking—
hence his quick "death" and subsequent reincarnation thousands of miles away.

He didn't want this communication to go out as an emergency, so he used the contact listed only as Sam and wrote
and rewrote the brief message before hitting send.

*I'd like us to meet again in person as
soon as possible to discuss some
important questions.*

Short and to the point. God, but he was tired of games. He wanted answers, explanations, and a chance to decide for himself the best course of action.

CHAPTER THIRTY

Jackie's second return to work went far more smoothly than the first. She felt as if a great weight had been lifted, even though in truth, the weight she was now carrying was even heavier—or at least more cumbersome.

Still ignorant of anything even resembling facts, knowing that he was alive, and that he still loved her, had given her back a sense of optimism and peace she hadn't felt since that long ago March. She had decided to trust that he was being as honest as possible, at least for now.

The name Kolya fit the gentle boy she had loved. And the strength of the name Nikolai spoke to the years of deception and secrecy he had needed to endure, at least in the unceasing array of possibilities that played out in her mind.

He had asked her not to search, and Mr. Riga had agreed it was better to watch and wait. But that didn't stop her imagination from spinning out one irrational scenario after another.

During large chunks of the day, however, she was once again paying attention to details at work, fending off invitations from Nadine, and spending at least a solid hour every night working on her novel. And Jackie didn't hesitate for even a second at using her writing to counter Nadine's insistence that Jackie shouldn't spend time alone.

"You're wrong. This is really a good thing and a positive sign that I'm finally on the mend. I wrote all the time before Leo died. I was even convinced I was going to spend my life as a writer. Contacting Kiran helped me see that it was time to stop living in the past."

She and Leo had known a fellow student at UVA named Kiran. He hadn't been a roommate or a close friend, but his name had popped into her head when she invented the former-roommate-using-HarryAlfred-as-username plot line.

She made herself text Nadine when her fictional "first contact" came through.

OMG, Nadine. You and Russo were right all along! It WAS someone who knew us both at UVA. He used to sing with Leo and sometimes uses references to him in his gaming and other online stuff. I had forgotten all about him until he answered my email.

Sheesh. She needed a chart to keep track of her various real-life storylines as well as her novel's outline and characters.

Persuaded that Jackie was no longer pining for a dead/not dead former boyfriend, Nadine reverted to insisting Jackie "act her age."

"I just don't like you spending so much time alone."

Jackie knew Nadine's intentions were, as always, kind.

"Listen to me. I'm really, really, really doing okay. I'm still doing physical therapy on this stupid wrist on Tuesdays, so if I want to make progress on my book, I've got to use the hours I have. There's a writing contest I'm thinking of entering now, and another I'd like to enter in the spring, and with Christmas coming and everything, I don't have all that much time."

Nadine folded her arms across her chest and glared at Jackie.

"Before you were a stay-at-home old lady, and now you're a stay-at-home writer. If you're not careful, you're going to wake up and find out you've turned forty and never had any real fun."

"And you've got to stop being such a mother hen." Jackie laughed as she said the words and pulled Nadine into a hug. Her friend's last words, though, had made her think.

She truly was enjoying writing again. It might not be Nadine's definition of fun, but it worked for her. She couldn't quite comprehend how something she had loved so intensely had first disappeared completely and then returned so effortlessly, but she wasn't going to question her current enthusiasm. Even if nothing else changed further in her life, she was more content now than she had been six months ago. However the improbable events had combined, she had found a part of herself brought back to life that she hadn't even known to mourn.

Busy as she was, she dedicated all the brain cells not devoted to work or her book to churning over her primary preoccupation. Just because she couldn't "search" didn't mean she couldn't ponder. She tried to approach it like a story outline. People hid because they were good guys being threatened or bad guys trying not to get caught. Kolya's response had eliminated the amnesia possibility, so that only left the good guy/bad guy options. Except that he had come right out and said he was being threatened. Who were the bad guys threatening him and why?

If his name was Kolya, he was most probably Russian. He

was here in the U.S., hiding first as a Swedish-American and later a Mexican-American, so it was clear that he was trying to avoid other Russians. Such lifelong, or *intendedly* lifelong disguises were complicated. Was he acting alone, or was someone helping him? He had lived with his mother, and Jackie was pretty sure, despite all she had since surmised, that the woman she had met had, indeed, been Leo, or Kolya's mother.

He had left her bed that long ago Saturday because his mother had called him, meaning a conspiracy of at least two. But Jake Carpentero had supposedly had no family. Had his mother really died in that explosion, or had she disappeared in another direction? Was she perhaps right here in Austin?

Russians as bad guys. Now *that* was an original plot line, especially given the current geo-political tensions in the world.

Why would some Russians want to catch? punish? kill? other Russians? Jackie shuddered. She knew it was wrong to stereotype an entire people, but Russians did, indeed, make very good bad guys. How many stories had made the news over the last several years of one Russian or another being wounded, disfigured, or killed by other Russians hunting them down? Which meant, presumably, that the ones being hunted were good guys.

It was all so beyond her white-bread suburban experiences. They had been college juniors when Leo/Kolya "died." Had the explosion been an ambush or a ruse?

Either scenario could precipitate a need to drastically change one's physical appearance. As in a choose-your-own-adventure story, however, possibilities branched off in multiple directions. If there had been an ambush, and either Leo/Kolya alone, or he and his mother together, had somehow escaped and gone into hiding, then yes, creating totally new identities would make sense. Such a move would require tremendous luck, ingenuity, and financial resources. All theoretically possible, but Jackie remained uncertain.

What about a ruse? Anything on such a grand scale—Jackie shuddered at the memory of the horrible devastation left where Leo's house had stood—would require careful planning and some kind of outside help.

Wait. Jackie chewed her lip. Help would have been required in either case. Leo Jorgensson had been declared dead. That didn't happen unless there was either a body OR some sort of intricate coverup. Anyone fleeing an assassination attempt, OR faking their own death, couldn't simultaneously manufacture a coverup, could they?

Had bad guys covered up a botched killing or good guys covered up a pretend accidental death?

Her head spun with the careening what-ifs. She had taken meditation classes over the years. Some of that training could certainly help right about now. She mentally pulled up the instructions: *make yourself breathe slowly and evenly. Quiet your mind.*

She tried, but meditation had never really been her thing. She persisted, and memories of Leo singing quietly to her in their bedroom came to mind. She let echoes of his voice fill her thoughts.

Holy shit. He *had* warned her. It had all been there in his fucking song. She remembered now that the same thought had passed through her mind in the early days after the shooting, but now she struggled to make it fit as part of this incredibly complex jigsaw puzzle.

"I'll forever sing my song for you and cry that morning came."

He had flat out said—*sang*—that he would still be alive but separated from her. Had he only known that someone was going to try to kill him, he wouldn't have been stupid or egotistical enough to assume he'd stay alive.

A ruse. If he knew or assumed that he was going to survive the incident that called forth sirens, then it had, indeed, been a plan in which he was at least partially complicit. Such a plan would have required powerful help. No one had ever accused Russian thugs of being helpful, so that pretty much eliminated them. The Swedish government? Ha. The Jorgenssons might have known the Swedish language, but Jackie was close to certain they weren't, in fact, Swedish.

No, the incident had taken place in Virginia, a state amazingly close to the seat of the American government.

Was it actually possible that the U.S. government had helped plan a pretend death for Leo and probably his mother and then helped them transform into completely different identities and live entirely different lives in another part, or parts, of the country?

Holy Jesus. Why???? Who was he, or who were they?

Jackie was sitting on her bed, her good fist pressed tightly against her mouth. She had no recollection of getting there and wasn't sure how long that last line of reasoning had taken her.

Maybe Kolya had both their interests in mind in warning her off further searches. Poking at a wasp nest was always a risky maneuver. And this was one hell of a complicated wasp nest. How badly were they likely to get stung?

CHAPTER THIRTY-ONE

S am's response took longer than Kolya expected. Was he reluctant to face his questions or just busy with other work? Kolya had no idea what other duties Sam had or even what his actual job was.

Anger continued to seethe within him. Anger at the monsters who had killed his father and tried to destroy his mother, anger at his mother and Sam for keeping so many secrets from him, but most ferociously, against himself.

He was thirty-one years old. How had he let that many years of supposedly being an adult slip by without knowing or trying to learn anything about himself?

Finally, a text appeared.

I'll be in town over Veterans' Day weekend and arrive at your apartment on Saturday afternoon.

Kolya wrestled with his instinctive impulse to ask if Sam needed a place to stay. The hell with the lessons in hospitality his mother had always modeled. This wasn't his real uncle.

Kolya was Sam's assignment, whatever and however that had come to be, and nothing more.

Nothing more? That wasn't true either and Kolya knew it, despite his resentment. Sam had been a kind and steady presence throughout his teen years and a dependable resource ever since. As a non-thinking human robot, he should have absolutely no complaints.

His problem, and soon to be Sam's problem as well, was that he was no longer content to be that non-thinking robot. He had to have answers, and he had to be free to make his own informed decisions.

The buzzer rang at 1:43, which Kolya knew for certain only because he had been obsessively checking his phone for the time every two minutes all day.

Sam was dressed as he always was, in casual business attire. Slacks—never jeans—a buttoned shirt, and a nondescript jacket.

He reached out his hand and shook Kolya's warmly, looking him up and down.

"You're looking good. The wounds are fully healed, I hope? Are you feeling more yourself?"

Kolya took a step back and studied the man who had played such a major role in his life. He distrusted almost everyone and everything by this point, but he couldn't help believing that Sam's affection and concern were genuine.

And, he realized with a start, the firm handshake was the only physical touch he had felt in weeks, maybe more.

"I'm doing okay, Sam. But asking if I feel more myself is not wise, considering that's why I want to talk to you. But thanks for coming."

He gave a quick glance around the living room that was just a few steps from the entryway.

"Do you want to stay here, or are you up for a walk? I've

spent a lot of time walking the last few weeks. It seems to help me order my thoughts more clearly."

Sam put his hands on his waist and stretched his shoulders back, seeming to physically prepare himself for a challenging task.

"Walking is fine if that's what you'd prefer. I remember seeing there was a park not far from here when I was looking at the apartment."

Kolya closed his eyes, momentarily nonplussed. Of course Sam knew about the park. Sam had always seen to everything, been aware of everything, and prepared for any situation. But unless Sam was psychic, as well, Kolya was confident that he couldn't possibly know of his communication with Jackie.

They left the building and walked the four or five blocks to the park in casual conversation. It was in the high 40s, but people at work had mentioned that snow would no doubt be in the forecast again soon.

Once they entered the park, they could see people several feet ahead walking a dog and children playing in a designated area off to the left. Young people were tossing a Frisbee in between trees in an area to their right.

Kolya glanced at the man walking next to him, hands in his jacket pockets, a look of calm resignation on his face. He took a breath. *Just speak.*

"Last time I saw you, you dropped hints—no, you pretty much made clear—that there was a chance my father was not my mother's husband, but a rapist, instead."

He realized his own fingers were splayed out tensely at his sides, and he tried to relax them, finally putting them in his own jacket pockets and taking another slow breath.

"It kills me that neither you nor my mother ever told me what she went through, but I still find it hard to believe my father wasn't my father. Or at least I very much do not want to believe that possibility. But assuming for the sake of argument that he wasn't, it's not clear to me why you are obligated to hide me, to protect me, after all these years. Who exactly are you, and why do you have the means . . . the authority . . . the motivation to relocate me, find me a safe apartment, and a job? I'm thirty-one years old, and I'm shielded and protected as if I were the heir to the British throne. I need to understand what's going on, Sam. Who am I, who are you, and what is this really all about?"

Sam continued walking, his eyes glued to the path in front of him. Finally he sighed, and his eyes briefly met Kolya's.

"I wish your mother were here. We always did what we thought best at the time, but you're right. You should know more than you do, and it's unfortunate that you and your mother never got a chance to speak frankly together as adults."

He stopped speaking and after a moment, pointed to a park bench several feet in the distance.

"Let's sit for a bit. This is going to take a while."

They sat down, both angling themselves slightly toward the other. Sam's right hand was out of his pocket, his fingers running down his cheeks and chin as if stroking a non-existent beard.

"You were about ten the first time I laid eyes on you. It was all a mess—a chaotic scene, and if the Secretary hadn't been the kind of man he was, your fate would have never been known, at least not to anyone beyond your family's immediate circle."

"The Secretary?"

"Yes. I was part of the security detail covering the Secretary of State. He was on a secret trip to Russia in the fall of 2001 to meet with the foreign minister about Russian assistance in Afghanistan. The whole world had rejoiced when the Soviet Union pulled out of Afghanistan, and here we were, soliciting Russia's help in crushing Al-Qaeda.

"It was cold, and even though there was a wide security cordon around their meeting place, there was a small group of protestors outside the perimeter demanding the release of some Chechen prisoners. Your father was there, talking to the protestors. He was a journalist. I don't think anyone there at the time was aware of the Secretary's presence—it was just another day for them. But you were with your father because your mother was ill."

Discordant images flitted through his memory. Cold, people shouting, his father's hand, and then being alone among strangers.

"I don't remember my mother being sick, but I think I have vague memories of the day you're talking about. What was wrong with my mother?"

Sam's face curled up in discomfort.

"Again. This is why I wish your mother were here. I knew nothing of any of this at the time, but it turned out she had just had a miscarriage, and your dad, heartbroken, was trying to give her some peace. You were a good boy but still an active little kid."

He stopped speaking, but Kolya didn't notice. He hadn't known what to expect, but this brief introduction brought its own unanticipated pain. Memories of wanting a sibling, a brother, of course, came flooding back to him. He had been very young; his recollections were blurry but most definitely expressed in Russian, back when he had no inkling of the upheavals ahead of him and the other languages in which he would have to become adept at speaking and even thinking.

He dimly remembered pestering his parents for a baby brother and his mother making inadequate responses of it not being God's plan or some other such nonsense. Now guilt knifed through him as he realized how much he had probably added to her unhappiness.

Both men were silent, each lost in his own thoughts. Then Sam continued.

"The Secretary had the car slow down. He wanted to know what the protestors' concerns were. The Russian security cars following us indicated we should continue, and when we didn't do so fast enough for them, several armed men got out and began forcibly clearing the demonstrators away and shoving them inside trucks that appeared out of nowhere. Your father attempted to ask questions, and they pushed him along with the others, leaving you alone. The Secretary observed all this and had a fit. He made me get out and bring you into our car.

"It was completely outside of protocol or precedence. Dangerous and utterly insane to the rest of us, but he was that sort of man: kind, honorable, caring, and a grandfather to little ones close to your size. There was no way he would have left you on the side of the street alone when it had been his presence that caused your father to be taken.

"So there we were, driving back to the ambassador's residence just a few hours before our scheduled departure, with this unknown little Russian boy in the car while the adults you had been with had all been carted off. You were smart and spoke some simple English, telling us that your father had been working and begging us to bring him back."

Sam blew out a breath and looked at Kolya, his eyes showing tolerant and amused reverence that had obviously survived decades. "You somehow captured his attention completely. He put calls through, arranging for the bureau chief, as well as embassy security and political officers, to meet us at Spaso House.

"That's the name of the U.S ambassador's residence," he said in response to Kolya's raised eyebrows.

"So, again, there we all were, you and he chatting away with almost no language in common, the Secretary insisting that your family be found. He had to leave as scheduled, but he told me to stay behind and get a full report back to him ASAP.

"Your mother was eventually located. It turned out she and your father were already walking a very thin line, under constant surveillance and never feeling secure. The U.S. embassy's interest increased the strain they were under tremendously."

"But why?" Kolya interrupted. "What had they done to merit constant surveillance?"

"Not a thing, by any rational standards. If nothing else, I've learned enough over the years to say that much with absolute certainty. But the investigative work they were doing unfortunately left them on the wrong side of the powers that be, especially since it turned out there was a lot of history there, particularly between your mother and the new president. The intimate details she knew about so many at the top echelons of power put her life in constant danger."

"I'm assuming you mean the Russian president."

"Yes. The history is complicated, and of course it helped frame everything that happened later, but I assume right now that you want to know the specifics of how you got to the U.S."

"I want to know it all, but we can get back to the history later. It's why you're still protecting me some twenty years later that makes no sense to me."

Sam gave a tired laugh. "I hear you. But that history and the explanation you're looking for are inseparable. And ironically, part of the reason I agreed to come up here without trying to talk remotely is because my protection"—he made air quotes—"is likely coming to an end. In a nutshell: we believed you and your mother to be in grave danger and, probably more importantly from a bean counter's standpoint, your mother was willing and able to provide unique intelligence. From her own experiences and the work your father was doing before he was killed, she had insights and details that our people on the ground weren't privy to. And the Secretary felt a particular connection to her, believing that it was his actions that led to your father's arrest and eventual death.

"But he died recently, as you probably heard. And while he's had no official government position in years, his influence remained, and the directives he had laid down were respected, whenever possible. Everything in Washington has changed in the last several years, though, and even long-standing operations are being discarded. Your mother helped us tremendously for years, even from Seattle, whenever we needed her, but as we all acknowledged in her last briefing, her insight was out-of-date. Too much has changed, and she's grateful to have little first-hand insight into the current activity and personalities. That's why she's free to truly start a new life now with no remaining obligations or protections. I don't think even she ever imagined she'd do so in Switzerland, but life is full of surprises."

Kolya squinted at him, more confused than ever. Would he ever get to the bottom of this spiderweb of personal and political conflicts?

"I don't know about you, but my butt is freezing, and I think I understand less now than when we sat down. Let's walk a while."

They stood and walked several paces in silence.

"Okay," Kolya began. "You had me at the embassy, and you learned from my mother that the government didn't like us. The Russian government could fill entire libraries with lists of people they don't like and of the people they dispose of for that very reason. How did my mother know so much and what made us special?"

Sam's hands were back in his pockets, his eyes again on the ground.

"Well, that puts us back to the history part, unfortunately. Your parents, and your mother in particular, were well acquainted with the new president. He had personally recruited her to serve in the KGB while she was working as a tour guide at the Hermitage in Leningrad. Your mother was a gifted linguist and could converse easily in many languages. She and your father, who was finishing up his PhD at the time, wanted nothing to do with the KGB, but it's a job offer that doesn't usually allow for polite refusal."

He shot a quick glance at Kolya and then pointedly returned his eyes to the pavement.

"As it turned out, sadly, his interest . . . one might even say his obsession, with your mother, wasn't limited to her language skills. You were born in January 1991. The Soviet Union officially dissolved in December 1991, and your parents were able to move back to Moscow, where they'd both grown up, in the spring of '92. Your mother did translating, wrote for some literary publications, and tried to stay under the radar. Your father, who had studied history and economics, took advantage of the seemingly new era of real openness and democracy and began writing pieces examining all aspects of contemporary Russian society."

Sam blew out another tired sigh.

"But as we now know, that openness was fleeting, and the Russian people seem relatively content to live under autocratic rule. The FSB, the updated incarnation of the KGB, officially began operating in '95, and by '98, the current president had been named its director.

"Unfortunately, his interest in your mother had morphed into outright hatred, as your father's work continued to poke holes in the regime's pretenses towards democracy. And of course, he was interested in you."

Kolya's jaw ached from the pressure his grinding teeth were exerting, and he tried to force himself to relax. He looked at Sam's profile and then turned his own gaze ahead, seeing nothing.

"He thought I wasn't my father's child?"

"Apparently so, yes."

"What happened? You said she worked for the KGB and my father was a student."

"Apparently her performance reviews were less than satisfactory."

Kolya peered at Sam, trying to make sense of his sarcasm.

"A large part of your mother's job involved cultivating relationships with foreigners and reporting everything she learned. She failed to do so in a sufficiently complete manner, according to her supervisors, but instead of just throwing her in jail or doing away with her, they decided to have a little fun with her and put the fear of the Soviet version of God into her. She was brought in, told her professional services were no longer needed, and then several of the top-ranking intelligence officers, who later moved into political positions after the new Russian state was formed, raped her. They raped her and told her they'd come back for her and her loved ones and do more, unless she kept her mouth shut."

Kolya struggled to keep air moving in and out. He had asked. He had known life in the Soviet Union was harsh, but he had never imagined the hell his mother had obviously endured.

"She and my father were already married?"

"Yes."

"And there was nothing they could do?" Even as he spoke, he knew the question was stupid. Here in America there was a cute saying that you can't fight city hall, but words like that were no joke in other parts of the world.

"So they didn't know for sure who my father was?"

"No. At the time of your birth, reliable DNA tests for paternity were just becoming widely available in the west. Even now, it's not something you can pick up at the drugstore, at least I don't think so. Although I must admit, I've never tried. But obtaining a sample from any of the people in question would never have been an option, and unfortunately, we don't have your father around to prove a negative. As I think I mentioned last time I was here, in theory you'd want to find members of his extended family to test, but that was never a reasonable route we could pursue. Given the state of international tensions for the last several years, you can understand other issues—truthfully *all* other issues—were a higher priority. And as I said, your particular case is being closed."

Kolya's eyes moved to the Frisbee players. He remembered playing on an informal team in high school and again in college and had a sudden overwhelming desire to throw off his jacket and go running after a soaring disk, oblivious to the world around him.

There were no referees in Ultimate Frisbee. It was a game that depended on the honest camaraderie of its players. How ironic that such a game was so popular in a world more given to greed, treachery, and betrayal.

Turning his eyes back to Sam, Kolya rolled his shoulders. Every part of him was stiff from the tension coursing through him. He wanted to talk to his mother, to put his arms around her and hold her tight. He wanted to go home and crawl into bed and never come out. He wanted desperately to forget any of the harsh words Sam had spoken. But he had asked Sam for information, and he had to push on.

"It still doesn't make sense to me. Why should the U.S.

care about me or my mother? What difference could it make to international relations for another Russian or two to have their lives destroyed by the assholes in charge?"

Sam looked uncomfortable, as if simultaneously wanting to refute Kolya's words and acknowledge their honesty.

"Looking back, not even I can say any of it really made sense. I do know that in the initial weeks and even months following 9/11, there was a real sense of heightened awareness about almost everything. Warning signs had been there, and anyone even remotely connected to security or intelligence felt that we had dropped the ball. We couldn't let that happen again. We had to pay attention to the minutest details, to the words of individual people, no matter how seemingly inconsequential.

"I gave my report to the Secretary and his antennae went up. He realized right away both that your mother might have a unique perspective onto Russia's leadership and that you, yourself, might have significance down the road."

"You mean as a pawn."

Sam turned his head away, and there was a long pause before he continued.

"In retrospect, yes, that was likely part of it. But it was not the first, or second, or probably even the tenth rung of importance at the time. The Secretary and the agency staff at the embassy considered your lives to be in danger, especially after your mother learned that your father had died in an accident in prison."

He didn't bother with the air quotes this time.

"Your mother was highly intelligent and knew more about the president and his associates than anyone else we had come in close contact with. She knew, and we quickly came to understand that there was a good chance you'd both disappear if we didn't step in.

"And so we acted. We arranged for you to get out and

relocate under new identities. Your mother cooperated fully with our intelligence officers and provided extraordinary details and insight into how control was exerted from the top down."

"I don't remember her talking to anyone."

Sam laughed. "It was while you were at school, silly. Your mom was adamant you remain as sheltered as possible from the 'shadows,' as she called them. She said it was bad enough that you had lost your father and everything familiar. She wanted you to slip into a new normal as fully as possible. We were successful in convincing her that we could keep you both safe . . ."

Sam paused and shook his head slightly before continuing.

"And that was because we believed it, even though the spirit of cooperation that followed 9/11 deteriorated rapidly. The U.S. withdrew from the Anti-Ballistic Missile Treaty, Putin spoke against the U.S. invasion of Iraq, and then he blamed the U.S. for encouraging unrest first in Georgia and later Ukraine.

"Yet while there were tensions, we never got close to out and out confrontation. After a fairly short time, your mother understood that she truly was free to build an independent life for herself. She did, and you grew up to be a normal American young man. She was always cooperative if anyone needed to consult with her to better interpret official Russian communications, and she literally devoted years of her life to assisting U.S. intelligence. But by and large, her reinvention as a Swedish-American translator was successful.

"When you were in college, however, cryptic messages started surfacing about finding the man and the lady and her kid. They were in English but phrased just like that: *We know that man and the lady and her kid are out there.*' The State

Department and the CIA get all kinds of nonsense on a regular basis. It's all checked, and most of it gets filed as 'indeterminate.' Then a few arrived mentioning your father's name, specifically, and saying that his wife and the kid were next on the list, and I was called in. We had a meeting, and the Secretary, even though he was retired and had no political or military position by then, participated remotely.

"Relations between our two countries were doing better at that time. Medvedev was president, and Putin was prime minister, but tensions had lessened. Nonetheless, the threat against your mother and you appeared to be real and based on intelligence that perhaps included knowledge of your identities and whereabouts. We decided that faking your deaths was our best option."

Kolya stopped and looked at Sam, incredulous.

"On the basis of some anonymous bizarre messages, you decided our entire lives had to be uprooted, again?"

Sam met Kolya's eyes and held his gaze.

"I know it perhaps sounds extreme. But try to understand. The former Secretary had been personally involved in your rescue and wanted assurances you'd remain safe. He and the intelligence community were indebted to your mother for the help she had consistently provided. He had a good relationship with Secretary Clinton and filled her in on all the background. She came on board. There was this whole idea of resetting the relationship between our countries at the time, and no one wanted that jeopardized by the kidnapping or assassination of two people whom the U.S. government had taken great effort to protect. Don't forget your father died in prison. The prison he was taken to after being arrested in front of the Secretary. That left a strong feeling of responsibility among all of us."

They were standing, motionless, each man regarding the other intently. A mother pushing a stroller while holding a large dog on a leash said, "Excuse me," and they both snapped out of the paralysis those last few words had imposed.

"Jesus Christ." The words left Kolya with a frustrated hiss as he slowly began walking once more. "Why didn't you tell me all this at the time?"

Sam shrugged and shook his head slightly, as if trying to search for a response.

"I have no real answer. Your mother was adamant that you remain as untouched by all that had gone on in the past as possible. I suppose part of me still saw you as the young boy I had first met and not as the young man you had become. The plan was conceived and executed quickly. Until that week in March, the plan was still just one viable option, but then another message was intercepted that said, 'The man and the lady and the kid have to pay. They all have to pay.' It was decided that the best way to end things was to kill you both, decisively."

"'It was decided.' What a simple way of saying 'Time's up! The life you know is done.'" Kolya's words were bitter.

"We were trying to keep you alive."

"What man were they talking about?"

"We don't know. Your mother assumes there is someone else they want, but she has no idea who it might be."

They had stopped walking once more and stood looking upon a large, covered area filled with picnic tables, grills, and trash bins. They could either sit at one of the tables or turn back to their starting point, but no words were necessary. They turned and began their return walk, neither speaking for several minutes.

Finally Kolya spoke.

"So you gave us new lives, again, and you figured you were done. It seems my mother has more or less been released and is now living a life she's chosen for herself. Why in the world did you say when I was shot that you had been thinking of moving me again?"

For whatever reason, Sam seemed to find this part of the conversation less unnerving. He replied easily.

"There was no specific threat, and even if there were, this isn't the kind of work I do anymore. But I had been kept on your case at my request because I've known you most of your life. I watched you grow up, and I'm proud of how you handled situations that might have put lesser individuals into a complete tailspin. But you survived, and you thrived."

Kolya snorted in derision.

"You did," Sam insisted. "You did everything we asked of you after leaving Virginia, and when you settled in Austin, you were a model employee and citizen. I wish all young men lived as responsibly as you do."

Kolya rolled his eyes. "Yes, thanks. I've been a marvelously well-trained puppet. Perhaps you have a gold star you can glue to my forehead?"

Sam stopped. His eyes narrowed and the look he sent Kolya's way was exactly what a frustrated father would send his not-quite-adult child.

"We did our best, and it was always what we thought would keep you safest at the time."

Kolya shook his head, closing his eyes in irritation. They were speaking from opposite ends of decades of secrets, with Sam somehow still thinking that all the little boy needed was food, shelter, and a small American flag to wave. He meant well. Kolya understood that basic truth, and he knew that Sam's affection and concern were real.

"Do you have kids, Sam?"

The older man looked taken aback, and he hesitated before answering.

"Yes. I have two. One's a year older than you and the

other a year younger. Makes it easier for me to always know your real age, regardless of what your documents say."

"Do they like you telling them what to do in life?"

It was Sam's turn to snort.

"Of course they don't, Jake. But they've never lived under a threat to their very existence the way you have."

"A threat I was largely ignorant of and never allowed to understand."

"Yes, you're right. And I've already admitted we should have been more open with you. But your mother was in charge when you were young, and we were used to deferring to her. I'm sorry. I really am."

Continued recriminations would get him nowhere. Kolya needed more information now so that he could step away from Sam's control.

"Okay. Back to Austin. What happened that made you nervous?"

"You're in tech. You know about Google alerts and the like. I've had them set up as long as they've existed for all your names and for the explosion in Ruckersville. This past summer there were a few hits on both Leo Jorgensson and the explosion. It didn't necessarily mean anything, but it got my attention because there were also references to the man and the kid. Then there were several searches on Jake Carpentero. You're a young, talented, handsome man, so it makes sense that people might take an interest in you. At the same time, there are a fair number of people with that same name both in Texas and elsewhere around the country. But we were closing your mother's file. She's out of the United States, now, so we no longer have jurisdiction over her. I knew I was going to be officially detached from your case soon. There are the cutbacks I mentioned, plus I'll be retiring next spring. Given the searches, I thought one more complete change would make tracing you impossible. And while I don't think there's any danger, I do need to tell you that searches have not only continued, but increased, in recent weeks. You should be aware of them and perhaps set up your own alerts."

Kolya gave a rueful laugh.

"I'm not surprised, and I'm not worried. I'm probably responsible for many of the hits myself, and I doubt we need to bother about any of the others. But there was no threat from Russia, was there?"

Sam shook his head. "Not that we can identify, no."

"It doesn't even matter who my father is or isn't. It never really did, did it?" Kolya spat out the words, frustrated after learning so much to still know so little.

Sam put up both his hands, negating Kolya's words.

"That's not true, unfortunately. One of the reasons you took such a circuitous route to the States way back when you first arrived, and then lived in such obscure circumstances in Virginia, was that your mother received a message after your father died assuring her that she and all of her family would be next if you were to disappear from Russia."

"Fuck."

"Fuck, indeed."

"But were you ever aware of anyone searching specifically for me?"

Sam's hands were still up, and he widened his arms in a full-body shrug.

"Who knows? We never found out who sent the messages about the lady and the kid, although they stopped after the explosions. That in itself was a pretty good sign that either Russian intelligence or some unknown entity acting independently had somehow traced you that far."

"But there's been no concrete threat since then?"

"No. Nothing concrete."

"And it's just speculation on your part that searches for

Leo Jorgensson or the explosion indicate that someone thinks I might not be dead."

"Yes . . ." The word was drawn out, as if Sam didn't agree with his own concurrence.

"So how about I relieve you of duty? I declare myself emancipated, thank you for your service, and decide how to live my life for myself from now on?"

His tone was clipped, and the minute the words were uttered, he could see the hurt they had caused.

Sam was studiously examining the path again, his pace and his breathing deliberate and measured. Kolya reached out and grabbed his arm, stopping him.

"Sam. I'm sorry. That was a shitty way to put things. I've always known you had my best interests at heart. I just can't live like this any longer."

"If they find out you're alive, they still might come after you. You still might be valuable to those in power as a pawn. Or one of them might see you as an existential threat to his position. How would it look for the world to know that some Russian government big shot had a kid who was a red, white, and blue American? And if you were found, your mother probably would be, too. Or she would have been, until recently. But as a guiding principle, they're usually good at extracting information once they have someone they've been looking for."

They stared at each other and then continued walking.

"Do you have beer at the apartment?"

Kolya smiled. At least part of Sam acknowledged he was an adult.

"Sure. We can order a pizza to go with it."

———

THEY TOOK turns using the bathroom when they returned to the apartment, and Kolya ordered the pizza. He used the moments of solitude to do some quick thinking.

It was looking serendipitous that his declaration of independence was coinciding with Sam's retirement. It was exactly what he had wanted, but Sam's revelations had brought home how little he, Kolya, knew, and what a resource Sam was. How much should he confide in him? Could he trust him?

The questions were absurd. Sam had proven himself to be the most steadfast and trustworthy caregiver on the planet.

Would Kolya confide matters of the heart to his father, had he lived? He had no idea. He didn't even have close male friends his own age to gauge what a normal father/son relationship looked like.

A vision of Mr. Riga came to him. He had pushed thoughts of the massive loss his landlord had endured out of his head, unable to find a place for them in his tower of regrets. He didn't want to remember any of the people he had known, if even superficially, who had suffered from the Texas Tango atrocity. He couldn't do a thing for John Riga, or any of them, from his anonymous hide-out in Albany. But he had liked the older man and felt genuine sorrow for him when he lost his sweet wife. They had both enjoyed dispensing casual advice: "Bring a jacket; it will be cold tonight. Come and eat with us; you need to put meat on your bones. Be careful out there riding your bike in the dark."

He had even foolishly confided in Mr. Riga about his tattoo, admitting his continued sorrow over losing Jackie in words he had never uttered to another living soul.

Was that what a relationship with a father could be like? But a true son would not have left the man to suffer alone, as he had left Mr. Riga. Guilt washed over him as he realized he didn't even know if Danny's father was still alive. An unexpected searing wish to have children of his own with Jackie shot through him with such force that tears came to his eyes.

Could it ever happen? God, how he wanted it. Wanted to have her next to him and grow old together the way the Rigas had, wanted to raise children with her who never doubted their identity or their parents' ability to protect them.

If there was even the smallest chance of making any of that possible, he had to fight for it. Had to fight with all the strength available to him. And if that meant trusting in Sam the way a man might trust his own father, and persuading Sam to help him in ways that went against the lifelong security agent's training and instincts, then so be it.

"The pizza will be here soon. I think it's time I tell you part of the story you haven't been aware of."

Sam physically winced while listening to Kolya, his shoulders drawing together and his casually crossed legs uncrossing. He pressed his hands down hard on his thighs as he leaned forward and then abruptly stood and began pacing the room.

"You should have told me this before we left Texas."

"Told you what? That I had seen the woman I once loved in the midst of a horrifying display of senseless violence? When was I supposed to tell you, and what would you have done? Perhaps slipped some memory wiping serum into her hospital IV? Kidnapped her? Although, come to think of it, that might not have been such a terrible idea. At least that way I'd know she was safe."

Kolya raised his eyebrows and glared at Sam, waiting. The wait extended as Sam remained silent, still pacing, the expression on his face changing as he evidently weighed various ideas and quickly discarded them.

"You said you had two children, Sam. Are you married?"

Surprised, Sam halted and looked at him.

"Yes. Yes, I am. And before you ask, the answer is yes, I'm married to the mother of my children, to the woman I fell in love with when I was in my twenties. I'm not a monster, Jake. I was always trying to save your life, not ruin it."

"You did save my life, Sam. Many times over. And I will forever be in your debt. But the last nine years of my life have not constituted a life worth saving. I'm not being melodramatic; I'm just stating a fact. In saving my physical life, you took me away from everything I loved. I know my mother and I had to go in separate directions. I understand that. But she was the only family I had left. And that's not even touching on what it was like to abandon Jackie. Do you know what it's like to watch birthdays, Thanksgiving, and Christmas go by with only a television or video game for company, wanting to see the person you love most in the world for just one more minute? Do you kiss your wife on New Year's Eve, Sam?"

The room stayed silent for several minutes.

"Are you confident she's not telling people you're alive?"

"The girl I fell in love with was already the smartest person I knew. She was observant and sensitive. All of that has probably only grown stronger over the years. Plus, it's been more than ten days since we communicated. If she had wanted to make a fuss, you would have heard about it by now. The world's a lot smaller than it was even nine years ago."

Sam continued to stare off into space. When his gaze finally turned back, his countenance was calm.

"I have a plane to catch. I figured you were itching for a better understanding of what . . . of everything you've been through, but I didn't foresee this. My mother-in-law is quite ill, and I promised my wife I'd be back tonight."

He gave a tired nod to Kolya's tilted head, its expression

211

clearly conveying an "oh, you have family commitments?" look.

"I get it, Jake. I do. And I'm sorry. Give me a few days. Let me think about all this and see if I can come up with any ideas. I know you've been thinking, too. The room practically reeks of it."

He gave a tired laugh.

"We'll come up with something. How about I plan on flying up again next Saturday? We'll compare ideas and see what looks the least dangerous. Does that sound okay?"

"It does. Thank you, Sam. And if you could manage it, I'd prefer to be called Kolya when it's just the two of us. Or Nikolai, if that's easier."

Another moment of silence while Sam studied him. He pursed his lips as if trying to choose the best response and then nodded.

"I understand, Kolya."

Kolya was surprised to find tears welling up in his own eyes, and he struggled to regain control. He reached out his hand, and Sam took it, squeezing it firmly.

"We'll figure something out." Then he smiled and shrugged. "We'll make things right again, or die trying, as the saying goes."

Kolya gave a tired laugh. "Well, after all we've been through, at this point I'd kinda like to avoid the whole dying part."

CHAPTER THIRTY-TWO

Jackie worked. She worked, she wrote, she exercised her fingers, wrist, and arm, and she checked her email. She made herself go out a few times with friends from the office, although even the fun-loving Nadine seemed temporarily content with dinners in quiet restaurants and didn't push for any nightclub visits. Jackie always took pains to steer the conversation quickly to her developing novel, and Nadine seemed genuinely interested and happy for her.

"I can't believe I'm going to be able to say I'm friends with a famous author."

Jackie laughed. "Hardly. Unless you know some other famous writer you've been hiding from me."

Nadine smiled, her eyes opening wide in an "I know more than you do" look.

"You read me that first chapter. I know good stuff when I hear it."

Jackie laughed again. "You never read. How do you know it's good?"

"Pfff." Nadine shook her head, exasperated. "I have

discriminating taste, that's all. I read only good stuff. I read the *Bridgertons.*"

Now Jackie was giggling. "You read the 'from the hit streaming sensation' shortened edition. The actual *Bridgertons* books go on for eight or ten volumes."

"Ewww. I hope you're smart enough to say it all in one book."

"I'll keep Mr. Riga's story to one book. Who knows what I'll do after that."

"Well, as long as you remember who was with you in the beginning, AND who brought you to his house in the first place."

Now Jackie's smile was filled with love.

"Oh, I'll never forget that. You got me through a dark place in more ways than you'll ever know."

Nadine's eyes drew together as she assessed her friend.

"You *are* in better shape now. I'm glad. I was so afraid for a while when you thought your old boyfriend was still alive and hiding from you. And I was really afraid you'd be devastated if it all turned out to be a wild goose chase. But you seem fine."

"I am fine. And I'm going to stay that way."

Underneath the table, Jackie's fingers were crossed. He was trying. He'd said as much, and she believed him. She'd keep checking her email and she'd keep writing. And she would be ready in case a miracle occurred.

CHAPTER THIRTY-THREE

K olya made a conscientious effort at work that week. He chatted with fellow employees, and he completed every task as quickly and expertly as possible. When his work required collaboration with others, he made an effort to come across as less of a standoffish asshole. He didn't know what his brainstorming with Sam might produce, but he had a gut feeling he wasn't destined to remain much longer at Today and Tomorrow Tech, and he didn't want to leave any loose ends or hard feelings.

At home, he gave up trying to search for information about his father. He would ask Sam for copies of all the biographical details they had and try again later. Besides, Sam had mentioned that he had asked friends to look into finding his father's family. Kolya would leave it to the experts to get the ball rolling, at least for now.

Instead, he focused his attention on Jackie and her friends in Austin. He made up new accounts yet again, with innocuous usernames, and hovered. Nadine posted regularly on Instagram and Twitter, and some of her pictures included Jackie, so Kolya became a frequent stalker, waiting for pictures that he could screenshot and save. Jackie had all the usual social media accounts, including the same Facebook account she had used in college. She didn't post often, and he had to be careful not to draw attention to himself as she had far fewer followers than Nadine.

The pull to "friend" or "follow" her was strong, but he had a renewed sense of hope after confiding in Sam, and he didn't want to jinx anything.

Idea after idea ran through his mind. If he—David Hilderman—and Jackie Bourne could meet somewhere, accidentally, or even online through a dating app, they could pretend to get to know each other the way any other couple might, right? Plenty of people relocated after becoming romantically involved, so that wouldn't seem out of the ordinary.

It would probably be unwise for him to return to Austin. Would Jackie be okay with moving? Not to Albany, but maybe they could pick a location together where they'd both be happy? One of Nadine's recent posts had pictured the two of them, and Nadine had written, "Me and my soon-to-be-famous best-selling author bestie." Jackie must still be writing. The thought filled him with quiet joy. He had loved her ability to bury herself in her work, fingers flying across her keyboard with occasional pauses, during which she gazed up into space, seeing nothing, her mind wherever her words had suspended her.

For the first time in years, he found himself wishing he had a guitar or a keyboard. Looking at pictures of Jackie, imagining her sitting before her laptop, a cup of coffee by her side, somehow brought lines of melody into his own head. She had said she had his guitar, and even now, the thought filled him with joy and longing. She had kept the most essential part of him close to her. But he couldn't reach across cyberspace and ask her to hand it to him.

Why shouldn't he have a guitar or keyboard here, now? Or both, for that matter? He wasn't spending his salary on anything else. He did a quick search and found, to his surprise, a few brick-and-mortar music shops still left in the area.

He stopped at the closest one on the way home from work one afternoon and mentally kicked himself when a young man approached, eager to help. Kolya was briefly frozen: was he there for something cheap and easily discarded, similar to everything that had been part of his life for the last decade, or did he want to invest in something worth keeping?

He stood, indecisive, and the sales attendant cocked his head.

"Are you looking for yourself or for a child?"

Of course. Parents were probably the store's primary customers, wanting to get their children involved in worthwhile pursuits beyond their computer screens.

"For me, but I haven't played in a while. Could you show me what you have in keyboards and acoustic guitars?"

The choices were overwhelming, particularly in keyboards. Display items were limited, but the eager young man detailed all the different models they could order.

Overwhelmed, Kolya began to regret his impulse. He should have done his own research online. Hell, he didn't even know if the urge to play again would still be around tomorrow, let alone long-term.

He finally settled on a simple guitar. Not the cheapest model, which came with everything included for a teenager likely to stay interested for only a few days, but a brand he found he remembered and had once admired. Amazing what details could stay buried for years and surface again with only a small crack in the ice.

He walked the long haul back to his apartment, annoyed

with himself for not having thought to drive. Darkness came early now, especially with the end of Daylight Saving Time, but he was so used to walking that he had set out not even thinking about having an instrument to carry back with him. He might have called for a ride, but he didn't have the energy for even that limited social engagement.

He switched the case from hand to hand every few blocks, thinking about Jackie, thinking about music, and wondering if he was on the precipice of a new life or another crashing disappointment. Lines from the lyrics and tunes he had composed long ago came back to him, and he found himself singing softly as he walked.

He loved her. He loved her still and knew in his heart he would love her always. He didn't know if he could find a way for them to be together, but he could tell her in music how he felt and send it to her. His pace quickened, and for the first time in years, there was a new song in his heart.

CHAPTER THIRTY-FOUR

Jackie's entire body tingled with anticipation, impatient for the file to open. And then it did, and she stopped breathing, spellbound.

A man sat, facing the camera, a guitar in his lap. He began to sing. His words were simple but direct, and he looked at her—looked at *her*—as he sang them.

> *The storm clouds came*
> *and stole the sun*
> *My days were bleak*
> *and I had to run*
>
> *How do we live when hope is gone*
> *Force our feet to move*
> *And our hearts to beat*
> *Without the sun to light the path*
> *Only darkness lives*
>
> *But then dawn burst through the night*
> *Routed darkness and returned the light*

Your presence once again a star
Bringing back to life a once-dead heart

AGAIN AND AGAIN SHE played the file, pausing only to find a box of tissues as the tears coursed down her face.

How was any of this possible? Here she was, more than nine years after saying goodbye forever to the only man she would ever truly love, and here he was, right before her on the screen.

She had found him, or chanced upon him, only because a monster had chosen to shoot and kill innocent people. Was she getting a second chance at the cost of their lives?

Fragments of stories she had heard over the years came to her: tales of people who had met working at Ground Zero and fallen in love, spouses of dead cancer patients meeting through their grief and finding joy again, an earthquake victim meeting his soulmate in a shelter.

She would most likely never know or understand it all. Probably never fully understand the mystery and intrigue surrounding Leo's disappearance all those years ago, and most definitely never understand the mixed tragedy and blessing that had brought them back together.

But he was alive. He was alive, somewhere on this earth, and he was singing to her again.

Her eyes moved greedily over each pixel on the screen, studying every aspect of his appearance. He wore no glasses, and the eyes that stared into hers were his eyes, the beautiful blue gray she remembered so well and not the dark eyes that had met her own the night of the shooting. Other parts of his face were different, and his hair had an auburn tint she didn't recognize and doubted was real. His fingers, though, were the same: long, lean, and strong, and she yearned with an intensity that made her curl up upon herself in her chair to reach out and touch those fingers, to intertwine them with her own and bring them to her lips.

Each time the song concluded, she heard the words he spoke in his own, still beautifully familiar, voice: *"I'm still trying, Jackie. Don't give up on us, please. I love you."*

CHAPTER THIRTY-FIVE

He prepared for his meeting with Sam, mentally laying out the various facts and obstacles that had to be discussed.

If whoever had sent those menacing messages almost ten years ago had zeroed in on his and his mother's identities, then they might have known about Jackie, as well. But Jackie's boyfriend had died, and her grief and the subsequent path she had chosen in her life had no ties whatsoever to him, David Hilderman.

His mother was now living an existence so entirely removed from who and what she had been previously, that he himself had trouble believing it possible. He sincerely doubted anyone else would question her background, or if they did, tie it to a long-dead Russian refugee.

He fervently hoped to see her again, someday. She had given up everything to keep him safe, and he missed the close, easy affection they had shared that had never waned, even during his obnoxious teenage years. He would love for Jackie to have the chance to spend time with her again as well, since they had seemed to enjoy each other's company during the short time they had spent together.

But such dreams could wait. For now, he had to come up with a believable plan that would enable Jacqueline Bourne of Austin, Texas, and David "Jake" Hilderman, currently of Albany, New York, to meet, fall in love, and begin a life together. A plan that would keep them both safe and allay Sam's fears.

This time when Sam arrived, they stayed in the apartment. The temperature had dropped significantly, and even the always dapper bureaucrat looked cold and tired as he took off his jacket and hung it on the hook by the door.

"The older I get, the less tolerant I am of winter weather. I'm beginning to understand why so many people not all that much older than me move to Florida, although I've always mocked the idea myself."

As if struck by the thought, he tilted his head at Kolya.

"Do you remember Russian winters?"

Kolya shrugged. "Sort of? I have vague memories of lots and lots of layers. In Virginia, in winter, my mother always tried to get me to dress warmly when all my friends were ignoring the cold. She never got the fact that it was dorky to be caught wearing a hat or gloves."

He pulled two of the chairs out from the small table and motioned for Sam to sit. "I can't do anything about the cold. You're the one who picked this town, remember? But let's start with Russia. We have a lot to talk about."

An hour later, they were still seated at the table, each with a paper and pencil and numerous jottings noted down as one topic after another was chewed over.

Going for broke, Kolya had almost laughed at Sam's physical reaction to learning of the video he had sent Jackie.

"You just sent it? Via email? No encryption or . . ."

He looked totally nonplussed, and Kolya tried to reassure him.

"I told you last week that my goal is to be with her. She has to know I'm still me and learn to trust me again."

"Yes, but . . ." Sam turned his pencil compulsively right-side up and upside down, his eyes unfocused as he no doubt cycled through all manners of monsters in the closet.

"There can't be any more 'buts.' I've thought about everything you told me. I understand the enormous effort and expense that were invested in keeping us safe, and I'm grateful. I really am, Sam. I know my mother and I would both probably be dead by now if the Secretary hadn't stepped in, and if you hadn't been so thorough and kind. But as you admitted, we've got to wrap everything up."

Sam continued to stare at the paper in front of him, the pencil still on its tilt-a-whirl cycle. When he finally looked up, his eyes looked suspiciously reddened and moist.

"If things all work out the way you want them to—and I hope with all my heart that they do—then maybe you'll someday understand what it's like."

Kolya raised his brows, uncertain where Sam was going at the moment.

"My son started out pre-med. He did well, and while we worried about the costs of that many years of education, we were happy he was building a solid future for himself. Then he announced at Christmas of his junior year that he was switching his major to art history. Art history, for Christ's sake. Because the whole world knows what a lucrative field that is."

He shuddered theatrically and continued.

"Now he's out in Seattle on a postdoc something or other, living on rice, beans, and the cheapest, most obnoxious beer you can even imagine. He probably only manages to keep up with his expenses thanks to the money my wife sends him that they both think I know nothing about.

"My daughter went to law school. Phew! At least she was sensible, right? But the besotted do-gooder has now switched to mostly pro-bono work and is writing romance novels on the side. Romance novels! And my wife, who's in publishing, is encouraging her."

Sam dropped his pencil and reached his hands up to clasp the back of his head, stretching his elbows out to the sides. He tilted his head from side to side and took in a deep breath before letting it out in a whoosh and glaring at Kolya.

"And there you were, right in the middle. A kid I cared about almost as much as one of my own. Your life was as complicated as hell, but at least, I thought, with every precaution we had taken, you were safe. Not only safe, but sensible."

He narrowed his eyes at Kolya before shaking his head in surrender and smiling an exaggerated evil smile.

"So if everything works out the way you want, you and your Jackie will reunite, marry, and start a family of your own. And then you'll really learn what worry and fear feel like."

They stared at each other in silence for a minute or two, and then both began laughing.

"Your wife is in publishing?"

Sam stared at him, astonished.

"That's what you heard out of everything I just said?"

Kolya laughed harder. "No, of course not. I heard it all. But you may have just hit upon a solution I couldn't find. I think Jackie is working on a book—she may have written a few by now, for all I know. What if she had to fly east to meet with your wife and discuss a book deal, and I was there at the same time to discuss a book of my own?"

Sam looked both confused and horrified. "You've written a book?"

"No! Oh, for God's sake, Sam. You've spent my entire life concocting imaginary details about me. Can't you see haphazardly crafted deceit staring you in the face?"

Now it was Sam's turn first to stare open-mouthed, and then to double over in anxiety-propelled laughter.

"Jesus. You got me. I hope you still have beer in the fridge. I think I need one. And it better be tastier stuff than the crap my son drinks."

They tossed around various ideas and timelines and finally agreed upon a plan.

"My wife, of course, knows nothing about my work in general or you in particular." Sam uttered the words in a measured tone, looking intently at the table. Kolya understood instantly that it was utter nonsense.

"Of course."

"But I'm certain she'll agree to meet with this exciting new writer to discuss her work. Sorry, with these two exciting new writers." He chewed on his lip for a moment.

"Thanksgiving would be pushing it, time wise, but if Jackie is planning on flying to the D.C. area around Christmas, we could make it happen then. You could both have meetings scheduled at my wife's office and then be invited to a holiday get-together. We can find somewhere in the area where we can all meet up, and then my wife and I can make a discreet exit.

"That would give Jackie a plausible storyline for meeting someone new and falling in love. You could keep up a long-distance relationship for a few months and then decide to relocate somewhere agreeable to you both."

He looked assessingly at Kolya. "I think it would be best if no one who knew you in Austin got a good look at you. The changes we made are minimal, and someone observant still might catch on. You said she had confided her suspicions in other people there?"

"Yes. I think so. I'm pretty sure she had some help finding me on the video game, but I think she understands now how careful we have to be. And now that we have a plan, I don't see why Jackie and I can't communicate freely, at least on email. Right? People meet online all the time, in all sorts of bizarre circumstances. I can find out who knows what, and we can figure out what to do about it. And there won't be any connections between our email accounts and the people who will meet for the first time in the D.C. area in December."

Sam blew out his breath in defeat.

"All of this sounds like a textbook example of how *not* to handle an identity protection case. Good thing I'm retiring soon. And by the way, when I do, I'll be fine with you continuing to call me Sam, or you can use my name, Bill. Whichever you prefer."

Kolya looked up, a strange sense of relief sweeping over him. Sam—Bill—was implying they'd have contact going forward. He was retiring, and his responsibility for Kolya would be over. But it sounded like Kolya might get to keep his trusted "uncle."

Sam looked back at Kolya, his expression showing affection and concern. "With luck, you two will have everything worked out just about the same time your file is officially closed, and then I'll just have two young writer friends to worry about. Let's just hope no new surprises crop up between now and then."

In the hours after Sam's departure, Kolya worked on his email. It would be his first chance to convey real information, and he struggled to find the right words.

Dearest Jackie,

I'm pretty certain it's ok for us to email, but we still need to be careful. I know I can say this much, even though I said it earlier: I am sorry. Sorry for all the years of pain I caused us both, but especially you. I have no right to ask your forgiveness, but I beg it anyway. I didn't choose the lies that tore us apart, but neither did I ask enough questions at the time or trust you with the most important truths. There is a man, whom I'll call Sam, who has been a source of protection and guidance to me throughout my life. He, too, is now sorry for the pain he put us both through, although he is unshaken in his belief that it was the right thing to do at the time to keep us all safe.

I have only recently learned important details that help explain Sam's long-ago decisions. He knows I am emailing you but asks that we be discreet: not to telephone or video-chat, and not to discuss specifics. He also feels strongly, and I agree, that no one besides you should know of the links between me and other people you knew previously. I've told him that you most likely already understand this restriction, infuriating as it is.

I promise you, when we meet, I will tell you everything. I do not want there to ever be secrets between us again.

As for meeting, Sam is volunteering to help. I saw a picture on a social media post referring to you as an author. Sam's wife is in publishing, and she will be reaching out to you to propose an in-person meeting during the Christmas holiday season. I believe she works not far from where your family used to live. I desperately hope you'll be able and willing to meet with her, as I hope to be there, as well.

Until then, I remain, now and forever, yours. That sounds so old-fashioned, but it says exactly what is in my heart. God, how I miss you and want to hold you again. Know that I'm sorry. Know that I love you, and know that I am doing everything I can to be with you, this time for real and for always, if you'll have me. K

CHAPTER THIRTY-SIX

Once again, Jackie found herself staring open-mouthed at her screen: shock, bewilderment, and elation chasing each other through her thoughts.

It was just a few weeks ago that he had written they should not communicate, and only a few weeks before that she had still believed him long dead. Now he was not only reaffirming his love, but also laying out tentative plans for a future together.

Christmas. A meeting. It was already mid-November. Thank God she had already bought a ticket to fly home. Would she really see him then?

Her eyes darted around the tiny apartment. It was nice, small as it was, and she liked her job well enough and enjoyed Austin's weirdness. But she could say good-bye to it all in a second. She would miss Nadine, but Nadine had lots of friends and was no doubt making new ones at that very minute.

And she'd miss Mr. Riga. In only a short time, she had come to care deeply for the dear man.

Kolya had written that no one should know about them.

He had good reasons, undoubtedly, as the cloak and dagger existence he had led had to be based on real danger. But Mr. Riga had legitimate needs as well, and he was not only all alone in the world, but he was also the only living person who knew them both well. People needed allies to survive in this world; the last few months had taught her that, if nothing else.

Would she ever be able to tell her parents or her sister the truth, supposing she herself ever came to fully understand it? Perhaps not. But maybe, just maybe, she could help create a happily-ever-after for the real-life hero of her book and the one person who had first given her hope.

She would have to tell Kolya she was breaking his "no one should know" rule, but she hoped he would understand. She was pretty sure the Leo she had loved would have agreed with her decision.

She'd stop by Mr. Riga's place on Saturday. In the meantime, she had a book to write. After all, it sounded like she had an appointment with a publisher.

The physical note arrived in the mail two days later.

Dear Ms. Bourne,

Thank you for entering our debut author contest. I'd love to meet with you in person to discuss your work. Please confirm if an appointment on Wednesday, December 22, would be convenient. After we talk, I hope you'll join me at the Commonwealth Emporium for a casual holiday gathering of emerging authors.

Yours Sincerely,

Brenda Macken

HOLY CRAP. It was actually going to happen. In just over a month, she'd be in the same room as Leo again. Except this time his name might be David or Kolya, or who knew what, but it would be him, the boy she had loved and the man she had longed for these many years.

Mr. Riga reacted with delight when she told him. His kind face was still too thin, but Jackie saw genuine pleasure, maybe the first he had shown since the shootings. Impulsively, she reached out and took his hands in hers.

"We're probably going to have to move. I don't know where, and I don't know when, but we'll have to start over somewhere where no one knows us. Will you come with us?"

His eyes widened, incredulous.

"Come with you? Don't be silly, girl. You don't want an old man hanging around while you start a new life."

"But I kinda do, Mr. Riga. If you hadn't mentioned that tattoo, I would have spent the rest of my life lonely and doubting my sanity. And the fact that Leo . . . Jake . . . I think his real name may be Kolya, but we'll stick with Jake for now —I think the fact that he told you about it meant that he trusted you. And I never, ever, would have thought of trying to find him on an online game. That was all you. You gave him back to me. If we ever have kids, they'll need a grandpa who is close by, since I doubt we'll be near my parents in Virginia. I can't think of anyone who could do a better job than you."

He turned his face away, but not before Jackie saw tears in his eyes.

"Please, Mr. Riga. Think about it. But just don't talk about it to anyone, cause I think we'd both be in trouble, then."

She made an exaggerated grimace, and he laughed softly, swiping at his nose with his fist before pulling her against him in a hug.

"My name's John, my dear. No more Mr. Riga. I'm not saying yes, but I'll think about it."

CHAPTER THIRTY-SEVEN

ecember 22. December had historically proven to be a good month for him, so he'd have to stop griping about cold weather. He knew he'd grown soft, climate wise. Would it look too wussy to ask if somewhere like Santa Fe or San Diego would appeal to Jackie? Maybe Flagstaff? He'd go wherever she wanted, though, if it meant they could be together.

He'd have to find a job. He'd never done that before. Should he create a LinkedIn? Go on Craig's List? Would he be David Hilderman applying for a position in a new city or someone else entirely? Could he possibly *be* Nikolai Polivanov? The idea both fascinated and terrified him. A month ago he had sat, seething with indignation. Now that he had theoretically "won" and received answers to many of his questions, a whole new horizon of uncertainties lay before him.

Who was he? Leo Jorgensson had been a budding historian, linguist, and amateur musician. Jake Carpentero and David Hilderman were computer scientists—both men who went to work and did little else with their lives save keep their bodies in shape and play video games. But who was *he, Nikolai Polivanov?* Could he be a real man once Geppetto was out of the picture and no longer pulling the puppet strings?

He wanted desperately to talk with Jackie—to hold her hand and walk for miles talking to her and hearing her thoughts.

What would Sam's carefully orchestrated meeting at his wife's office entail?

Forty-eight, forty-nine, fifty. He was on his living room floor, once again resorting to push-ups in a desperate attempt to rein in his panic. His chest muscles screamed, but he persisted.

He was a Russian-American with a decidedly foreign sounding name. How would it be to function in society as Kolya? With all that was going on in the world, he doubted his existence, regardless of his progeny, made any real difference to anyone, anymore. But would he stick out too much in whatever world they tried to immerse themselves in? Would he be better off branding himself as a Nick, rather than a Kolya? How he wanted to just be himself, whoever that turned out to be.

Would Jackie be happy finding herself linked to a Russian-American with a murky background? *Fucking A.* He'd be anyone she wanted him to be if it meant they could be together again. For two and a half glorious years they had been everything to each other, shared all of college life's little ups and downs, and dreamed of a forever future together. And then he had died.

He hadn't seen the site of the explosion after it happened, but every cell in his body had been changed by its aftermath. With the now familiar twist of guilt in his gut, he knew Jackie had been changed as well. The sensitive, poetic, and curious young woman he had known would never have aspired to a marketing position with an international corporation. Her joyful perspective on life had been snuffed out with his physical life.

No. They weren't who they had been. But if he believed in anything in this world, he believed in love. It was the force that had driven his mother into exile in order to keep him safe. It was what had propelled him across the nightclub floor, regardless of consequences, when he had thought Jackie in danger. Hell, it was probably what lay behind Sam's mother hen-like supervision of his life these many years. And, as unlikely as he ever would have anticipated, it seemed to have turned mild-mannered Jackie Bourne into an internet detective with relentless determination.

He pushed himself up from the floor and went for his guitar. Maybe his incoherent thoughts would make more sense as music.

CHAPTER THIRTY-EIGHT

It was one thing to turn giddy with excitement and delight every time a new email appeared in her Kolya-only account, but it was quite another to maintain appearances as her regular, boring self at Home Pantry. Again and again she had to push breathless speculation about seeing Kolya out of her head and focus on product placement and hype. The big holiday issues were behind them, and the bulk of her work now centered on Valentine's Day, Mardi Gras, and Easter.

Nadine's mother invited her to Thanksgiving dinner, and for the first time in years, Jackie declined, with gratitude, and then found herself having to deal with a suspicious friend.

"You probably won't believe this, knowing how limited my cooking skills are, but I was planning on going over to Mr. Riga's house and preparing a meal there just for us."

"No! We can invite him, too. The more the merrier!"

Jackie smiled at her friend. The world needed more of the effervescence that seemed built into her family's DNA.

"Thank you. I'll let him know you offered. But my guess

is, he'll say no. He's doing better, but I don't think he's quite up to 'merry' yet, and I'm not sure I am, either."

Nadine peered at her, assessing.

"I thought you said you were feeling better."

"I am. I really am," she hastened to add at Nadine's tilted head.

"But we're spending a lot of time talking about his early life and family stuff. The whole idea of giving thanks is complicated for someone who's lost everyone dear to him. I think he'd be more comfortable if no one tries to force him to get in the holiday spirit. It'd be nice if you could maybe drop in on him while I'm home at Christmas."

"Of course I'll drop in on him. It's a little strange how the two of you have grown so close. It's like Danny and Jake brought the two of you together even though Jake didn't turn out to be your old boyfriend, after all." Nadine's gaze was gentle as she paused.

"I'm sorry, you know. Your crazy certainty almost had me convinced for a while there that some kind of weird miracle had come out of that horrible night. But I guess if Mr. Riga has a new friend, and you've found your way back to writing, then maybe something good came from it after all."

Jackie nodded and smiled. "That old stuff about a door closing and a window opening might be true after all."

God, please let it be true.

CHAPTER THIRTY-NINE

O*omph.* The sound of his breath leaving his throbbing chest wasn't pretty, but he felt like he was beginning to make progress. He had enjoyed the challenge of martial arts in Austin, and as his mood improved with the pace of his email communication with Jackie, he decided to give it a go again in Albany. Why not? So what if he was only short-term? The anger and ennui that had engulfed him upon his arrival had receded, and he now felt he had to do something to take his mind from the never-ending hamster wheel of thoughts and plans. So much was hanging on the precipice: after years of every life decision being made for him, he was finally going to attain some form of self-determination. And, God willing, he was going to do it with Jackie at his side—an idea that would have seemed unthinkable even six months ago. But for just a few weeks more, he had to remain in limbo, so whatever discipline he could assert over his mind and body would be to his advantage.

A Jiu Jitsu academy was nearby and highly rated, and Kolya—still David for now—began taking classes. The practice was very different from the Tae Kwon Do and Tai-Chi he had studied previously, but he found the ground-based grappling a good outlet for his pent-up energy and anxiety.

Three more weeks. Three weeks until he'd see Jackie again. See her, hold her, and *please, please, please* find a way for them to be together.

They emailed constantly now, words flying back and forth across the miles almost as seamlessly as they had done across campus grounds all those years ago. Jackie was bursting with enthusiasm over the novel she was writing about John Riga, of all people.

Kolya had frowned at his screen, bewildered, when she first described her book. Jackie was writing about Danny's father? How in the world had that happened? How had they come together? The shooting, obviously, but . . . wow. Talk about coincidences. He could focus on Jackie, but pangs of angry impotence hit him whenever he thought about the others who had been injured, killed, or left grieving. When thoughts of that horrible night crossed his mind, he pushed them away. Mr. Riga's loss in particular haunted him, and he tried to ignore mental images of the elderly man sitting alone in his empty home.

The past decade had taught him not to feel, not to dwell on his own pain or anyone else's. His role had been to function, nothing more. Now, during the cold morning and evening walks to and from work, he tried to work through the waves of sorrow and regret he had steadfastly avoided. Danny had been a good guy and a better friend than the jerk named Jake had ever acknowledged. Always generous, welcoming, but never demanding, he had steered Jake into living arrangements that had been exactly what he had needed. The Rigas had looked out for him almost as parents might, he now belatedly realized. They had been parental figures he had never thanked or even acknowledged as being important to him.

He sensed from Jackie's words that she had grown close to Mr. Riga, and while a small part of him automatically shouted "DANGER, WILL ROBINSON," another part of him felt a surge of joy that the lonely man was not completely alone. John Riga was the one person from Austin, besides Jackie, of course, whom he would truly like to see again.

Three weeks. Three weeks until they could talk about everything. He had a return ticket to Albany booked for January 2, but who knew what would happen after they all met up?

"Good job, David." The Jiu Jitsu master, who said to just call him Matt, gave him a hand up. "You're catching on fast."

"Thanks."

The exhaustion felt good. The smell of sweaty mats here wasn't all that different from the smells he had known in Austin. He inhaled deeply and prepared for the next roll.

CHAPTER FORTY

Bill Rousch couldn't shake the feeling he was missing something. A lifetime in security and intelligence had taught him to trust his instincts, but all those instincts were telling him now was . . . he had no idea. He felt like he was being followed, but of course, he wasn't. He'd been doing primarily desk work for years now. And even if, somehow, he was being targeted, it shouldn't have anything to do with the Polivanov case, one that he was supposed to be closing up.

He was spending more hours than necessary going over everything in the boy's files. The boy, who was most definitely no longer a boy, and who wanted to be called by his true name, Nikolai.

Brenda had laughed in delight when he asked for her help arranging a meeting.

"I'll finally get to meet him, our third child! And his girlfriend, too! I just may have to write a book myself, if this all turns out as well as I'm hoping."

He glared at her. "Do you want me to get sent to prison? Lose our retirement? You shouldn't even know he exists."

"Don't be silly. I'd be creative enough to change all the incriminating details. But you have to admit, darling, if this works out, it will, indeed, be a love story for the ages."

"Let's just hope it's a love story more akin to a Hallmark Christmas movie than Romeo and Juliet."

"What's the matter with you? I thought you said it was all looking good? There haven't been searches of their names, the mother is safe and sound living her own happily-ever-after, and God knows the assholes in Russia have other things on their minds right now."

He smiled at her in tired bemusement. "How you manage to keep straight so many details of a story you know nothing about is beyond me."

"And," she paused for dramatic emphasis. "Who knows, maybe you're introducing me to a great new writer. This Jackie may have the next bestseller tucked away somewhere. It's a win-win, no matter how you look at it."

Bill nodded. She was right.

Then why was his gut telling him she was wrong?

CHAPTER FORTY-ONE

"Having a face-to-face meeting with an editor is such a huge step, Jackie-love!"

Her mother's bubbling enthusiasm filled the car as they drove home from the airport.

"And if she wants to publish it, there's no reason you can't move back here and write from home." She breathed out a contented sigh, confident that all her maternal dreams were coming true.

"Mom, I told you this is just a preliminary meeting, if even that. It's only because it's Christmas time and I did well enough in a contest they were running. It's most likely more of a courtesy thing that's part of a program to encourage new authors."

Would she be struck by lightning for spinning out one whopper after another to her well-meaning parents? She had to figure out a way to keep them unsuspecting and supportive without building unrealistic expectations.

"It's still a wonderful sign. A harbinger of good things to come, like the Christmas star."

Jackie bent her head and kneaded the area above her eyes.

The more she fretted over how she was deceiving her parents, the less she feared that her excitement about seeing Kolya would light her up like a neon sign on Broadway. She loved her mom and dad dearly. But she also understood at a cellular level that even the barest outline of the complicated twists she was following would put them into a tailspin of worry.

They had been vocally supportive when she had switched majors, gone into business, and then followed increasingly promising career options around the country. But passing remarks had slipped out at regular intervals throughout the years: "It's such a shame you can't find a good marketing job closer to home." "That nice boy, Mark, from high school, got a job teaching in Chantilly. With your background, you could probably get certified to teach in no time." And, dropped most often with an accompanying dramatic sigh: "How sad that your niece and nephew only get to see you once or twice a year."

She knew they loved her, and she loved them. They had been good parents while she and Britney were growing up: neither crazy strict nor totally oblivious, and they had offered nothing but comfort and a safe space to heal first when Leo had died during college and again when she had been injured this past year in the shooting.

Who knew what she'd be able to tell them once she understood the complexities of Kolya's situation? And that was assuming she ever understood it all, herself.

She'd just have to cross that bridge when she came to it. For now, the best, least upsetting thing that could happen, was that she would end up telling them that the editor—and Brenda Macken *was* an editor, Jackie had confirmed that much online—had told her she had potential and to keep writing. Because she could easily say that regardless of what else happened.

Her head still bent in the backseat where her father couldn't see even peering in the rearview mirror, Jackie felt a smile spread across her face. Less than forty-eight hours now. That was all. One of her parents would probably insist on driving her to the address in Crystal City, but she'd convince them to leave her to make her own way back.

A shiver of excitement ran through her, and she bent her head lower to keep her glee to herself. Forty-eight hours. Added to the nine plus years, what was another two days? An eternity, that's what it was.

CHAPTER FORTY-TWO

The office was on the 12th floor. From where he stood, Kolya could see the Washington Monument in the distance. The thick windowpanes kept the noise from the nearby take-offs and landings to a minimum, but Kolya's eyes briefly followed each plane. Were there other lives inside those air-borne vehicles as convoluted as his? Was anyone on board one of those jets as nervous as he was at this moment?

"Are you sure you don't want some water, David?"

He hadn't been surprised when meeting Sam's wife, Brenda. Somehow, she looked exactly right. Not tall or short, fat or thin, she was a woman probably in her late 50s who didn't look like she was trying to hide that fact. Instead, she exuded a quiet beauty and ease in her own skin and carried herself with a gentle demeanor. Her eyes expressed nothing but kind intelligence, exactly what Sam had shown him all these years.

"I told her to be here at 3:30, so she should be arriving any minute. I'll leave you alone when she gets here, but I am interested in meeting her." At his startled look, she laughed.

"I'm sorry, my dear. You won't get to keep her all to yourself, at least not for this evening. We have reservations at the restaurant for 6:30."

"I'm not sure he's hearing anything we say to him."

Sam's voice came from the conference table where he had been working on a laptop. "Try telling him that this is all just a reality TV pilot and see if he reacts."

"I heard that, Sam, just as I've heard every word your more understanding wife has said. Thank you, Ms. Macken. I appreciate everything you're doing here today."

"It's our pleasure. And for heaven's sake, call me Brenda. I know the rest of you change names as frequently as I get my hair trimmed, but I'm Brenda, now and forever."

A knock sounded and a young man opened the door.

"Your 3:30 is here, Brenda."

"Thanks, Andrew. Send her in."

Kolya caught his breath—panic, anticipation, and hope sweeping over him.

She came in, and it was at once the same beautiful woman he had seen standing in line for the bathroom months before in Austin and the same girl who had stolen his heart all those years ago in a university library.

"I'm so glad you could come, Jackie. I'm Brenda Macken, and I look forward to speaking with you later. But for now, we'll leave you two to talk."

He heard Brenda's words and was dimly aware of her pulling Sam toward the door.

"God help us all."

Sam's words were quiet, but they hung in the air as Kolya and Jackie stared at each other. Jackie's head was slightly tilted as she studied him.

"Kolya?"

So many uncertainties were conveyed in the breathless upward intonation of his name.

"That's my real name. It's short for Nikolai, which is actually my real name." *Don't babble, idiot!*

He moved from the window and walked slowly towards her. A jacket lay over her arm, pressed tightly to her side. Her nose was turning a pale pink color, but he knew it wasn't from the cold.

He pulled the jacket from her unresisting hold along with the small purse strap hanging from her shoulder and tossed them on the nearest chair. Then he reached out and took her hands in his.

"I'm sorry. I didn't want to leave you. And I never wanted to hurt you." His voice cracked as he struggled not to break down.

She nodded silently, and he saw her teeth bite down on her quivering lower lip.

"Please don't cry, my angel. Please." But he was crying too, tears running down his face.

And then she was against him, her head burrowing into his chest, and his arms were around her, holding her as tightly as he dared.

"I'm so sorry." He whispered the words over and over, pressing his lips against her hair.

"I'm sorry, too. I should have looked for you."

"No, sweetheart. You have nothing to be sorry for. You had to believe I was dead. But I wish I hadn't had to hurt you like that. I never wanted you to suffer."

They were both still crying, but somehow her face was turned up to his, and he was talking into her mouth, his words interspersed with soft kisses as their lips tentatively became reacquainted.

"You feel the same and taste the same." Her words were half-laugh, half-sob as her head once more buried against his chest. "You even smell the same."

The last sentence was muffled, but Kolya understood and

held her even tighter. With a twinge of guilt, he realized he had a raging hard-on pressing into her midriff, as well.

Jackie obviously noticed because she made a muffled snort against his chest and smiled up at him through her tears.

"That feels the same, too." But as she looked at him, her brows drew together, and her smile faded.

"So much of you is different, though. Your eyes in the video were your old eyes, but these are different, and they're all different from the eyes that looked at me during the shooting.

"Who are you, Kolya, that I can't even know what your real eyes look like?"

He blew out his breath and squeezed the offending eyes shut while keeping her pressed securely against him. After a moment, he loosened his hold and took a step back, once more holding her two hands in his.

"My eyes are the ones you used to know—the ones you saw on the video when I sang to you. All the rest are colored contacts. Could we sit down? I can try to explain the basics, although I myself still don't understand some parts of it."

She looked at him, tears still glistening. Her gaze moved slowly as she examined each tiny segment of his face, perhaps creating a map for future reference.

"Is it okay?" He regretted the words the moment they came out, but he wanted her not to hate the face he had now.

She gave a shaky laugh. "It's fine. You're still beautiful, just different. But I don't care, as long as you promise me you won't disappear again."

Tears ran more quickly down her cheeks, and once more he held her pressed to him as tightly as he could without hurting her, wanting to absorb her into himself so they could never be parted again.

"I promise. I'll do whatever I have to. I want to be with you as long as you want me."

They stood quietly then, each breathing in the other's essence. His groin ached, but he would gladly stand this way through all eternity if it would give her peace.

Finally she pulled back, sniffling.

"Okay. Let's talk for a few minutes. Ms. Macken will probably want her office back soon. Was the man who was here with her the Sam you wrote about?"

"Yes. That's Sam. He's the hero and the villain behind everything that's happened in my life."

"Which is he—a hero or a villain?"

"Both. But definitely more hero, fortunately. Which means I can't hate him for everything that's happened to me. He's only ever done what he thought best to keep me safe."

"But keep you safe from what?"

He led her to the small couch that was against a wall covered with framed collages of book covers. The couch was set kitty-corner to a large desk, with two upholstered chairs at the other angle: a small office within a larger office.

They sat, hands clasped together, and as he struggled to decide where to start, he noticed the red scars running along Jackie's wrist and up her left arm. Pain shot through him at this visual reminder of how much they had endured, both individually and together. He lifted her arm and tenderly kissed the skin that was obviously still not completely healed. He had to remember to go gently whenever he touched her on the left side. He took a slow, steadying breath and began to regurgitate the synopsis he had worked at as a roadmap to the absurd twists and turns of his life.

Jackie's eyes were half-closed, her brow furrowed as she attempted to make sense of everything he was telling her. Her questions came out randomly, and he tried to answer each one as simply and honestly as possible.

"You were never Swedish?"

"No."

"But you speak Swedish, right? I know I heard you speaking it with your mother."

"Yes, we did. I haven't spoken a word of it in almost ten years, though."

"Is your mother alive?"

"Yes."

"So no one died that day in Ruckersville?"

"No."

She stayed silent a moment or two, and then she gave him a piercing look.

"Did you know I was right there, at Home Pantry, the whole time?"

He shook his head, still not completely believing the strangeness of it all himself.

"No. Yes, I saw a name, a name just like yours on the staff list, but I rejected any possibility that it could be you. It wouldn't have made any sense for you to be there, working in that kind of position. The first time I knew we were in the same city was when I saw you standing in line for the bathroom that night. I couldn't believe it was you. And I don't even know what I would have done—what I should have done. I ran. I acted like a stupid coward, and I ran because I was terrified you'd recognize me. But then I had to come back to the bar, after all. And then the shooting started, and all I could think was that I couldn't lose you."

He looked away, unable to speak for a few seconds.

"But then I lost you again, anyway. I was shot, I lost consciousness, and when I woke up, you were gone, Sam was there, and I learned I had died again."

He closed his eyes and felt Jackie's fingers tighten around his.

"Yeah. I remember that part. I woke up thinking I had

seen *or heard* a ghost, only to find out that whoever the ghost was or wasn't, he was dead."

She had been rocking back and forth ever so slowly as she spoke, and Kolya felt another wave of guilt sweep over him.

"I'm so sorry, Jackie. So very, very sorry."

"Why did Sam decide Jake Carpentero was better off dead? Was it to keep people from looking into your background? I'm pretty sure no one checked out my background once they realized the shooters were just angry nut-jobs."

"That's a valid point. But he made a split-second decision, not knowing anything about the shooters at the time. And he told me later that he had wanted to move me one last time, anyway."

"Move you one last time. Like you were some kind of piece on a gameboard. Do you have any idea how bat-shit crazy that sounds?"

"Fuck yes, I do. And it's part of the battle I've been waging with him these last few months. I think we've finally reached an understanding of sorts, though, which is why we're here now, you and me."

"And tomorrow? Or next week? What if he decides you're in danger again, and poof—you're gone?"

"There won't be any more disappearances, at least not from you. Anything I do, we do together, as long as you're on board."

Her gaze was intense and more than a little skeptical.

"So does that mean a house and a dog and a white picket fence, or changing identities and eye color at the drop of some mysterious hat?"

"A dog would be nice."

The hand not holding hers had gone to her face without him consciously moving it, and his fingers lightly traced over her cheekbones and lips as he tried to take in all the tiny changes a decade had wrought.

She reached up and pressed his palm to her lips, kissing it. Then she heaved a long, quiet sigh.

"I guess I could manage contacts if I had to."

He laughed.

"No colored contacts for you. Your eyes are beautiful just as they are." He leaned forward and kissed each closed eyelid and then the irresistible soft spaces under each eye before finally reaching her mouth again.

He drank in the taste of her, the familiar but so long-denied shape and texture of lips that seemed to have been designed uniquely for him. Their kiss deepened, and he felt her tongue dancing with his. An overwhelming sense of joy and completeness filled him, and for the first time in years, he felt whole.

They clung to each other, devoured each other, and then somehow Jackie was straddling him there on the office loveseat, and their kisses were wet with the salty taste of their tears and hot with their growing urgency.

"I have a hotel room right nearby. Stay with me tonight, Jackie, please?"

"Of course I'll stay with you."

"We'll figure everything out. Nothing matters to me but you. I've stayed alive these last nine years, but the only thing I've learned is that life is meaningless without you."

Her reply was cut off by the knock on the door. It opened, and before they could right themselves, Brenda and Sam came in.

"I knew it was a good idea to keep that couch here. It makes heart-to-heart talks with my writers so much easier."

Brenda moved purposely towards her desk and then turned and gently tossed them the box of tissues that had been sitting there.

"And thank heavens we found the right Jackie. I can't wait to hear about your book, my dear."

She prattled on, allowing them a few moments to put themselves in some kind of order and mop up their faces.

"I'm going to step out for just a few minutes more while Sam goes over a few things, and then we'll head over to the Emporium. I've been told their holiday menu is sensational this year."

She walked out, closing the door once more behind her. Sam looked from Kolya to Jackie and then gestured for them to join him at the conference table. He took a seat on one side, and Kolya and Jackie took seats next to each other facing him.

His countenance as he looked at them was at once resigned, cautious, yet kindly, his eyes, too, showing signs of emotion.

"As Brenda said, I'm glad you both turned out to be the one the other was looking for. We might have had a real mess on our hands, otherwise."

They all smiled. The room was quiet for a moment, save for the sound of now three noses sniffling. Kolya held Jackie's hand firmly in his, his thumb caressing her fingers reassuringly. Sam was trying. And he was doing so much more than had ever been officially required of him, as always.

"Sam, allow me to officially introduce Jackie—Jacqueline Bourne. Jackie, this is Sam."

Sam stood up and extended his hand across the table.

"My name is Bill Rousch, Jackie, and I'm truly glad to meet you. But for simplicity's sake, it's probably best that I remain Sam. It's a name I've grown fond of over the years."

He looked down at the table, and Kolya was touched at how Sam, too, was overcome by the improbability of this reunion.

They had gotten to this point, however, because of Jackie's conviction that he was alive and his determination to take control of his own life. He needed to help Sam let go.

"I've told Jackie most of my story. We only had a few minutes, so there will obviously be holes to fill over time, but I'm determined not to hide anything from her going forward."

Sam nodded, keeping his gaze on his steepled fingers. When he looked up, it was evident he was picking his words carefully.

"Everything that constitutes Kolya's story here in the United States is considered classified information. As you're both perhaps aware, classified information can only be shared with employees holding security clearances. You are not government employees, and neither one of you holds a clearance. As the subject of a classified protection project, Kolya is in a gray area—obviously he knows his own history, but it is essential for the success of his protection, for other people that have worked on his case, and other figures that are still under government protection, that details not be shared. And I, accordingly, of course, can never disclose classified information to anyone without a clearance."

The smile he gave them was rueful.

"Yet here we are. As Kolya perhaps mentioned, Jackie, I'll be retiring soon. It is my dearest prayer and intention that Kolya remain safe. But selfishly, I'd like to remain out of prison, as well. So I'm clinging to the hope that discretion will prevail.

"Going forward, I hope the three of us, and most importantly, the two of you, always remain conscious of what you discuss in public and even what you speak about in private unless you are certain your location is secure. You will need a convincing story to explain your identities, your relationship, and your histories. I'm available if you want suggestions or my take on your own ideas, but I realize that you need to build a foundational story together that will hold up over time. Of course, I can help with any logistics such as documents, résumés, and the like that you may need before I retire.

"On the other hand . . ." He stopped, and the smile he gave Jackie was wide and full of admiration. "The sleuthing you did to find Kolya was worthy of high-level intelligence in and of itself, so I'm not overly worried. If you ever consider applying for a job that does require a clearance, don't hesitate to use me as a reference."

They all laughed then, and the tension eased.

"Kolya's told me a little about the book you're writing, and I told Brenda. She's genuinely interested in hearing about it. We won't discuss any of this serious stuff at dinner, but business is light here this week, so she's said we can meet up again in this office tomorrow if it's convenient for you both after you've had a chance to talk more privately. Does that sound reasonable?"

"Of course."

"Yes."

They spoke simultaneously, and Sam smiled before continuing.

"And then of course, there's that one last obvious issue. I've been acknowledging you as Kolya," he nodded in his direction, "at your request. But you're still David, at least for now. That's who you need to be until some other plan is implemented."

They agreed, and Sam texted Brenda that they were ready. She appeared almost immediately.

"The Emporium's only two blocks away, and they're holding a nice quiet table for us in the back."

CHAPTER FORTY-THREE

They stepped out into the cold December twilight. Brenda and Sam walked a few steps ahead, and Kolya's arm was wrapped tightly around Jackie's jacketed waist.

"I wish now I hadn't agreed to dinner," Kolya whispered against her head. "But it seemed a perfectly reasonable arrangement at the time."

She looked up at him, still not quite believing they were together again.

"It's fine. They obviously care very much about you. You said your hotel was nearby?"

"Yes. This whole area is in the middle of a building boom since Mr. Amazon's empire came to town."

Jackie laughed. "Is that why the restaurant is called the Emporium?"

Kolya smiled back at her. "Who knows? Brenda's office has been here for a while, according to Sam, and she says the place is good. That's all I know. You're so beautiful. I pictured you in my imagination so many times over the years, but you're more stunning in person than in any of my fantasies."

He bent his head back down towards hers, and she felt his kisses land on her hair.

"That is perfect. Just stay close together like that. Keep moving, and no one will get hurt."

Kolya's head whipped around, and Jackie heard his "What the fuck?" before he was pushed back against her. Two men in long coats now flanked them.

"I said to keep moving."

An icy shiver shot down her throat, immediately forming a cold ball of horror in her middle. What was going on? Were they going to take Kolya away? Was all their convoluted secrecy over the years proving warranted, now that they had finally thought it was coming to an end?

Maybe, if they were lucky, it was a simple mugging.

"I have money. And a credit card. I'll give you everything I've got." She tried to pull away from Kolya to reach her purse, but she was pushed roughly back.

"You have trouble with English? Keep moving."

The man's own English was heavily accented, but he apparently liked sarcasm.

Through her rising panic, she realized that two different men had fenced in Sam and Brenda a few steps ahead of them, as well, and were propelling them all forward.

"Oh God, oh God, oh God." The words came out of her in a quiet whimper. She'd never see her parents again or get to give her niece and nephew their Christmas presents. She'd never see Nadine again. And poor Mr. Riga. The thought of leaving him all alone, heart-broken once more, was almost worse than her fear for herself.

The group in front of them had turned a corner to the left, and Jackie was pressed more closely to Kolya as they were moved in the same direction. She chanced a quick glance to the right where she saw bright lights and Christmas decorations. There it was, the Commonwealth

Emporium, shining brightly in invitation. The street they had turned on was smaller, still well-lit, but with no other pedestrians in sight. They were herded several feet along before Jackie saw Brenda and Sam being maneuvered through a glass door held open by a woman in a long gray puffy coat.

What did they want? Why was this happening?

Automatic lights had come on as they moved into the building, but they were pushed through the foyer of wherever they were and down first one corridor and then another. The woman moved past them and pushed open an exit door with a horizontal crash bar.

Lights came on here, as well, and Jackie saw they were in what was most likely a loading dock, on the edge of what seemed to be part of a parking garage.

The man holding on to Sam's arms pulled him away from Brenda, turned him around, and punched him so hard in the face that Sam fell to the ground, blood spurting from his nose.

Jackie and Brenda both screamed, and Kolya tried to jerk away but was held firmly by one of the men who had first taken them.

"That was for my brother, Mr. Rousch." The bearded man who had hit Sam spat out his words in heavily accented English. "But do not worry. There is much more waiting for you." He mispronounced Sam's name, making it sound more like "Roosh," but no one attempted to correct him.

"What is going on? What do you want?"

Kolya spoke the words clearly, conveying none of the panic that was suffocating Jackie.

The man turned to Kolya and pulled off the ski cap that had been covering his balding head. His eyes were cold and merciless.

"This is not your concern. But you are, as I think they say

here, in the wrong place at the wrong time. As my brother and father were when he took that boy."

"What boy?"

"What are you talking about?"

"Let me go, you animal!"

Their words came out in a mixed jumble: Sam's in a pained gasp, Kolya obviously striving to remain calm, and Brenda hissing as she pulled furiously against the man holding both her arms. Sam had rolled to his side and was holding his head against his arms and trying to use his sleeve to staunch the blood flowing from his nose.

The bearded man said something unintelligible to the man holding Brenda, and he loosened his hold. She ran to her husband, falling to her knees and pulling him to her.

Every part of Jackie's body was trembling: her knees, her arms, and her hands. She forced herself to try to breathe and still her twitching limbs. There had to be a way out of this nightmare. She was sick of being a piece of jetsam tossed about by currents beyond her control. Should she try to reason with them? Before she could speak, Kolya's voice rang out.

"Please tell us what you want." Kolya spoke slowly and calmly, but Jackie could hear the steel in his voice. Having spent hours surreptitiously watching his avatar play video games, she realized he was assessing and reassessing with computer-like speed, trying to gain an advantage over the enemy.

"What I want is for Mr. William Rousch to pay for the twenty years of suffering he has given my family."

Jackie had absolutely no idea what the crazed man was talking about, but she saw immediately that she was not the only one. Kolya's head was tilted ever so slightly, and Sam was peering at the man in confusion.

"How did I hurt your family?"

259

The kick was fast, hard, and unprovoked. Sam cried out, and Brenda screamed again and moved to block her husband's body with her own. Jackie and Kolya both tried to run to him but were held back by their respective thugs.

"You, with your big car, and your important secretary. All the world must move out of the way for the important Americans. Did you ever stop to think of the people who were moved out of the way for your important car and its important people? You took one child and maybe gave him a nice life. How noble of you! They took all my family and destroyed it."

"I'm sorry." Sam's words were whispered, and Jackie winced at his obvious pain. "There was nothing we could do. The boy's father was taken away, too. He died in prison."

Jackie's head was spinning. What in the world were they talking about? Whatever it was, it seemed she and Brenda were totally in the dark, but she had a sense from Kolya's stillness that he had at least some insight into the madness.

"Nothing you could do. What rubbish. Did the mighty American Secretary try to do anything to help my people? No. You took a little Russian boy, and you went home."

"That's not true." Sam had pushed himself to a sitting position, one hand pressed tightly to his side where the kick had landed, and the other against his still bleeding nose. "We tried to help the Chechens. That's who you are? Whom you're talking about? They were part of the reason we were there."

"Bullshit." The man's accent made it sound like "sheet," and Jackie shuddered. How were they going to get away? The man was obviously insane and blind with pent-up rage. He had a gun in his hand, as did the man who had first pushed her. Did these fanatical people intend to kill them, or were they expecting Sam to wave some kind of magic wand?

"It's not bullshit. The Secretary spoke to President Putin

about the Chechen prisoners and urged him to recognize their call for self-determination and show them leniency."

"I do not know this word. I do know that my father and my older brother were taken away that day and never came back. I know that my mother died because her brothers—my uncles—were already in prison, and she had no heart to live when her son was gone. Your car stopped, you got out, and they were taken. You are responsible. I have spent many years trying to find you. First, I tried to find the boy, but he maybe died. Maybe not. I keep looking. I watched the Secretary, but he became old and weak. When he died, I saw you on television at the funeral. Finally. I have found you. My friend, the TV man, helped me learn your name."

"TV man?" Sam asked, while at the same time Brenda said, "A guy on TV?"

Jackie felt a chill creep up her spine. These people, whoever they were, had obviously lost touch with reality.

"Yes. Montgomery Fergusson, from the TV show. He is a true friend."

"Holy fuck."

"You've got to be kidding."

Once again Sam and Kolya's words overlapped.

Jackie looked at the man who had been speaking and tried to understand.

"I'm sorry, but are you saying that the news anchor, Montgomery Fergusson, is helping you kidnap an innocent man?"

He took a menacing step towards them, and Jackie tried to back up, but the man holding her arms prevented her from moving. Kolya's eyes bored into her with wide-eyed intensity, and she knew he was begging her to stay quiet.

"William Rousch is not an innocent man. Perhaps you are his family? The family he could keep while my family was destroyed?"

"No." Sam's voice was raspy, but Kolya's forceful "Yes," drowned it out. "We are his family, but he has done nothing wrong."

"Listen to me." Sam's damaged nose gave his words a nasal quality. "They were not with me in Russia. Let them go, and you can do what you want with me."

Jackie gasped and saw Kolya stiffen. Sam was obviously trying to save them, but what else was going on here?

"Does Mr. Fergusson from the news know you are Chechen?"

What was Kolya doing? Who cared what somebody named Montgomery Fergusson thought?

"No. He thinks I am Russian. He loves Russia, loves President Putin. But he understands people were unfairly arrested because of U.S. Secretary, and he says he will help. I have talked with him many times, and he understands how U.S. pressure makes Russia feel in corner. He told me name of Mr. Rousch and helped me to find him. Now I think we all go back to Russia and maybe more U.S. pressure will bring my brother home."

Holy Jesus. This man was insane.

For a moment no one said anything—each of them probably trying their best to sort through the ridiculous torrent he had been spewing.

The lunatic studied them, looking at each in turn.

"I plan to take only Mr. and Mrs. Rousch, but four is better."

Jackie spoke up amidst the stunned silence, shocking even herself with the shaky defiance in her voice.

"You can't take us to Russia. No one will let you take us on a plane against our will."

He glared at her. "Stupid girl. Who said anything about plane? We will go on boat and then another boat before we go on plane. But first, we will go in car."

He pointed to a van that was parked not far from the area near the door where they had all been congregated for several minutes—or perhaps several hours. Time had lost all meaning.

Jackie's mind raced. Every thriller she had ever read, every true-crime story she had ever listened to, had taught her that the first twenty-four hours were critical, and that the more victims were moved, the harder it was to trace them. They were four people, one already badly injured, against four strong men, one woman, and God knew how many weapons. But they could not get in that van.

"I have to pee." The words were out of her mouth before she had time to weigh their wisdom. Would stalling and perhaps splitting up help them or put them in more danger? She couldn't bear to be separated from Kolya now that they were finally together, but neither could she do nothing and let these terrorists do what they wanted with them.

Kolya strained to pull himself away from the arms that held him, shaking his head at Jackie with an expression of horror on his face. Jackie answered him with a look of what she hoped was reassurance and mouthed, "I love you."

The bearded man said words that she guessed were ugly in any language and then jerked his head at the woman. Whatever he said to her had her grabbing Brenda by the elbow and pulling her up and then coming over to take Jackie's arm.

"Come," she said and pulled them back towards the door they had exited what now felt like hours earlier.

The man said something else, and their minder stopped and yanked the purses from both their shoulders, tossing them on the ground near the bearded boss. He looked quickly inside them and pulled a phone from Brenda's leather bag. Then he looked at Jackie.

"Your phone."

Reluctantly she handed over the phone she had in her coat pocket.

"Go," he said. "You have five minutes." The woman took their arms and pushed them through the door. Jackie shot a last look at Kolya, willing him to understand. Whatever happened, she would always love him. But this couldn't be the end. Not after all they had gone through. She could not lose him again.

CHAPTER FORTY-FOUR

"I need to go, too." Kolya kept his eyes down as he spoke. "And my father probably does as well. Let me take him to the bathroom before we go anywhere."

He had to do something—follow Jackie, try to protect her. *He couldn't lose her again.*

The bearded man looked at them both suspiciously.

"Fine. We will all go to the toilet. Give me your phones."

They handed them over, and the asshole allowed Kolya to help Sam to his feet.

"Tengo un arma en mi calcetín, y mi esposa en su sostén."

Holy shit. Maybe they'd have a chance after all. Not much, but maybe. Sam's words had been barely audible, whispered between his much louder groans as Kolya tried to help him up. But he had said that he had a gun in his sock and Brenda one in her bra. If Sam could cover him, maybe he could take out at least two of these goons. There was no time to waste. He adjusted his stance so that their captors' view of Sam was limited and shot a quick prayer into the universe.

"Then let's roll," he said, helping Sam into a standing position, and then he proceeded to do just that.

To a foreigner, the words were perhaps innocuous, but to any American who remembered 9-11, they carried meaning. Kolya had not been in the States when the attack occurred nor even seen it on TV at the time. But having spent years alone, often with only a television for company, Kolya knew well the bravery shown by the passengers on board Flight 93. And after all the misery his life had involved up until now, and the happiness that just an hour ago had seemed finally possible, he was damned if he was going to let this fucker take it all away without a fight.

And so they rolled. But he did so literally.

A shot went off, and a howl of pain echoed. *Please let it be Sam doing the shooting and not the one shot.* But there was no time to look.

His years of Tae Kwon Do had taught him elaborate kicks and blocks, but his few months on the mat with Jiu Jitsu had taught him to use the ground. The head honcho and one of his helpers were standing next to each other, and Kolya somersaulted into their legs, knocking them both down. With adrenaline-driven speed he hauled one of the struggling thugs on top of the other, using the second one's weight to hold the first in place while he put a strangling choke hold around the man on top. He hoped to hell the move he had only ever done in practice could deliver sufficient pressure to incapacitate and not kill, but he had no time to second think his moves. He had also never performed any of the motions wearing a jacket, and the guy under him had a coat and winter scarf on, as well.

The man underneath was struggling, and Kolya was using the full strength of his legs to hold both men down. The top man finally succumbed, going limp as he lost consciousness.

Kolya growled as he pushed the body to the side and immediately slammed his bent arm under the chin of the struggling man still beneath him. "Roll, goddamnit," he panted, as his opponent wriggled and bucked. Finally he got the man turned enough that his hold increased pressure on the windpipe. Agonizing seconds passed before this one, too, at last stilled.

Kolya hauled himself to his feet. Was Sam all right? And where the hell were Jackie and Brenda?

Fucking A. Sam might be retiring, but he obviously still had what it took. The two remaining kidnappers were standing back-to-back, heads bent submissively, and Sam was binding their feet and hands together with the men's own belts even as blood dripped from one man's coat.

Glancing up at Kolya, Sam gave an approving nod.

"Well done. Get their belts and secure them tightly. Check them for other weapons, including their socks and the thigh area. We don't want them to come to before we've got them tied up." His voice was still muffled due to his swollen nose, but his words were decisive.

Kolya moved back to the two men he had brought down, securing them as Sam had instructed but still frantic. *He had to find Jackie.*

They had been after Sam. Sam! Had he, Kolya, ever been in danger? Why in the world were they blaming Sam for anything?

"Sam, do you understand any of this?"

Sam shot him a quick glance, shaking his head as if trying to clear it. "I'm not certain, but it seems we—I—may have spent the last decade protecting the wrong person. If I understood this son-of-a bitch, I'm the one they wanted all along."

Kolya forced his open mouth to close and finished his work quickly, finding just one gun but an assortment of knives and switchblades. He handled the gun gingerly. He had grown up in Virginia and then spent years in Texas, and somehow, he had never before touched a firearm. He stared at the weapon in his hand. His friend Danny was dead, and Jackie, too, had been shot. Even now, his own chest ached from his exertion in the spot where he had been shot in Texas. *Please, dear God, let Jackie be okay.* He couldn't go on without her.

"You fired the shot?"

"I did. This one here," Sam jerked his head at the shorter of the two bound men, "pointed his gun in your direction as you went for those two. I was able to shoot him in the arm before he could get off a shot. They both lost the will to fight amazingly fast after that."

"Then I guess I'm really lucky you were armed. But take this. I think I'm better off just using my body."

"Which you did, remarkably well." Sam was now tying one of the men's scarves around his bleeding arm, ignoring the whimpers and mumbled invective. He took the gun from Kolya's hand and did something to it before slipping it into his waist under his belt.

"What about Jackie and Brenda? We have to find them."

"They haven't showed up yet, but don't panic. Brenda's a trained marksman, and from what I've learned of Jackie, she's a damn smart cookie." Sam's words were uttered evenly, but Kolya could hear the worry in his voice. Sam stepped back to check the bindings on the men Kolya had secured, then motioned with his chin to the bag the bearded man had held and where he had put their phones.

"Get a phone and dial 911 while I look for Brenda and Jackie. Their odds were better than ours, so I'm sure they're both fine."

Kolya didn't catch the words Sam mumbled after that "fine," but he was pretty sure they were an echo of his own worry and fear. His fingers trembled as he found his own phone and fumbled with his passcode, and he had to repeat it twice. The adrenaline rush had subsided, but fear for Jackie was quickly rising to take its place.

He stared at the phone in his hand once the screen was active, his fingers hovering over the keypad. He hadn't even needed to sign in to dial 911. The useless thought flitted through his mind as he tapped in the three numbers and paused for just an instant before he touched the phone icon. What in the world was he going to say?

"911. What is the nature of your emergency?"

"Uh . . . I'm in a parking garage, I think. It's in Crystal City, and my . . . my family and I were taken here at gunpoint." *They've got Jackie. I've spent my whole adult life without her and those bastards have taken her from me* were the words he wanted to scream, but he fought to keep his voice under control.

"Are you in danger at the moment?"

"No. We were able to . . . to stop them. Except yes, we're still in danger because one of them has my fiancée and her . . . book publisher."

"Hold just a moment, sir."

There were a few endless seconds of silence, and then the operator returned.

"The police are already on their way. A message came in from your location several minutes ago, and help should be arriving momentarily. Are there any injuries?"

Several minutes ago? What the hell?

"Yes. The guys who took us—two of them were . . . were knocked unconscious and one of them was shot."

"You're going to need to put all weapons on the ground and have your hands in the air. Officers are making their way to you as we speak. Do you understand what I said? Make sure all weapons are on the ground in plain sight."

The next few minutes passed in a blur. No sooner had the

woman on the line finished her last sentence than Sam came back through the door, flanked by three uniformed policemen, all with guns drawn.

"Where's Jackie?" He didn't even try to hide the panic in his voice.

"There are more police with Brenda and Jackie and the girl these guys had with them. They're all fine."

Kolya caught his words and was afraid for a moment that his knees would buckle in front of them all. Tears came to his eyes, and he struggled to catch his breath. One of the cops was frisking him, telling him to spread his legs and keep his hands up. He didn't care. They could do whatever they wanted to him. Jackie was safe. That was all that mattered.

One policeman was photographing the scene, a female officer was on the phone, her eyes moving around the premises as she spoke, and a garage door in the distance that Kolya hadn't even noticed before was opening to let in an ambulance.

"How were the police called before I called them?" He spoke to Sam, who was standing nearby. He had known for years that the man seemed at times to have superpowers, but he hadn't counted telepathy among them.

Sam laughed.

"It was my newest recruit, of course. I think Brenda and I may end up in a bidding war to win her allegiance."

At Kolya's look of total bewilderment, Sam laughed again, spreading his hands wide while shrugging his shoulders.

"Jackie had a second phone. Who would have guessed? She texted 911 from the bathroom stall and gave them the details, her phone on silent. They were on their way before she even flushed."

"A second phone?"

"Yes. It turns out she had one she used just for texting and emailing with you. It was in her pants pocket. They demanded her phone, and she gave them one. That's some girl you've got there. I'd hold on to her if I were you."

Kolya nodded slowly, still in shock.

"That's the plan, Sam. That's the plan."

CHAPTER FORTY-FIVE

Hours later, they were back in Brenda's office, boxes of delivered pizza spread out on the conference table. Sam had walked to a nearby convenience store and brought back a six-pack of soda, some beer, and a bottle of wine.

He flipped back the aluminum pull tab on a soda and held it up. "Not quite the gourmet celebratory meal we were planning, but I think we have much to be grateful for. Here's to being alive, and to you two finding each other."

Jackie was sitting next to Kolya in the same spot she had sat hours earlier. Their fingers were once again laced together, but this time their grip was almost hermetic, the strain of the last several hours still cresting over them in waves. Jackie's head was angled slightly back and her eyes closed. She lifted her head at Sam's words and picked up her wine glass with her free hand.

"If this is how book meetings go, I might stick with marketing." She smiled ruefully and saluted first Sam and then Brenda with her glass. She turned her head and dropped a quick kiss on Kolya's mouth before taking a sip and narrowing her eyes at Sam.

"I know you gave us that talk earlier about secrecy and not sharing classified information, but do you think you might be able to explain what the heck happened this afternoon?"

Sam blew out a prolonged sigh and shot a calculating look in Kolya's direction before turning his gaze back to Jackie.

"As I told you earlier, I'm retiring from a lifetime in security. But it seems conceivable—likely—that my highly superior and finely honed intelligence may have been totally ass-backwards these past twenty years, if you'll pardon my language. We've spent that whole time believing we were hiding and protecting Kolya, when it's just possible that I may have been the intended target all along."

He put up his hands as all three made various sounds of confusion and incredulity.

"Nothing's certain, and we have an awful lot of details to investigate and check out. Kolya's not in the clear, at least not yet, and yes, this is all still completely off the record and not to be discussed outside of this room. And sadly, I've got to leave you all, right now." He paused and shot a theatrical frown at the can of soda he was holding. "Otherwise, I'd most definitely be joining you in a more authentic toast. But I've got to get to the office. Today's little incident will add reams of updates to a file we were hoping to close. And no doubt open new ones."

The last sentence sounded tired and defeated.

Jackie cocked her head. Her mouth opened, but it took several seconds before she could force coherent words out of it.

"If you were the one being pursued all these years, then Leo never had to die? And Jake didn't need to leave Austin? And Kolya never had to hide out in Albany?"

Sam pursed his lips and his head lowered slightly as he first turned away but then looked back to them.

"That's what it looks like. There's obviously nothing I can say to undo what was done, but we always—*always*—had his and his mother's best interests at heart."

Jackie's eyes narrowed as she tried to process the magnitude of what they all had experienced and learned.

"Why couldn't they find you? The bad guys. Not that I would have wanted them to hurt you, but if they had gotten close earlier—like maybe ten years ago—we could have avoided a decade of misery."

Kolya's fingers tightened around her own, and he rubbed his face against her hair. Sam's breath came out in a frustrated hiss.

"I guess what they say about faceless bureaucrats is true. I was a nameless man surrounded by important figures. They could focus on Kolya, the boy," he made quotation marks in the air, "because he was more easily identifiable within the domestic population, especially after his father permanently disappeared."

"And you never had any sense at all that anyone was looking for *you*?"

Sam's eyes met Brenda's, and she shrugged, obviously as nonplussed by the day's surprises as the rest of them.

"Brenda was carrying a gun today because our house was broken into several weeks back. We weren't home, but there was a cryptic message spray painted on the garage, which until today, was totally mystifying. It said 'you will pay.' I've had a concealed carry permit all my adult life, but after that, Brenda got one, too."

All four of them remained silent for several minutes.

Sam's shoulders straightened, and he gave them a brief nod. "We'll talk more, obviously, but I do have to leave."

Brenda moved from where she had been standing near

the window and walked with Sam as he headed towards the door.

"Let's stick with our original plan and meet back here tomorrow afternoon—that still okay with you both?"

Kolya and Jackie nodded, and Sam gave them a last tired smile.

"You were both terrific today. I can't think of anyone right now I'd rather be kidnapped with than you two."

"Hey! What about me?"

They all laughed and the tension lessened as Brenda stepped back from Sam, shooting him a look of dramatic outrage.

"That goes without saying, my love. I was scared shitless when the two of you left to go to the bathroom, but the part of me that's watched you handle one problem after another all these years knew you'd be fine." Sam pulled her back towards him and hugged her fiercely before they walked out together through the door.

Kolya and Jackie looked at each other, and their breathing slowed as they stared into each other's eyes. The silence grew as the weight of all they had experienced and learned washed over them.

"I was pretty scared, myself. You left to go to the bathroom, and I was afraid I might lose you again."

She heard the catch in his voice and squeezed his hand tighter. "And I hated leaving you with those four creeps, but I knew we couldn't get into that van. All I could think to do was stall."

"Thank God you did. And thank God you had a second phone hidden. Sam's right. You'd probably make one hell of a spy."

"I think I prefer writing books. I heard the gunshot and was terrified." Tears slipped once more from her eyes, and they both were quiet as he held her again, his hand caressing her hair.

"So all of this—your death in the explosion, the years of hell we both lived through—it was all a mistake."

His shoulders moved in a slow shrug, and he nodded. But he said nothing. His intense gaze—from eyes still not the right color—nevertheless expressed thoughts too intense for mere words. They had loved each other completely and then been forced to go on alone. But they had survived, and they were together once more. The past couldn't be changed, but they had a chance to build their own future.

Tears were still running down her cheeks, and her lips trembled, but she managed a weak smile. They had gone through hell, but that didn't mitigate her current joy.

"I guess it's a pretty good thing we both didn't die during the shooting in Austin. Or today, for that matter. It would have been horrible never to have found each other, or to have lost each other again over a stupid grudge that had nothing to do with us."

His own lips formed a rueful smile.

"That's true."

"I never thanked you for saving my life that night. Thank you."

He pulled her head against his chest and held her to him tightly.

"You're most welcome. It was my pleasure."

She sniffed and looked up at him.

"Sam and Brenda seem like really nice people. Or whatever he said his name is."

"Maybe we should make name tags optional at the wedding."

His words were quiet, but the look he gave her was both questioning and overflowing with hope.

She smiled through her tears and tilted her head up to kiss him, a quick kiss filled with promise.

"Did you already check in to your hotel?"

Kolya nodded again, wary.

"Can you take out your contacts when we get there?"

Kolya smiled back at her. "I think that can definitely be arranged."

His face was different from the one she had known so many years ago, but it had its own beauty. The soul of the man inside was the part of her that had been missing, and now she had it back. His name or the color of his eyes was immaterial.

He brought his face close to hers and she felt his breath against her lips. "Anything else you'd maybe like me to take out or off?"

She moved the fraction of an inch it took to touch his lips with her own. "We'll think of something."

CHAPTER FORTY-SIX

W as such happiness possible? Jackie's head was on his
chest, one bent leg resting atop his own. He didn't
want to sleep, didn't want to miss even one second of having
her in his arms once more. But waves of suffused contentment spread over his exhausted body, and his eyes closed.

———

A PHONE WAS RINGING in her dream, distracting her from her
crazed search through an immense desk drawer for a tiny
key she desperately needed to find.

Jackie pushed herself up, confused, hearing the phone and
feeling Kolya's arms trying to pull her back down.

"Stop," she said, laughing as she broke free. "It's got to be
my parents or my sister. Those are the only calls that come
through when it's on 'do not disturb.'"

Kolya grunted his disappointment but let her go.

Where was the damn thing? The bathroom. She'd plugged it
in after the long and most delicious shower she and Kolya
had shared sometime last night.

"Hey, Mom." Her voice was breathless as she managed to catch the call just before it went to voicemail.

"Jackie, love, what's going on? We've been dying to hear how your talk with the editor went, and you didn't even mention it in your text."

Jackie had sent a quick message telling her parents that she'd met some old friends in Crystal City and was spending the night.

"Ummm . . . It went well. She was encouraging." Brenda had never gotten around to asking about her book, but that was certainly understandable given all that had happened.

"Are you coming home soon? I've got Bethanie and Stevie today so your sister can get some last-minute Christmas shopping done."

"Uh . . . Let me call you back in a bit. No one else is up yet." She glanced at the time at the top of the screen. 8:42. Early for some, but late for her mother. "We stayed up late catching up. I'll call you back in a little while . . . Love you, too."

Kolya had come into the bathroom while she talked and now wrapped his arms around her naked body, pulling her back against him, his erection pressing eagerly against her hip.

She looked down at the forearms and hands clasped under her breasts. They were larger and stronger than she remembered, but they were indisputably his. One of those beautiful hands moved down to press against her pussy while the other moved up to cup and tantalize her breast. She squirmed, trying at once to push herself more closely into his hands while pressing against his straining cock. How had she survived so long without him?

She turned in his arms, reaching up to pull his head down to hers. She needed him now, this instant, and somehow, thank God, he understood. Wordlessly, he lifted her up and rested her bottom against the sink. Her legs wrapped around him, and she reached between them to guide him into her.

A whoosh of absolute rightness escaped her lips.

"Leo." The name came out without thought, and she winced, even as her inner muscles clenched more tightly around him.

"Shh . . ." he whispered, his own breathing accelerated as he grasped her buttocks, the tips of his fingers reaching close enough to caress where the friction was greatest. "It doesn't matter. As long as we're together."

It took only a few thrusts to push her over the edge, and she buried her head against his collar bone and sagged against him as he found his own release with a cry.

He held her then, her legs wrapped around his hips, their heartbeats slowly returning to normal as they both tried to prolong their contact. Kolya finally loosened his hold and let her feet slip down to the floor.

"We didn't use a condom. Again. I'm sorry, Jackie. I brought a box, hoping you'd want me, but it's still in my bag."

She snorted. "Wanting you was obviously never in question. But it's okay. At least I hope so. I went back on the pill before I flew out here. My alarm is going to go off any minute reminding me to take it. And I can pretty much guarantee I don't have any STDs. I've never been with anyone else." The last words were mumbled against his chest, and Kolya lifted her chin with his hand to peer into her eyes.

"Did you just say what I think you said? When you're so beautiful, and I was dead?"

She arched her brows and tried to twist her face away, a little embarrassed.

"Are you developing a hearing problem, or are you suddenly less fluent in English?"

Kolya laughed and clutched her to him in a ferocious hug.

"I just have trouble believing you didn't have men fighting over you."

She laughed and then assumed a theatrical coy smile. "I never said I didn't." But her smile faded as she shrugged. "I couldn't get into it. Part of me always held back, watching, like a spectator. I figured that part of me was finished."

"So that makes us both 30-year-old virgins or something crazy like that."

She pulled back, her look growing mockingly wary.

"I'm pretty sure I remember us taking care of that whole virgin thing long, long ago, so is it your memory that's going now?"

He laughed again.

"No, silly. My memory's just fine. That was always the problem. I never wanted to go to bed with anyone else. Sometimes—okay, often—I desperately wanted sex, but any time I started to get close to someone, I found reasons to end things. I never wanted to actually lie in bed with another woman. The memories of us were too good. And I never wanted to cheat on you."

She stared at him, stunned.

"You honestly never slept with anyone else?"

He shrugged. "I guess I never got around to it? I thought about it at times, but I knew it wouldn't be like it had been with you. And my hand worked, so . . ." His cheeks reddened slightly, and he looked away.

"Leo. Jake. David. Kolya—whoever the hell you are, you're crazy. We're obviously both crazy, and I love you."

"I love you, too. And I don't care what you call me, especially if you call me Leo. I was him for so long, and I was happy being him. So happy being him with you."

His look was serious once more.

"I can't ever give you back all those years, and I don't know how I can make it up to you."

281

She ran her fingers through his still short hair and inhaled deeply. He smelled the same, a deep, musky scent that was all his. She jerked her head back. His smell. All those days and nights in Austin when she had argued with herself over whether she had heard his voice, whether the area around his eyes was the same, an awareness of having breathed him in, if only for a minute, had probably been the subconscious factor that made her pursue her crazy hunch. And thank God she had.

"We're here. We're together now, and that's all that matters." Reluctantly, she pulled away.

"I do, however, have to call my mother back, and we need a plan for what I . . . what *we* are going to do and say. Sam sounded pretty sure that the crazy cloak and dagger stuff may all have been unnecessary after all. That is what he was saying, right? I wasn't misunderstanding things? Can my parents know I'm with you, and if so, which you are you?"

Kolya shook his head.

"I honestly have no fucking clue. I think we have to wait and see what he says later today. Could you maybe tell them I'm a different old boyfriend?"

Jackie laughed. "That would be a stretch, but we need to be careful in any case. My mother has a bee in her bonnet about more grandchildren and will have a deposit down on a wedding location before she gets a chance to take a good look at you. And once she does . . ." She trailed off, staring intently at him. "Everything's all muddled in my head now. I can't tell if you still look like Leo, or if you're different enough that other people wouldn't notice. And we don't even know for sure if you'll have to stay David, or if you can be you, whoever that is."

Kolya grimaced. "That last part may still be the kicker." He paused and bit his lip.

He was nervous. What else was going on?

"Kolya? That is your name, right? That's how you signed your email, so I thought you were telling me who you really were . . . are."

His eyes turned up to the corner of the bathroom ceiling as if seeking guidance, and then he took her hand and pulled her back towards the bed.

"Let's sit for a minute. That's how old-fashioned Russians do it, or at least how they used to do it. Before a voyage, or an important event, they sit quietly together. It maybe used to involve praying, but that probably got washed out of the tradition, at least for some, by the Soviets."

What in the world was he going on about?

He pulled the sheet from the bed and wrapped it around her.

"I can't look at you and think straight. You're so beautiful." His fingers caressed her face, but his frown showed he was still nervous.

She grabbed his hand.

"Stop. Look at me. We just found out that we were both bonkers enough to stay faithful to each other all these years even though there was absolutely no 'us' left. So whatever it is, we can handle it, together."

She gave him a stern look, tucked the covers around herself more securely, and held out her right hand.

"Let's start with introductions. My name is Jacqueline Bourne. I come from northern Virginia, I have a job in marketing and am working to become a writer, and I love you, whoever you are."

He reached out his own right hand and took hers and then pulled so she was nestled against him.

"My name is Nikolai Gregorievich Polivanov—Kolya for short. I grew up in Moscow, Russia, until I ended up in the U.S. when I was just turning eleven. That's when I became a Swedish-American named Leo Jorgensson. There's more, obviously, which I promise I'll tell you, but the problem is defining just who exactly Nikolai Gregorievich Polivanov is."

The way he was holding her prevented her from seeing his face, but she felt his hands stroking her hair and was aware of a strange rigidity in his posture.

"My parents . . ." his voice broke, and he cleared his throat. "Both my parents wanted desperately to help create a strong and democratic country even before the Soviet Union broke up. They both made enemies, thanks to their ideals, and were targeted in different ways. The people trying to wrest control were barbarians, and many of them are still around today. They raped my mother sometime around the time of my conception and facilitated my father's death in prison years later."

Her gasp was involuntary. She started to pull away, but he held her close.

His fingers continued to caress her hair. She could feel the tension throughout his body. *Jesus Christ.* His poor mother. How had either of them survived? He had stopped speaking, but now even his breathing was quiet, as if he were struggling to keep his emotions under tight control.

Jackie, too, sat still. This was all so much bigger—so much more convoluted—than anything she had imagined while sleuthing in Austin. She didn't give a fuck who his parents were or weren't, but she cared very much about the burden he was obviously carrying. She imagined a young boy being taken from everything he knew and forced to adapt to a new culture—no, *two* new cultures and languages—with a mother who was probably barely able to cope, being overcome with grief herself. That such a child had become her Leo was a miracle. And that he was here with her now was even more wondrous.

She pulled away and turned to straddle him, tilting his face up so he met her eyes. Could she come up with words sufficient to reassure him of her love? The bond between them had survived time and space, so surely it was strong enough to put past ghosts in the past.

"Kolya is a beautiful name. So is Nikolai. I now have so many choices of what to call you when you turn my mind and body to mush. But none of it matters. You are you. You are the smart and talented and incredibly kind boy I fell in love with. You are still smart and talented and kind, but now you've proven to be strong and brave, helping to save my life at least twice, and you're a fucking sex god. I'm the luckiest girl in the world to even know you, let alone sleep with you."

Kolya's eyes were fixed on hers as if trying to see straight through them and divine her deepest thoughts.

"You really don't care? That I might be the offspring of a monster?"

"My God, Kolya, did you listen to anything I just said? I love you. YOU. You are a wondrously unique human being." She closed her eyes and struggled to come up with words that might convince him.

"If I made a cake—a delicious, moist, rich cake, that tasted better than any other cake you'd ever eaten, would any of us give a shit if the hen, who laid the eggs I used to bake the cake, was a real bitch to the other chickens?"

He stared at her, dumbstruck, and then began to laugh. And so did she. They laughed until tears ran down their faces as they rocked back and forth in an anonymous hotel room in a city neither one of them knew. They had each other, and nothing else mattered.

EPILOGUE

SIX MONTHS LATER

Jackie gazed out at the breathtaking view visible from her kitchen window and started slightly when she felt water against her hands. *Whoops.* She had once again overfilled her kettle. Should she blame her distraction on the baby or the beautiful mountains that surrounded their valley neighborhood? Maybe a little of both. But since they both filled her with utter delight, she wasn't going to complain.

Exactly one year ago, she had been a boring, uninspired marketer who did her job, read her books, and shared her seemingly limited capacity for affection and enthusiasm with a few close friends and her far-away family.

Now she was reunited with the love of her life and gloriously happy that they were due to welcome a baby boy in three short months.

Yes, she had wisely? optimistically? thought to go back on the pill before her trip at Christmas, but the week's worth she had taken before their reunion had obviously been insufficient to withstand their explosive passion. The first stirrings of nausea had begun drawing her attention just as she came to the break in her pill regimen, a break that

—surprise, surprise—had not included the onset of her period.

Instead of misgivings or fear, however, she had felt only joy. Joy, and a burning impatience to be back in Kolya's arms and for their long separation to finally and permanently come to an end. Their reunion had taken more time than either of them wanted, but looking back, they had truly pulled off miracles.

Sam had been a tremendous help, somehow making seemingly unsurmountable bureaucratic hurdles disappear.

Jackie and Kolya had both been adamant that they preferred Kolya reclaim his true name and identity, if at all possible. Their argument was strengthened after Sam's embarrassed and gut-wrenchingly apologetic admission that extensive interviews with their attackers had confirmed that he, indeed, had been the target all along and not Kolya. Case workers were examining the evidence, trying to find holes, but so far had found nothing.

The many references to "the boy" over the years had been the result of Timur Dudaev's conviction that finding the child the Secretary's car had stopped for would lead him to Sam, the man on whom his warped mind had laid blame for all his family's pain.

Why Sam and not the Secretary of State? Unbeknownst to Sam, Kolya, or anyone from Western intelligence, one of the protesters on that long ago day had snapped a photo before running away that clearly showed Sam kneeling down to speak with the bewildered Kolya. Thus had begun an obsession that festered over twenty years.

Timur had grown up without a father or uncle and with a mother crazed with grief and intent on retribution. Timur had taken that rage and determination to heart, learned multiple languages, and clawed his way into economic strata that allowed him to travel and recruit followers. He had coerced other Chechen dissidents to join his crusade, and his four most devoted companions had assisted in the kidnapping attempt. A folded up and enlarged copy of the twenty-year-old picture of Sam and a newer shot taken during the Secretary's funeral had been carried by each of the arrested, who were all now being held on a variety of charges including overstaying their temporary visas, attempted kidnapping, and assault.

And contrary to what both Sam and Kolya's mother had feared, the Russian leaders, as far as anyone could tell, had apparently grown indifferent to Kolya's existence. After disposing of Kolya's father and effectively silencing his mother, they had focussed their attention on other forms of despotism.

Given the increasingly erratic behavior of the current leadership, moles were now more numerous than ever in Russian intelligence. One of Sam's close friends currently stationed in Russia had called in a favor after helping to secure a visa for an informant's family member. His informant verified that there was no active file on a Nikolai Gregorievich Polivanov or any of his extended family. Kolya's mother had long ago given Sam a list of family members still living in Russia, and Sam now felt comfortable passing that list to Kolya, who was beginning to reach out to his father's relatives.

And so finally, despite still deeply-ingrained reservations, Sam had assisted in the official rebirth of Nikolai Gregorievich Polivanov—Kolya, for short. On a beautiful spring morning, Nikolai and Jacqueline were married at a winery in Northern Virginia. Jackie had introduced Kolya to her family as a distant cousin of Leo—someone she had known at college and immediately fallen in love with when they had run into each other in Crystal City after being friends on social media for years.

They came up with the idea on the spur of the moment on that cold December day. Unwilling to part, Jackie had stared long and hard at Kolya, holding up an old photo of Leo from her phone in comparison. She shook her head, trying to concentrate while Kolya ran his hands up and down her torso.

"If I didn't know you, I'm pretty sure I'd never guess you were the same person. I recognized your voice that night in Austin, and I realized this morning that I remembered your scent as well." She rubbed her nose into his chest near his armpit and inhaled deeply, a smile of sheer contentment spreading across her face.

Kolya theatrically held up his arm and sniffed, putting on a look of exaggerated dismay. "I smell bad?"

Jackie laughed and pushed her nose all around, snorting and giggling as she tried to tickle him.

"No, you idiot. You smell delicious. But you smell like you, and somehow my terrified senses recognized you in the middle of all that craziness. And I'm so glad they did."

"Me, too," he whispered, and conversation had again fallen off for a while. But Jackie had picked up the thread once more as she lay curled into his chest, her hand resting against his gradually slowing heartbeat.

"I still think no one else would ever think you were Leo just by looking at you or even talking with you. And there better not be anyone else walking around out there who remembers your smell like I do."

Kolya had laughed softly, his hand resting on her head.

"I'd say that's a definite no."

"Then let's make you Leo's cousin." Her mind had flown, instantly creating a believable scenario.

"Part of the family left Russia for Sweden around the time of the revolution—that's where Leo grew up—but great-grandparents and grandparents stayed in contact, and the two of you met up when you were both students at UVA."

"How did I get to the U.S.?"

"Your parents came over as guest musicians in the late 90s and were able to get long-term positions here. Your mother moved to Europe after your father died and has since remarried, but you stayed because you're a U.S. citizen and this is your home." She paused and shot him a curious look. "Are you a citizen?"

"I think so. I asked Sam years ago, and he said yes, but that my status wasn't registered under my name and that I shouldn't try to vote. I'm not sure now which name he was even talking about, but that's something we can try to get straightened out. I've always hated not being able to vote."

Now Nikolai Polivanov was a registered New Mexico voter, looking forward to voting in the June primaries. They were both comfortable in the south-western climate and had easily settled into positions in the tech-focused city. Best of all, they had succeeded in persuading John Riga to come with them.

When Jackie first confessed that his former landlord knew everything, Kolya had been shocked. But as she spoke, Jackie watched a change come over him. His instinctive wariness faded, and a look of genuine happiness replaced it.

"It means that something good beyond us came out of all this. We weren't responsible for Danny's death, and we can't bring him back, but we can be a family to his father. I thought about him when I was in Albany. I hated knowing he was alone."

She laughed. "I guess I knew in my heart you would think that way, but it's a good thing I was right, since I already asked him to move with us."

Sam's eyes had bulged when he learned that Jackie had

confided in someone else, but he gradually calmed and muttered something about doing a security check.

Mr. Riga had been her first stop upon returning to Austin in January. He opened the door, looked at her face, and broke into a huge grin.

"You found him. I can see it on your face. This is amazing. Is Jake really still alive? And is he truly your long-ago dead boyfriend? He must be, given how your eyes are glowing. Come in, my dear, and tell me everything."

She had. And she had ended her story with a sales pitch she and Kolya had worked on together.

"We need you to move with us. You're the closest thing to family Kolya has left in this country, and my family is too far away. Please come with us, John."

At that point she still hadn't known she was pregnant, but perhaps premonition had guided her words.

"Our children can only benefit from an on-site grandpa, and we want you to be that person. Please say you'll come."

Arranging a wedding, giving notice, fending off her parents' worries that she was rushing into a relationship, making up a convincing timeline to once again persuade Nadine she wasn't crazy, and preparing to move—it had all been at once exhausting, demanding, and ridiculously easy.

Nadine stared hard at Kolya at the wedding reception. "He looks a little like Jake. You must have a particular type, when all these years you just acted like no guy really appealed to you." Her eyebrows had been lifted almost to her hairline as she spoke, but then she shrugged and smiled and reached out to hug Jackie tightly to her.

"I'll miss you, Jackie. I'm really glad you found him, this Kolya of yours." And she winked.

Sam helped Kolya find a position in Albuquerque, and David Hilderman had resigned from his job in Albany, moved into a short-term rental, and set to house hunting.

Sam had even assisted in the transfer of all Kolya's scattered finances into consolidated accounts under his "new" real name, eyes widening again at seeing the profits from Kolya's numerous wise investments.

Kolya posted alerts and searches in ways that bewildered Jackie and found a house with a detached in-law suite that had been under contract but was now unexpectedly available. He put down a deposit, and Jackie and John Riga had flown out to look at it and fallen in love. Jackie now had a part-time job she enjoyed and spent the rest of her time finishing up her novel and planning for the birth of the baby they were all anxious to meet.

Now she stood and marveled at the exquisite vista surrounding her and smiled as the baby stretched and poked out her belly with a tiny foot. She had never lived so close to mountains before, and their startling majesty continued to take her breath away. But so did the wild one constantly cavorting inside her.

The water boiled and she filled the waiting teacups. As she carried them into the living room, the baby kicked once more and she laughed. Happiness washed over her in waves. Kolya was sitting on the edge of the couch, guitar in his lap, eyes closed, and head tilted slightly skywards as he experimented with chords.

He looked at her as she walked closer, and the smile on his face filled her with joy.

"I'm working on a lullaby," he said. "Come listen."

And she did.

ACKNOWLEDGMENTS

As always, it takes a village, and I am so very grateful to my wonderful village angels. Thank you to all my fellow writers, angels every one: to terrific authors Kathleen Gilles Seidel, Susanna Eastman and Pru Warren for giving **Second Stanza** an early read, unending thanks to Sharon Wray for her limitless patience and for sharing her unparalleled knowledge and experience, and thank you to Keely Thrall and all the morning writers who make getting up and getting to it a joy, rather than a chore.

Kudos to my cover designer Jaycee DeLorenzo, of Sweet 'N Spicy Designs, who took my inarticulate babbling and nonetheless created a terrific cover. I am in awe.

Thanks also to best-selling author Gayle Forman, who kindly and quickly acquiesced to my request to use a line from one of her beautiful books, and to the phenomenally talented Sherry Thomas, who has been a mentor and friend. Read their books; they will change your life, I promise!

ABOUT THE AUTHOR

Meg Napier is a book worshipper, married to a bibliomaniac, (his word, sadly!) and the mother of book fanatics. They love reading them, collecting them—even smelling them. But Meg loves writing them, as well, and sharing stories with the world that will ultimately bring a smile of joy to readers' faces and a warm sense of homecoming to their hearts. Novels **SECOND ACT** and **SECOND SIGHT** have brought excitement and joy to readers worldwide. Visit her at MegNapier.com or any of the social media links below, and look for her books at Books2Read.

And now a plea: if you liked this book, please leave a review wherever you feel most comfortable. It is the greatest gift you can give an author.

NEWSLETTER SIGN-UP

When you visit my website at MegNapier.com please sign up for my newsletter and receive a free short story, "Second Draft," just for signing up. Thanks!

Made in the USA
Middletown, DE
23 October 2022